Tl

RANSOM STRIP

THE
RANSOM STRIP

To Norma
Best Wishes
Richard Leng

— Richard Wedgwood Leng —

Disclaimer

The Ransom Strip is entirely a work of fiction. Any similarities to persons alive or dead are entirely coincidental.

A CIP catalogue record for this book is available from the British Library.

ISBN 978-1-7399810-0-6

Cover artwork by Richard Leng

Book layout by Clare Brayshaw

Prepared and printed by:

York Publishing Services Ltd
64 Hallfield Road
Layerthorpe
York YO31 7ZQ

Tel: 01904 431213

Website: www.yps-publishing.co.uk

To my family

About the author

Richard Wedgwood Leng spent most of his working life as an architect based in Manchester. His first book "Painting The Village" was a collection of drawings, histories and portraits of the people and places of Mellor and Marple Bridge, the village where he lives with his wife Margaret. The Ransom Strip is his first novel. He has two daughters and four lovely grandchildren.

Acknowledgements

Richard is grateful for the help of numerous friends and family members for their practical help and support without which the Ransom Strip would not have seen the light of day.

Thanks are particularly due to Anthea, Jenny and John for agreeing to take the risk of reading the first draft. Their generous encouragement and practical advice were invaluable. Thanks also to Richard Smith for his proofreading of the final manuscript, and to York Publishing Services for all their help in producing the finished book.

Finally, my grateful thanks to my wife, Margaret for her patience, love and support in this project and so many others.

Chapter 1

1965

"Revival ran along the hedge
And made my spirit whole
When steam was on the windowpanes
And glory in my soul."

John Betjeman had it right, Adam had not been
expecting glory, and he did not know he had a soul.
He had gone to the Welbeck Road Congregational
Chapel in Halifax that Saturday afternoon in secret.
He had only agreed to be there on condition that no
one else knew – his friends at school, his teammates
at the rugby club and especially his mother and father.
The secrecy was to save his embarrassment, save him
from ridicule and preserve his reputation, but most
of all, it was to avoid having to explain to his liberal,
agnostic and impossibly tolerant parents what he had
been doing.

Adam Rowntree was much the same as any other
17-year-old boy living in West Yorkshire in 1965, a
reluctant grammar school pupil, who liked rugby and
tennis, both of which were readily available to him.

He also enjoyed underage drinking and girls, which, sadly, were not. Yet here he was on a Saturday, yes, a Saturday afternoon, squeezed onto the end of a hard pitch pine pew at the back of the upper balcony of a chapel, with three hundred assorted Evangelical Christians, all engaged in some kind of uproarious Victorian revival meeting.

He was familiar with church for high days and holidays, Christmas and Easter, but he had experienced nothing like this. The chapel, built to accommodate vast congregations of 19th century nonconformist, working-class men and women, was these days rarely a quarter full. But today it had been hired by this 'wacky' group of evangelicals and was packed to the rafters.

It was a vast, towering space with tall lantern windows down either side, rising up to the plain queen-post trusses in the vaulted roof. The afternoon sun slanted in through the misted glass, picking out small clouds of dust as the congregation took their seats. The stark simplicity of the interior with its horseshoe balcony along three sides, was more like a concert hall than a church. The space was dominated by a majestic organ occupying most of the end wall, in front of which, where one might have expected to see an altar, was a large, elaborate wooden lectern, the focus of the whole interior. Its significance and presence was reinforced by two sweeping staircases giving access to the grand affair, all made of the same treacle brown pitch pine of the polished pews. The lectern was midway between the ground floor and balcony, as if hovering between heaven and earth. Devoid of stained-glass, statues and memorials, and without an altar or choir stalls, the chapel was designed for just two things, music and preaching. The organ for music and the lectern for preaching the word. The chapel may not have belonged to these people, but they certainly knew how to use it.

As a child, Adam had reluctantly attended the local church with his parents, where the regular liturgy, led by the same regular priest, with the same small regular congregation, went through the same motions Sunday after Sunday. His father had once joked that when the vicar was asked to speak up, he would apologise, saying he was very sorry, he had no idea anyone was listening! Adam certainly never was. To his parents, the Church of England was a little like the piano in the front parlour which nobody knew how to play, but did not have the heart to throw out. To his mother, religion was a casualty of the enlightenment, education and the scientific age; it was harmless, useful for weddings, funerals and Christmas, but definitely not to be taken regularly or seriously. The country was supposed to be full of people who believed in God but never went to church, but Adam's mother probably belonged to a more select group which did not believe in God, but occasionally went to His house.

The occupants of the Welbeck Road Congregational Chapel certainly believed in God. They were not going through the motions and were taking the whole thing incredibly seriously. The hymns, the readings, the lengthy and passionate preaching were a revelation. The building would have been impressive with no one in it, but filled with three hundred believers, all singing John Wesley's hymns in four-part harmony, at the top of their voices and with the organ going at storm force ten, the atmosphere was extraordinary. This was sensory overload to the uninitiated Adam. The preachers were inspiring and one, in particular, was decidedly charismatic, able to hold the whole congregation with humour, passion, and to Adam, some very original ideas. He was listening, and he never listened to sermons in church. But here, he found the experience overwhelming. If he thought he had one, he would have said his soul had been stirred.

This of course was the most disturbing aspect of the whole afternoon, for he had come reluctantly and sceptically to please his friend. Yet here he was – impressed, moved even and he could not deny it. He was not sure what he was moved by, but you don't have to know the name of something to know that something is there.

This was all Matthew's fault. There was one member of the Whitwood Rugby Club, more specifically a member of the front row, who would not need to be told of Adam's secret attendance that Saturday afternoon. Matthew, otherwise known by his nickname 'Slim', was the large presence sat by his side, innocently crushing him against the end of the pew. If Adam was the silent assassin, the blindside flanker from hell, then Slim, all sixteen stone of him, was the wrecking ball of the scrum, the unguided missile of the forward drive, running through or over opposition defences. The two were used to close personal contact. During last week's match Adam had, in the time honoured fashion of rugby forwards, bent over and reached out between Slim's legs, grabbed his shirt just above the crutch and forced his shoulder into the prop's left buttock at the moment the ball had come in. When they got this right, which they often did thanks mainly to Slim's knowledge of the dark arts of scrummaging, they would trample the opposition back row into the mud.

On the field, if Slim was the terror of all before him, off it, he was by common consent one of the nicest blokes you could wish to meet. He was easy going, generous and had a heart of gold. No one disliked him because there was nothing to dislike. But he was different. No one disliked him, but nobody really knew or got on with him either. It was the religion 'thing' that kept everyone at a distance. It was no secret, either at school or in the rugby club. Slim did not hide it. He did not find his religion at all embarrassing, although almost everyone else did. His friends tended to treat it like someone with a bad stammer; they tried to ignore it, pretend it was not there to protect his feelings, but really it was their own embarrassment they were protecting.

Slim was happy, eager to tell anyone about his religion and 'the brethren', the assembly and the assembly hall where meetings took place. He spoke about what the teacher or the speakers had been saying at the Sunday night lecture, who was the leader of the Mutual Improvement Group this weekend and how they took the Bible very seriously. He invited everyone to come to their gatherings and obviously, no one ever did.

This was one of the strange things about Slim's religion. It had its own lexicon, entirely different from any church language Adam was used to. In fact, the word church was entirely absent from their vocabulary, as were the words priests, vicars, sermons, altars and parishioners. There were brothers and presumably sisters, although the sisters did not seem to get much of a mention. They had assemblies at the hall where meetings or lectures took place, led by teachers or speakers who took to the platform. There would be gatherings, where folk would come from miles around on a Saturday night.

The trouble was, for all Slim's eccentricities, Adam liked the bloke. Playing rugby was a great bond, particularly among the forwards, where eight individuals have to operate as one. But it was more than the rugby, there was something about that oversized personality, contained within his oversized frame, that exuded a generosity of spirit and Adam, in spite of Slim's weird religion, found it compelling. Who knows what it is that draws two souls together, but both were relaxed in each other's company, and their friendship was strong.

Adam's problem of course was that you could not have Slim without the brethren, the assembly, and all the rest of it. It was not that Slim was trying to convert him, it was just that whatever the subject, news item or argument, he always had an answer or solution that came from religion, usually the Bible. It was like the third person in a relationship, Slim's imaginary friend. From time to time he would say in his easy-going way, "Why don't you come along sometime, you never know, you might find it interesting?"

And so it had happened, late one Saturday afternoon. The game had gone well and they had won convincingly, on a cold wet day, perfect for a hard game of rugby. The forwards were invincible; the ball rarely got out of the back of the scrum, much to the disgust of the three quarters, standing out wide, in the cold wind with nothing to do. They were now sitting outside the clubhouse, licking their honourable wounds, happily reflecting on the match and drinking an illicit beer. If they asked discreetly, Jerry, the elderly Steward, would let them have just the one pint. It was early spring, the season was nearly over, and the low sun, at last breaking through the grey clouds, was sinking behind the poplar trees. There was a feeling of well-being that comes after a game of rugby, exhaustion, a few cuts and bruises, and a pint. Endorphins mixed with alcohol. Paul Simon's Homeward Bound drifting over the still night air from the club radio.

"No game next Saturday" Adam commented with clear regret "what am I going to do with myself?"

"Big day for me "said Slim, "I'm off to Halifax."

"Halifax? " Adam laughed, "What big days do they have in Halifax?" He looked across at the large, bruised frame of his smiling companion, "Don't tell me, it's church…sorry, not church, I should say assembly."

"Why don't you come along mate, it'll be a grand do, we have got the biggest chapel booked, you never know you might even like it, there'll be some lasses there, and a free supper."

Perhaps it was the mention of the girls or the mistaken assumption that supper would include beer, or just the desire to please his mate, but Adam relented and said,

"Okay, how do we get there?"

"Easy, I'll pick you up at 2 o'clock. Let's see if we can get another half out of Jerry." Halfway back to the clubhouse, Slim turned around, and with the true understanding of a friend said, "Don't worry mate I won't tell a soul." Adam nodded and thought to himself, you had better not.

He spent the following week trying to work out what he should tell his parents about where he was going next Saturday night. He certainly was not going to tell them the truth. He would have been more relaxed saying he was going out to trash the town centre and vandalise cars. The rest of the time he spent wondering what he had let himself in for. The only thing he had not anticipated was what had happened, and it was all very disturbing.

When the service was over, with a thundering rendering of God Be With You Till We Meet Again, and the organist had finished his rousing show off voluntary, they slowly made their way down the upper reaches of the chapel balcony. It was like getting out at Elland Road after an unexpected Leeds win. The heavy slap on the back he was familiar with, "Well" said Slim "what did you make of it?" Nothing came back in reply. Slim gave his usually talkative mate a quizzical look as they were swept along with the rest of the crowd of brothers and sisters. "Come and have some supper, it's free." Adam, he noticed, looked uncharacteristically subdued and reflective.

By the time he caught up with him, Slim was in a large hall surrounded by a crowd of people he clearly knew well. Most were his own age, and included some of the promised lasses, and very nice they were too, one in particular. Straw coloured blonde hair, curling out under a demure similar coloured hat, cute nose and freckles, not too many to distract but enough to charm, a floral dress, no doubt Laura Ashley, and some fine curves indeed. You would not have called her pretty, handsome was a better word. She had a presence, she was a part of the group, but somehow separate. The prospect and the challenge brought him around.

"Here you are mate," Slim pushed a paper plate, piled with porkpie, sandwiches and pickled onions into his hand and started the introductions. They were a good group, friendly, more friendly on first meeting than most people he met, but like Slim, they were different. There was lots of shaking of hands and kisses on cheeks. All of the girls wore hats and dresses and all the blokes a suit, or jackets and ties. No trousers or jeans for the girls, and fewer of the shorter miniskirts than he might have expected or hoped for. They could have been going to a young Conservatives Club twenty years ago, except for the Bibles under their arms. Some lads were even carrying smart briefcases, but they were friendly, open and welcoming. Adam realised these were Slim's other friends and this, his other life.

Eventually the crowd wandered away leaving the two of them alone.

"Where's the drink? "demanded Adam. Slim handed him a cup of tea and noted the look of disappointment.

"I promised you lasses, I never mentioned booze." Yes, the lasses. He could not remember the names of everyone, but he had remembered one.

"Rachel seems very nice," he volunteered.

"I thought you might think that, most people do, that's cousin Rachel. It was her father you heard speaking earlier, inspiring, didn't you think?" Adam nearly said,

Rachel or her father? He had certainly been inspired by something!

Before he had time to reply, Rachel, arm in arm with her father, a large and jovial besuited figure, were heading their way. He was no less impressive now than he had been earlier when commanding the attention of the assembly from his elevated position in the grand lectern of the chapel. "How are you?" He greeted Slim with a vice-like handshake and the same substantial smack on the back that Adam was used to receiving. Turning, he offered the same hand to Adam. "Is this the famous Whitwood assassin, the blindside flanker from Hades? We have heard a lot about you Adam, haven't we Rachel?" Rachel smiled politely but without conviction, looking down, a little less sociable than she was earlier. "Have you enjoyed yourself Adam, it is a grand gathering always is Halifax, what did you make of it?" Again, the question was asked, and again Slim noticed his usually voluble friend strangely hesitant. It did not matter because Harry Sunderland, or Uncle Harry, as he seemed to be known to everybody under the age of twenty-five, was one of those amiable interlocutors, who in any two-way conversation was more than able, positively willing, to fill both roles. "You must come around for Sunday lunch sometime soon, you must bring him along Slim." Turning to Adam he continued, "It's a big deal Sunday lunch in our house isn't it, Rachel?" Again, there was a polite smile, even less convincing this time and a slight tensing of the shoulders as Uncle Harry put his arm around her and led her away to hail another group, presumably of admirers and supporters.

The hall was beginning to thin out, the food on the trestle tables had all but gone and no one was serving tea anymore, not that Adam wanted another cup of tea. Slim said they had better find Ken. Ken and the grey Ford Anglia van had been their unlikely means of transport earlier in the day, but on investigation, he appeared to have now left without them. "Don't worry," said Slim in his usual relaxed manner, "we will get a lift from somebody", and headed for the exit.

They stepped out into the cold spring evening. The sky was now clear, but the yellow sodium street lamps reflecting off the grey millstone grit of the chapel's high walls, denied any possibility of starlight. But the moon was up and the chill of the night was beginning to take hold, with the promise of a frost before morning. And standing there, nonchalantly leaning on the white roof of a gleaming blue Mini Cooper, her breath slowly rising in the cold night air, like the heroine of an old black-and-white movie, was the beautiful cousin Rachel.

"Hi Rach," said Slim, "any chance of a lift home, Ken has done a runner."

"Sure, Roger will be out any minute, he is deep in conversation with Dad." Roger, who the hell is Roger? As the question formed in Adam's mind, a rather short, bespectacled, almost comic figure stepped awkwardly onto the uneven cobbles of the pavement, dressed in unkept cloths that looked like they belonged to someone else. Adam had noticed him in the group earlier and paid him little attention. He seemed insignificant then, but the car keys in his hand and the presence of his arm around Rachel were clear indications of ownership and signified a greater significance altogether in Adam's increasingly fevered imagination.

"These two reprobates want a lift home Rog", said Rachel, clearly in a better mood than earlier with her father. The two lads piled in the back. Rachel dropped into the seat in front of Adam, her perfume filling the small, enclosed space and, throwing her head back so that her hair almost enveloped him, asked, "Where should we drop you?" Adam thought to himself... anywhere you like love, anywhere you like...Slim, knowing that the bar would still be open, suggested the rugby club, and with that, Roger dropped the clutch of the Cooper, spun the front wheels and shot off down the cobbled street. As a young 17-year-old, Adam knew little about driving, enthusiast though he was, but he was certain that Roger had the coolest of cars. He was also certain he was the worst driver he had ever seen. It was not so much the speed, as the frenetic driving style. Rachel, no doubt used to these displays of machismo, seemed entirely relaxed in the front seat. Roger clearly was not long for this world thought Adam, a thought which hardly troubled him at all.

It was a relief to finally scramble out of the back of the car in the club car park. Rachel elegantly stepped aside to let them out of the back, a good night kiss for cousin Slim and one for Adam? A moment's hesitation and yes, only a peck on the cheek, but oh yes, a peck on the cheek. She dropped back into the passenger seat with the grace of a dancer and slamming the door shut, glanced up and waved them goodbye. Roger sped off in a shower of gravel, almost over steering into the club gates.

"What's with Roger?" demanded Adam.

"Oh, Rog hasn't been driving long, it's all a bit new to him."

"It looks like he won't be driving for much longer if he carries on like that, some car though."

"Oh that, that belongs to mummy."

Sitting in their usual spot at the back of the clubhouse, looking out over the unused second team's pitch, they could hear the folk night reluctantly winding down. A group of Irish lads had done a decent impression of the Dubliner, a good fit for Saturday night drinking in a rugby club. The ballad of Danny Farrell drifted out into the night air, *He's a loser, a boozer, a me and you user, still though Danny Farrell he is a man.*

"Great song" Slim commented as he took a last swig of his pint and leaned back easily on the bench; it creaked beneath his considerable frame. Judging that the beer and the music might have rendered his friend a little more chilled out than he seemed to have been earlier, he asked in his usual casual way,

"Well, what did you make of it all, you were strangely quiet." This time it was Adam who finished off his pint, then turning to Slim with a mischievous smile said,

"Well, I did like Rachel."

"Good grief," said Slim who would never use 'God', or 'Jesus', "I know that! What did you make of the service, was it what you expected?"

The music, the alcohol and the night had had the anticipated effect. Adam leaned across and slapping his friend's massive shoulders said, "Well…I'm not quite sure what I expected, but certainly I was not expecting me. It makes one think." Slim leaned forward placing the empty glass between his great feet,

"You were impressed weren't you, I was sure you were?" He could not conceal his pleasure.

"Oh, impressed certainly" said Adam, "never experienced anything quite like it in my life before."

"Moved?" asked Slim.

"I suppose so, but I'm not sure by what. Just at the moment I'm not sure about anything."

"Except Rachel" Slim offered, "Except Rachel" Adam admitted. "It's time I got off home, and time to think of a credible answer to the inevitable parental question that awaits, what did you do today?"

"You could always tell them the truth," suggested Slim. "The truth's no good" replied Adam, "I want something I can tell my mum and dad!"

Slim slowly rose from the bench and began to amble towards the gate. For such an athletic figure on the rugby pitch, he was strangely awkward off it. Adam called out, "Don't forget your promise." Without turning, Slim waved his arm in the air and said "Don't worry Christian, your secret is safe with me."

Adam was alone on the bench, trying to make sense of the day.

If he had had some understanding of the history of the chapel he had spent the afternoon in, and the nonconformist revolutions of the 18th and 19th century that created these citadels of religious dissent, he might have better understood what had happened to him. These magnificent, austere, undecorated buildings, with their lecture halls and Sunday school rooms, were the product of radical religious, social and political change. Harold Wilson had said that socialism owed far more to Methodism than it ever did to Marx. He should have known, brought up as he was amongst similar chapels, in the working-class areas of Milnsbridge in Huddersfield, not far from where Adam had spent his seminal Saturday evening.

As the Industrial Revolution transformed the English landscape, and vast numbers of agricultural workers migrated to the mill towns of the North, many working-class men and women moved away from the Anglican churches that had dominated their rural existence. They saw them as part of the establishment, maintaining the established order and trying to keep them in their place; singing hymns like, "the rich man in his castle the poor man at his gate, God made them high and lowly and ordered their estate." In places like Halifax, Huddersfield and Bradford, they had had enough of that. The chapel became the instrument of working-class emancipation and social change. They were the first to offer free primary education and mutual improvement classes for working men. The reason the brothers and sisters that afternoon in Halifax had taken their Bibles and followed the lengthy readings, was not because they did not trust the reader to get it right, but because that was how many working people learnt to read in the 19th century. Others learned how to study. They taught themselves to be students, scholars even. The authority of the clergy was gone, authority lay only in scripture, and that was open to all. That was why the pulpit was at the centre of the building, why Bible study was so important, and why preaching was the centre of worship. Such liberties of course lead to differences, divisions and schism, but was not always the price of freedom, progress and democracy.

And if the word and the preaching was the people's, so was the music. No need for choir stalls and a choir, the congregation could sing, tenor, bass, alto and soprano, in beautiful four-part harmony, led by the mighty organ. Charles and John Wesley provided the inspirational hymns, with radical themes. And when not singing in chapel, they formed their own choral societies, performing Handel's Messiah, Stainer's Crucifixion and Mendelssohn's Elijah, to large audiences of their own, in the local town halls. They were exciting and transformative times, that changed the lives of working people for good. By the mid twentieth century the chapels were victims of their own success, the process of emancipation all but complete. No longer would three hundred people fill them every Sunday. The weekly congregations were gone, but the cathedrals of the revolution remained. Adam, who knew nothing of this history, had just been caught up in the brief afterglow of the glory that had once been. A late transformation perhaps, "as of one born out of due time."

He was left trying to decide what to say to his liberal, undemanding parents. Spent the afternoon in a revival meeting with a bunch of fringe fundamentalist Christians? Even their liberal values would have struggled with that. The trouble was, Adam had decided that whatever his parents and his sister might think, it was not going to be the last afternoon he would spend with Slim, Rachel, or the rest of the Bible-based fundamentalists.

Chapter 2

Sunday lunch may have been a big deal at Harry Sunderland's house, but it was no less so at 39, Lumley Street. It probably was in most of the neat semi-detached houses in the street, or anywhere else on the Yorkshire coalfield if there was a family to feed, a mother to cook and, of course, enough money to buy a piece of topside of beef. At 39 there was just enough, even if it had to spread to Sunday night sandwiches, cold meat and chips on Monday, and something creative on Tuesday. Adam's father played a significant role in this trick. He could cover half a plate with raw roast beef, so thin you couldn't have done better with a spokeshave. His mother's unspoken rule was to do what you want at the weekend. Whether she imagined that might include attending a revival meeting of a group of religious fundamentalists was unknown, though unlikely. But she did ask them to be at home from 2 o'clock to 4 o'clock for Sunday lunch.

Even Julia, Adam's older sister who was away at university, would make an effort from time to time, no doubt combining the chance of at least one good meal a week with the laundry facilities included. The piles of dirty washing hanging on the stairs and in the back kitchen informed Adam of such a visit, as he made his way down the stairs. He greeted his sister with the usual, "Hi Sis." Then, sinking down onto the sofa, received an inaudible acknowledgment from the figure next to him enveloped in the Observer. "Give us the sports page, love." A crumpled sheet of paper was passed across without further comment. Both would be fully occupied for the next hour.

Julia's presence had two minor consequences: Morning church had been given a miss, probably to everyone's relief and, as she had already commandeered the Observer, her Father retreated to his shed. This was his preferred location on Sunday mornings or, indeed, at any other time of the week. It was the shed of a frustrated engineer. It was filled with all the appropriate tools, a small lathe, numerous drills and stands, shelves covered in spanners, nuts and bolts, and everything else the practical engineer might require. It was a hive of the engineering industry, yet rarely produced any finished products. He was something like the pure mathematician, studying and practising the subject for its own inherent worth.

It's difficult to say when the ritual of Sunday lunch begins at the Rowntree's house. Was it the peeling of the vegetables early in the morning, (the only task which might be allocated to other members of the family), the oven being turned on, or removing the meat from the larder for it to be anointed with salt and pepper and a lump of dripping? The most important aspect of the ritual was that Mother, up to a point, was in complete control of the timescale.

The point being , just before midday, Father would appear from his shed, pull on his Harris tweed jacket and cheerfully announce that he was just off for a stroll, the clock was running. Wife and daughter smiled at one another, and Mother said, "They will be out by two o'clock". The assemblies of Christ were not the only ones with an esoteric lexicon of their own, this household had its own shorthand. *They'll be out by 2 o'clock* had nothing to do with cricket or industrial relations. 'They' were the Yorkshire puddings and 'two o'clock' was when they would be taken out of the oven ready to eat. It was around the Yorkshire puddings that this quasi-religious ritual, officiated over by Mother, revolved.

It's a simple thing, a Yorkshire pudding. A couple of eggs, some plain flour, salt, pepper and milk, with a splash of water, beaten in a bowl and finally, placed into a hot oven. But, whereas the beef can and should be left to stand, the vital gravy may be made in advance. The vegetables can be kept warm in the bottom drawer of the oven. Yorkshire puddings must come from the oven at the summit of their rising and be eaten with only the gravy, almost immediately. They are essentially the best way of consuming the Sunday gravy. It's the gravy that contains all the flavour of the meat and the vegetables to come. What follows then is something of an anti-climax, it's the puddings and the gravy that matter.

Puddings will not wait. They must be eaten three or four minutes after they are out. They may be left in the oven to turn black, as the air in the kitchen turns blue, or they may be thrown into the sink, into the bin, or

20

onto the back step. All this may have happened in the dark days of the past when the children were younger, stresses were greater and the ritual had been less well understood. But today, Father would be back from his stroll just before two.

His pint of bitter was on the bar almost before he walked through the door of the Black Horse Tavern. Hector was a man of regular habits, and this was one of the most agreeable. Years ago, when recovering from kidney trouble, his GP had advised him to drink a glass of beer every day. It was probably the only medical advice he had ever followed. When Hector's wife asked the doctor some years later whether a glass of water would've done the same job, he replied, "Almost certainly, but I doubted the bugger would've drunk it."

Hector timed the ordering of his second pint to perfection and sat there in great contentment, thinking what a splendid institution the English pub was. There was now a crowd of people around the bar waiting to be served. It's incredible, he thought, a pub was the only place where no one came to serve you, yet nobody forms a queue. The English will happily form a queue at a bus stop, even when there's only two people there, but they never form a queue at the bar of a pub. Yet with a landlord like Les at the Horse, everyone gets served in the right order. Les could let you know with a nod or a look that you have been noticed, are in his virtual queue and will be served as and when. Heaven help anyone who tries to jump the queue. The only exceptions to this rule being the regulars, whose pint may be pulled simultaneously with the others, without being asked for, and without interrupting the flow.

Hector's pint had appeared on the bar according to this amended rule. Friends and strangers alike were chatting around the bar. In the Black Horse, or any English pub, you may speak to complete strangers at the bar, join the conversation without invitation and leave it without comment. Furthermore, you were free to talk about any subject you choose: sport, politics, gardening, even religion. This was on the one, absolute condition (usually enforced by ridicule or sarcasm from the regulars), that you must not, under any circumstances, expect to be taken seriously.

The best landlords, like Les, made little effort to ingratiate themselves with their customers or try to please them in any way. Les would give the impression that you were there under sufferance and should be grateful for his forbearance. The worst of his cruel and withering wit was reserved for his most faithful and regular patrons. Disturbing changes were on the way, with food offerings going beyond the basic meat sandwich, pork pies and pickled eggs, but, so long as the bar and the area around it remained sacrosanct, all might be well.

Finishing his pint and checking his watch, he said to Les, "My lad's seventeen soon. I must bring him with me some time and introduce him to you lot." The landlord struggled to contain his mirth but the regulars around the bar did not quite manage it. Fortunately, Hector was out of the door before the laughter got entirely out of control. "He's in for a big surprise one day, that one," said Les to his regulars around the bar. Recently, they had seen more of Adam than they had of Hector!

Later, as the five diners sat around the discarded plates and cutlery, an atmosphere of calm relaxation permeated the dining room. The ritual had been observed. "You may say it was, satisfactory." Mother sat contented in the chair closest to the kitchen, enjoying the moment. There was invariably one or two additional diners at the table. They were waifs and strays, identified by Mother to be in need of food and fellowship. Today it was Albert, affectionately known as Pop, who had been a regular visitor at Sunday lunch for some time, and almost part of the family. He lived on his own, just a short walk around the corner. Looking at him, Mother felt he was beginning to show his age.

Adam had got involved with Pop over the last four or five years. He cut his grass, trimmed the hedges, and helped him with the endless and usually unsuccessful repairs to his ancient MG. It had initially been Mother's suggestion, but he was happy to go along. Adam kept an eye on Pop, for it was he who had introduced him to the pleasures of underage drinking in his back garden.

After Pop had left, Adam commented that he had looked particularly smart in a nice three-piece suit. Usually, he wore an old threadbare jacket and a pair of gardening trousers.

"Did you notice Dad, Pop did look very dapper today." Adam said with a wry smile, glancing at his sister. "Didn't you used to have a suit like that Dad?" Julia picked up the narrative. All eyes turned to Mother, who busied herself getting the coffee. Adam mumbled, "Not anymore, he doesn't." There was a long, pregnant pause…

"You've got plenty of suits Hector, and it never was a good fit." Mother shouted from the kitchen. Hector looked at his wife with deep affection and, smiling to himself, took the last piece of Stilton.

Mother thought it advisable to change the subject. "And where were you all day yesterday, young man? I can't imagine you've got much revision done this weekend. Your exams are closer than you think."

To avoid the questioning, Adam stood up, "I have the rest of the afternoon. I'll go and make a start now unless you want a hand in the sink?"

"Oh, go and get on with it. Julia and I will do the pots."

Got away with it, he thought to himself, heading for the stairs.

"So, where were you all night then?" Julia asked mischievously, no doubt in revenge for being saddled with the washing up.

"Slim and I looked in at folk night at the rugby club," he said truthfully, but was through the door and halfway up the stairs before any further interrogation was possible.

Collecting the dishes and plates from the abandoned table, Julia asked, "Isn't Slim the one involved in that group of Christian fundamentalists that have taken over the old village hall?"

Hector, glancing over the top of the Observer that he had now managed to get hold of, said, "Is he really? Seems a nice enough lad to me, and from what I've seen, he's one hell of a good front-row forward."

"Oh well that's okay," Julia replied, "so long as he is capable of trampling his fellow human beings into the mud and inflicting actual bodily harm on all and sundry, he must be fine. You won't be too happy if Adam comes home with a broken arm one day."

Hector mumbled, "If he does, I doubt it will be his own" and returned to a disturbing article about local government reorganisation, which caused him far greater concern than his son's Saturday night activities. Mother, however, with her hands deep in the sink, had listened to these exchanges with concern, but without comment, and retained them for future consideration, investigation and, if necessary, interrogation.

Adam was stretched over his chair in the back bedroom, staring down the long garden, towards the greenhouse and well-tended vegetable patch at the far end. Beyond, he could see the tennis club, enclosed on all sides by almost identical gardens, a much more appealing prospect than the neglected maths and chemistry books spread out over the mahogany table in front of him. He didn't find schoolwork difficult, certainly not maths. Mental arithmetic was his specialty. Physics and chemistry required a little more effort, and there was the problem, making an effort. None of the work was hard, but he just didn't find it interesting. His history teacher had wryly observed in one school report that Adam displayed, "A remarkable lack of any intellectual curiosity." There was an offer from Sheffield University to do applied maths, subject to some decent grades, but the prospect of another three years sat in lecture rooms and classrooms did not fill him with any enthusiasm. No doubt the sport would be great, even if university rugby was a big step up, but he was horrified at the prospect of spending a further three years of his life doing little other than studying and sitting for exams.

Perhaps Julia's promise as a future academic, if indeed that was what she was promising, would be sufficient to satisfy parental ambitions. She had definitely embraced the whole university thing – socially, politically and intellectually. No lack of curiosity there, intellectual or otherwise, in C.N.D., civil rights, and the Young Socialists. He wondered if she ever got round to doing any actual studying. Surely that would be sufficient to satisfy Mother. Hector, of course, was not a problem. His aspirations, if he ever had any, were entirely satisfied. Contentment was Hector's great gift. The title, 'Municipal Engineer' suited him perfectly, like a made-to-measure Burton suit, a good fit, without much style. Highways and drainage he knew and understood, local and office politics he would leave to his bosses. Hector would keep everything flowing, above and below ground, permanent and pensionable, which suited him very well. With the garden, his shed, the pub and family, he asked for little more. An occasional golfer, he would sometimes observe that the secret of a happy life was much the same as a secret to happy golf, low expectations. Hector would be happy whatever Adam chose to do. His mother, however, was another set of problems altogether.

As the brightest girl in the family and with three younger brothers, there had been a cruel, though common inevitability about her adolescent years in the 1930s. After matriculation, the head teacher had pleaded with her mother to let her stay on and go to university. But the family business needed a secretary and her mother needed help around the house, so that had been that. Secretarial college, marriage and children were her past, present and future. It had not been a bad life, she told herself. She had married a good man, which Hector undoubtedly was. They had been lucky. He was away in North Africa during the War but came back in one piece. Secretarial skills were always useful, but increasingly these days she wondered, what if? What if the teacher had been more persuasive? What if her mother had listened? What might have been? She was certainly determined that her children, Julia in particular, would get every opportunity and every encouragement, not that she needed either. She had picked up the baton and run with it, much to her mother's delight. Adam knew he was his mother's next project. Mother always had a next project.

She was content to lose the men in the house for a while – Hector to his paper and sleep, and Adam, hopefully, to his revision. It would give her time alone with Julia, where she aimed to get up to date with what was happening at Leeds University, or at least anything that Julia was prepared to divulge. Julia probably underestimated the degree of lurid detail that her mother could cope with. What some middle-class parents of the time may have been alarmed at, CND, sit-ins and civil rights marches, her mother was anxious to hear about. As the final dishes were being stacked away and the table cleared, Julia returned to the subject of Adam. With a sister's intuition, and more empirical evidence than was available to either of her parents, she asked, "Mum, are you sure that he really wants to go to university next year?"

It was the elephant in the room question, so it came as no surprise. Her mother, leaning on the folded tablecloth, looked up at her daughter with a characteristic smile. She was a large attractive woman, in her late 40s, not fat, but big, a strong woman, energetic and determined. She loved her husband and her kids and cherished the little house they had lived in since the War. The only frustration, and it was a growing frustration, was that the arena in which her life was being played out, was too small. She folded the tablecloth and dropping it into its usual place in the dining table drawer said, "Well, he's going whether he wants to or not."

"And if he won't go?"

"Well, there's always an alternative."

"What's that?"

"He can always leave home and find a job. Now you get off, back to Leeds, I have things to do."

On Sunday afternoon, like many other afternoons, the dining table became Mother's study where she spent time on her own various good causes. This afternoon, it was the accounts for the Family Planning Association and when that was finished, the rota for next week's Meals on Wheels. Hector often said that she was incapable of getting involved in anything without finishing up running it. She was always the secretary, never the chairman. Secretaries do all the work while chairmen and presidents take all the credit. She was beginning to lose patience with the W.R.V.S. and its patronising approach to their elderly clientele. Charity worker she may be, but Lady Bountiful she was not.

Putting such unworthy thoughts aside, she turned her attention to the account book. The Family Planning Association was much more to her liking. Here she believed they were making a real difference to women's lives. The pill, she mused, would be transformational if she had anything to do with it.

If the dining room table was a hive of industry for Mother, and the shed an area of quiet, though purposeless endeavour for Hector, the back bedroom was the most unproductive area in the whole house. The books and folders lay scattered across the table as Adam had found them. The view down the garden had not changed, except for two more fortunate teenagers who he could just spot, knocking up on the tennis courts. In fact, the only literature that had been consumed in the bedroom during the last hour was Adam's ageing secret copy of Playboy magazine. This had been passed around the rugby club in recent months. Needless to say, Slim was not included in the list of subscribers. Adam was the current custodian of the codex erotica and kept it carefully hidden next to his copy of Lady Chatterley's Lover on top of the wardrobe. The copy of Playboy was highly prized, but he found Lady Chatterley something of a disappointment. It seemed an awful lot of turgid reading for very few thrills. Carefully returning both illicit documents to their hiding place, he returned to the view out of the window. He need not have been so careful, for his mother had found both documents while cleaning the room some weeks earlier and, smiling to herself, carefully returned them to their secret location. She made a mental note however, to make absolutely sure that her son had a full understanding of exactly how the pill was going to change everyone's life. Family planning she had thought, like charity, should begin at home.

Adam judged that it would be unadvisable to appear in the lounge much before six o'clock, and with Mother in the dining room, getting out of the front door would be high-risk, so out of desperation he tried to do some work. He easily ploughed through a few equations and something to do with non-Euclidean space, but the clock still crawled around the dial. The chemistry folder stared guiltily at him from the table, but it was too much of an effort to do anything with it, so he lay back on the bed, where, unbidden, the events of Saturday afternoon drifted into his head. It was just after five when he woke. He tidied up the books and papers on the table, trying to arrange them in such a way that it gave the impression of work having been done. He drifted downstairs and out into the garden to discover what strange engineering projects his father was working on in his shed. Mother noticed him passing with a look, but mercifully, no comment.

The Sunday ritual was not entirely over. There was the inevitable and wholly agreeable sequel. The ingredients were very much the same, although the personnel and location different. Both food and drink for Sunday night supper were Hector's responsibility. Indeed, it was the only meal in the week he prepared. At seven o'clock he would appear from the shed and ask with time honoured predictability, "Who's for a drink?" This did not involve opening some elaborate drinks cupboard, as might have been the case in the Sunderland household. Here, the choice was limited to sweet sherry or a bottle of pale ale kept under the stairs with various other bottles of pop.

"I will have a beer," said Mother, still sitting at the kitchen table, amongst piles of books, folders and ring binders.

"Really?" A disappointed Hector checked how many bottles of pale ale were left under the stairs.

"Yes, really, I never did like Harvey's Bristol Cream, I don't know why you get the stuff."

He got the stuff to preserve his stocks of pale ale.

"Isn't it time we introduce this lad to the delights of pale ale?" It was getting worse thought Hector, checking the stocks under the stairs again. "Would you like a beer Adam?" Unsurprisingly, Adam said he would.

The kitchen was left to Hector to assemble the ingredients and prepare the feast. For someone who didn't cook anything in the week, it was a task that he relished. Glass of beer at his side and cold, rare beef to carve, pickled onions and cucumber left over from the Yorkshire puddings. Added to this his speciality – warmed up mushy peas in the small glass bowl, with salt and pepper, a dash of vinegar and sugar sprinkled on top. There was a large round of sandwiches for each of them and a bowl of mushy peas to go with the beer. Not bad Hector thought as he brought the feast through into the lounge. As Adam sat there, eating his sandwiches and drinking his beer, his mother looked across and said "You seem to be enjoying that love." Adam looked down at his almost empty glass.

"It's okay."

"Is it really?" said Mother.

"It takes a bit of getting used to lad. It's an acquired taste." Hector suggested in sage-like tones.

"Oh, I don't know, he seems to be managing okay" she added with a knowing wink. Adam wondered if there was anything she did not know and attempted to change the subject,

"They were good Dad, any chance of another one?"

"Of which," Mother said, "the sandwich or the beer?"

"Both," he replied hopefully,

"Get him another sandwich, Hector." Hector strolled into the kitchen to carve more slices off the now diminishing joint of beef and to open the last bottle of beer for himself. Mother, having Adam to herself, broached the subject that had been on her mind since before lunch.

"Now tell me more about the famous Slim, and his born-again brethren that Julia is so preoccupied with."

Thank you very much sister, Adam thought to himself. "You know Slim, Mum, he's been around all year. We've had a great season with the under 18's, it's the best set of forwards they've had for years, Slim is a great prop and a really cool guy, I like him."

"It's was more his religious affiliations I was interested in, rather than his sporting prowess or his homicidal tendencies. Julia seems to think he's a bit of a loner, a bit odd." He was beginning to develop homicidal tendencies of his own towards Julia. Mother, like so many of her fellow liberals, was a great believer in tolerance, freedom of thought and a non-judgemental approach to life in general. That, of course, only applied to anyone who shared her liberal values. Tories, high churchmen and especially religious fundamentalists, were not likely to be offered the same degree of tolerance. And like many freethinkers, to Mother, freedom of thought probably meant freedom to think like her.

"He never seems to say very much about his religion to me," he lied. "Some of the other blokes give him a wide berth, because he doesn't smoke or swear, and he complains when he hears the others blaspheming."

Mother was clearly not reassured, "Well I don't want you getting drawn into some weird group of evangelicals, you've got other priorities, at least until the end of June."

Returning from the kitchen with extra rounds of sandwiches for everyone and a glass of beer for himself, Hector pleaded with Mother. "Leave him alone, Slim's a decent lad. There's nothing wrong with being a bit different. It's not as if he's dragging the lad off to vandalise cars or cause a riot in the town."

She looked at her husband reproachfully, "I suppose that's the last of the beer is it?"

Adam hoped that might be the last of Slim for the evening, as his mother finally took her turn with the Observer. Hector picked up the Radio Times to check the listings, although he was not sure why. It would be the usual issue; would he get to watch Sunday Night at the London Palladium or would Mother insist on the Sunday night play on the BBC. With Adam there, the two men would probably carry the majority.

Looking up from the magazine, Hector asked, "Will you be wanting another summer job this year lad, I think the street lighting department will want some casual labour. There is a big programme replacing street lamps and the money will be useful, whatever you do next year."

Before he could answer, the phone rang in the hall.

"I'll get it, "volunteered Hector, dropping the Radio Times on his wife's lap.

"You'll be wanting that job won't you? You can't expect us to keep you in the lap of luxury for the rest of your life" his mum added testily. She was interrupted by Hector's head peering around the lounge door with a cheeky grin.

"It's Slim for you, Adam. He wants to know if you have any time tonight to help him nick some cars down the town, and then there's an evening of child sacrifice with the brethren down at the village hall." He managed to get his head behind the door before the Radio Times came to the end of its trajectory. Adam picked it up on his way to the phone, closing the door firmly behind him.

"Hi mate!" came the welcome, cheerful voice over the phone. "What was that all about?" "Oh, it is just what passes here for family fun on a Sunday night." After all the tensions of the day it was good to hear a friendly voice.

"Listen!" Slim said, "No pressure, but thought you might like to know some of us get together on a Tuesday night at the hall. It is a bit of a social, bit of a study class and wondered if you might be interested? It is all very informal, no pressure." Adam thought that would be good, and strangely, when Slim said, "no pressure," he believed him. "I'm not sure mate, exams are looming and I should do some work."

"It is up to you, we are there most Tuesdays anyway, and before you ask, yes, I expect Rachel will be there."

"What time?"

"7:30"

"I will see what I can do"

"Cheers mate."

Putting the phone down, he called through the door, saying he was going to do some more revision, anything to avoid further cross-examination. Hector gave his wife the look which said, 'leave it'. Reluctantly she did, but got up from the sofa and in retaliation, laid aside the Observer and turned the television on.

"If it's just the two of us, we may as well watch the play."

"That's fine by me dear". Anything for an easy life. That was Hector.

Chapter 3

August 1965

Adam had arrived at the assembly hall early on Tuesday evening on his bike, a good twenty minutes before anyone else. The A level results were out at 9 o'clock the following morning. He couldn't endure the tension and expectation at home any longer. The school didn't think he had done enough work and nor did his mother. Only he actually knew how little work he had done. He'd had a good and profitable summer, thanks to his father, employed by the Street Lighting Department, digging holes for street lamps and cleaning traffic signs. He had even scared himself silly, riding the cherry picker to change street lamps throughout the town. The latter added significantly to his credibility on the street. The hours worked and money earnt had also added something to his credibility at 39 Lumley Street. He doubted it would endure much beyond tomorrow morning's results.

He sat on the bench on the grass verge, in the shade of three large ash trees. The evening sunlight was filtering through the tracery of the low hanging branches, with crazy patterns of light shimmering across the pavement in front of him. His back ached and his hands were covered in calluses, but his forearms and biceps were impressive. It was a pleasant enough place to sit on a summer's evening after a hard day's work, and undoubtedly less stressful than at home.

This week's work was supposed to be his last one before he went off to university. He had enjoyed the manual labour and the working men's company for whom this was their regular job. They gave him a hard time at the start, of course. The boss's 'privileged son', working the summer before going off to what they insisted on calling 'fornicating university.' They had seen students before and seen them off. But when Adam got stuck in and demonstrated he could graft as well as the next man, he was eventually accepted, even looked after, which he quite liked. It was a glimpse into a different way of life and a different way of work for him. He stood with the other men on the street corner, early in the morning, waiting to be picked up in the scruffy van and taken to the various sites. He learnt how to make strong tea in a tin brew can and drink it from a tin cup. He learnt how to fry bacon on a clean shovel over an open fire. He listened to the conversations in the grime, smoke-filled site cabins at dinnertime (dinner, not lunch), and shared their dirty jokes and prejudices. He learnt how they tried, and often succeeded, to beat the system and con the bosses. He was astonished by how much some of them could drink and still function. But after eight hours digging cable trenches by hand, in sticky clay soil, he understood why they did drink. He would work hard for most of his life, but would never be as tired at the end of the day than after a shift with the street lighting road gang. His mother would have approved of this addition to her son's education.

It kept him fit for rugby and, more importantly, gave him a pay packet at the end of each week. It was handed out by the foreman on a Friday afternoon in a transparent paper envelope that crackled in his hand. He could see the colour of the money; the green, and the red notes, and feel the weight of the loose change. He knew that it was his to spend as he pleased after Mother had taken her ten bob note out for board and lodgings. The money would find its way back to him at some point in the future, but she was determined he wasn't going to imagine he could earn money and live at home for free!

The assembly hall was on the very edge of town, just where the suburban landscape gave away to the rural. In front of him, he could see the winding gear of the local colliery and parts of the slag heap behind, but beyond the hall and its car park were farmers' fields and hedgerows as far as the eye could see. The broad river wound around the edge of the site on its slow, lazy journey to the Humber. The idyllic Constable like landscape was somewhat compromised by the multiple grimy coal barges, locally known as 'Tom puddings' being towed downstream, transporting opencast coal from South Yorkshire to Stanley Ferry on the Humber. Not quite as picturesque as the Hay Wain.

The building looked like any rundown village hall on the Yorkshire coalfield. It was single-storey, built of soft red bricks with an asbestos roof in poor condition, stained with coal dust. The whole building needed either significant renovations or, better still, replacing. It contained a large meeting room, schoolroom and a kitchen beyond. At the corner of the site closest to the river and linked to the grass verge was an overgrown triangle of woodland that had been neglected for years. It certainly lacked the grandeur of the congregational chapel in Halifax, and it was nothing like any of the churches Adam had ever attended. But over the summer, it had become an unlikely sanctuary and refuge. There was not much going on at the rugby club in the summer. When he wasn't playing tennis or helping Pop in the evenings, he now found himself at the hall. He would be playing table tennis, drinking coffee, or trying to chat up the lovely Rachel, though sadly, Roger was invariably around as well. Tuesday evening was study group and he knew his mother and sister would have been alarmed to learn just how much he looked forward it.

If someone were to ask him (though no one ever had), what the attraction was, he would have found it difficult to say. The best he could have come up with was that it was 'different'.

Everyone had been very welcoming, not in any formal or patronising way, but people had naturally allowed him in. There were not the usual obstacles to joining a new group, so he felt accepted. There was an absence of the usual peer pressure or competition. He sensed that there was a different set of values in operation, although nothing was spelt out. He felt comfortable and relaxed in their company. Sure, there were some oddballs amongst them, Roger being the prime example, but he was friendly enough in his own eccentric way.

If asked, his sister would claim that this was all deliberate and calculated, to draw him in, convert him, claim him for the group. Julia would insist that he had been 'love bombed' to make him susceptible to their ideas. Adam thought this a bit thick, coming from Julia, who ever since going to university was continually trying to convert Mother and him to her new radical left-wing ideology. Not that Mother needed too much persuading. Julia had certainly been claimed by the group. She had been very susceptible to the ideas of the Young Socialists or Socialist Workers' party. Whichever one, her conversion appeared to be entirely complete.

Adam would not have used this word, but what he had found among these different people was kindness. Kindness and generosity. Not sentimental or patronising, more a habit or an undercurrent of kindness. What they called fellowship, Adam experienced as kindness. The group at times just seemed an extension of Slim's generous personality. They were, in fact, filling the emotional and spiritual vacuum of his adolescent years.

Much of what they believed and taught was discussed on a Tuesday evening, and came something of a shock. He could be forgiven for thinking that whatever the established churches believed, they believed the opposite. In the back kitchen of the hall, he noticed a book in the library entitled, 'Where Christianity went wrong, erroneous doctrines of the Church.' Heavy stuff he thought and left it safely on the shelf. That subject wasn't particularly relevant to Adam, as he hadn't got much idea what the Church of England taught anyway. But the few things he did know something about, the Trinity, heaven and hell, christenings and confirmations, were, apparently, all 'tosh,' more accurately erroneous and false doctrines. The assembly's idea was, "We are right and everyone else is wrong!" He rather liked that. For a young teenager, this kind of radical dissent was stimulating and attractive.

There was also a certain simplicity that appealed to him. The basic rule was, if you could find it in the Bible it was true, and if you couldn't, it wasn't. None of the above ideas were in the Bible, so the assembly claimed they were not true. It was simple, or so he was led to believe, so he was happy to believe, hence all the Bible study on Tuesday nights and the other nights, when they all got together. It wasn't so much Bible 'bashing,' as Bible finessing or Bible reasoning. Reasoning, logical reasoning, Adam liked it, just as he liked his equations in Maths. No statement was to be made that was not a logical consequence of the previous statement. You were right, or you were wrong. 'Chapter and verse,' you might say. For Adam, it was all a surprisingly good fit.

He leaned back on the bench, anticipating the evening ahead, hoping that Rachel would make an appearance, and that Roger, would not. He was aware of the sound of the car before it came into view, and knew immediately who it would be. The blue Cooper came screaming over the bridge, breaking at the last minute to turn into the narrow gateway, attempting and failing to execute a handbrake turn on the loose gravel of the car park. The car finished up at an obtuse angle, in no particular place. Not an inappropriate metaphor for Roger's life in general. Four passengers, including Slim, squeezed out of the tiny vehicle and Adam noticed, with some disappointment, that there was no Rachel.

Roger was expecting to lead the study later in the evening. He was older than most of the group and clearly regarded as one of the leading lights – a future 'eminent brother,' so it was said. No one ever mentioned eminent sisters though, so quite what 'eminent brother' meant in this context, Adam had no idea. What he did know was, if it was going to be a long-term role, Roger needed to radically change his driving style. Slim came over and, dropping down on the bench beside him asked, "All ready for tomorrow morning, are we?"

In truth, Slim was as nervous as he was. He needed three good grades to go and study architecture at Leeds. Unlike Adam, he knew what he wanted to do. Slim was worried that he might not get the grades and be unable to go to university. Adam was worried that he might get the grades, and have to go. Failure would be the end of the university problem, but no doubt the start of another. Slim was reading his mind and said, "You could always go to plan B..."

"What's that?"

"Don't go home." He had been wondering about that himself. Standing up, he looked around and said with obvious regret, "No Rachel tonight then?"

"Oh, Uncle Harry is coming down later to do the study, so I expect she'll be coming with him." Almost on cue, a stately admiralty-blue and grey Rover cruised over the bridge and swung elegantly into the car park. The large, imposing car entirely suited the driver, which was no doubt the intention. While no one went to open the door, it felt as if someone should. Stepping out onto the gravel, Harry Sunderland greeted everybody with his familiar warmth and good humour, but still no Rachel.

Adam liked Harry Sunderland. Impressed would be more accurate, for he was an impressive figure. He wasn't in charge of the local assembly, (that role fell to his brother Walter, Slim's father,) but Harry was clearly a big cheese in the whole set up. Slim had explained that his father was local, while his Uncle Harry was national. Adam had once made the mistake of referring to him as the priest, only to be told, "We're all priests here lad. A kingdom of priests, a holy nation." The answer to any questions regarding Uncle Harry were nearly always accompanied by a quote from the Bible. The absence of any clergy or formal ministry was one of the peculiarities he had to get used to. It really was a 'do it yourself religion.' They claimed that, as there were no clergy in the Bible, there should be no clergy now. OK? Although it wasn't quite that simple. 'All priests' in practice seemed to refer only to the brethren and not the sisters, so while all were priests, some were 'priestlier' than others in an Orwellian sense.

There was more to Uncle Harry than the inspirational speaker and Biblical scholar though. He was clearly a successful man about town. In fact, to Adam, everything about him spoke of wealth and success; his style, charisma, the way he dressed and the easy air of confidence and authority all impressed him.

Slim had filled in the back story. The two brothers had inherited their father's small estate agent business in the centre of town. It was the usual thing – house valuations, sales, property surveys, and lettings. It dealt with some industrial and commercial property, but mainly domestic. It was a part of the community. Everyone knew the Sunderland's and the they knew everyone and everything that was going on in the town. Slim's dad still ran the agency, but Harry, although he retained an interest, had moved into property lettings and development. It had started with little old ladies coming into the office with odd pieces of land, asking if it was worth anything. Harry then found local people to buy and develop it. Doing developments with local builders seemed the next logical step. They now had a sizeable property portfolio, around the town and throughout the north of England.

All this was a new world to Adam, quite different from his father's life as a local government officer and municipal engineer. In fact, Uncle Harry's world was as different from that of his father's as it was possible to imagine. Perhaps that was part of the attraction.

If Adam was impressed with Uncle Harry, Harry had taken something of a shine to him in recent months. His own son, Damien, was now grown up and had been in the business since leaving school. Harry would sometimes joke, "I had to employ him as nobody else would've done." It is often said that we only jest when in greatest earnest. Unfortunately, the joke would sometimes get back to Damien and naturally fuel bitter resentment, something Uncle Harry was too busy, or too confident to notice. But he had noticed Adam, first at the rugby club when there to support Slim. It was Harry who had suggested inviting Adam to a meeting. He liked the way he played his rugby and he sensed in him a bright, intelligent lad who was looking for something. A lad with potential. Harry was generous enough, and vain enough, to see himself as something of a mentor to those like Adam. He was somebody he could help and see him realise his potential. He believed that divine providence was the precursor of everything that happened in the world, and was happy to see himself as a benevolent instrument in the process.

The study sessions were usually informal discussion groups with a leader. Roger had come prepared for the role and looked miffed when Uncle Harry took over. This evening would not be the usual dialogue, but a Harry Sunderland lecture on his favourite themes: the Second Coming and Israel in Divine Providence. He reminded them all that they were living in the last days, "A time of trouble such as never was," the Second Coming of Christ was imminent and certainly before the end of the century. They were to watch and look for the "signs of the times", and the most important sign, apparently, was the re-establishment of the Jews as an autonomous nation in Palestine. Israel was the miraculous proof that God's purpose, prophesied in the Bible, was coming to pass. To Adam, this was heady stuff.

At first, he had found it all very odd. They were a group of otherwise normal, mainly middle-class teenagers sitting in a little hall on the edge of an ordinary northern town, talking calmly and rationally about the imminent end of the world, the Rapture and the final battle of Armageddon. They were not a bunch of drug-crazed weirdos in caftans following some charismatic leader who demanded all their money. No-one asked them to go and sit on a mountain top waiting for the appointed day. After tonight's session was over, they would get their A-level results and go off to university or work. After telling them, "Seek first the kingdom of heaven", Harry would then go and disappear in his Rover, looking for the next property deal. He liked quoting the book of Hebrews, "Here we have no continuing city," and claimed that "They were all in the world but not of it." Perhaps the writer to the Hebrews was unfamiliar with the concept of a flexible property portfolio and the other financial instruments all too familiar to him.

What changed in Adam was that the unfamiliar became familiar, and the extraordinary, over time, became ordinary and reasonable. Reasonable because it was, in its own terms, reasoned. Everything had chapter and verse, and a logical argument to follow, like his maths. Adam liked that for it suited his mindset. And perhaps equally important, this group of young people that he had come to know and like, believed it, for they had reasoned it out for themselves. To anyone outside, casually listening at the window it may have all sounded extraordinary, even bizarre, but if in the room, it was all increasingly convincing. The belief of the group allowed him, encouraged him, to believe. Believing was no longer weird and incredible, it was natural and expected. It was what everybody else was doing.

Rachel finally appeared, just as Harry was concluding his exegesis. He glanced at his daughter over half-rimmed glasses, clearly indicating disappointment, if not irritation. Whatever her look might have communicated in return, it was hidden behind the straw blonde curls hanging down over her face. She went straight to the kitchen and began collecting the coffee cups in a way reminiscent of his mother dishing up the Sunday lunch when Hector was late back from the pub. Adam had come to understand that there were at least two Rachels, one when her father was around, and one when he was not. Adam wandered through to the kitchen with more dirty coffee cups.

"More empties for the workers," he offered. She turned with a look of pleasant surprise, but the smile the eyes began, failed to get any further. Clearly, the only company she craved at that moment was the sink.

"You missed your dad's talk," he said, immediately regretting his clumsy predictability. There was no look of pleasant surprise this time, more bored resignation.

"Adam, I have heard it many times before. I could do it myself, word for word, if I were allowed" she said, glancing through the kitchen door at the group surrounding her father, "besides, he's got enough admiring disciples without me." She turned to Adam, who was leaning on the dishpan, fixing him with those lovely blue eyes, "What about you? Are you going to become one of his admiring disciples?"

She returned to attack the washing-up with greater force than intended, splashing soap suds everywhere. The comic moment broke the tension and forced a smile on both their faces.

"Sorry, that was unkind, it's not your fault." She handed him a tea towel, suggesting he make himself useful. He took it and dried the suds from his own face, then, after a moment's hesitation and with a confidence that he didn't possess, dabbed the traces of washing-up suds from her freckled cheeks. This time, the smile in her eyes completed its journey across the whole of her beautiful face.

"Thank you, kind sir."

They returned their hands to the washing-up, and the conversation to themes more trivial and inconsequential, though not for as long as he might have wished. As a few minutes later Rachel's father and Slim had made their way over to them.

"Adam, Slim and I are going for a pint on the way home, why don't you come and join us, unless, of course, you've gone off beer, now that you can drink it legally?" Rachel's irritation at the interruption was obvious to everyone except him. Adam could think of a number of things that he would rather do later in the evening than go for a pint with the two of them, but Slim joined in the persuasion, "Come on mate, it'll take your mind off tomorrow." Rachel held out a resigned hand to take the tea towel. He handed it over with a look of an apology and guilt, but mainly regret. It was notable that there wasn't the slightest acknowledgement that Rachel was there at all in all the exchanges. It was only at the end, when, seeing Adam's hesitation, Harry said, "Don't worry about Rachel, Roger will see her safely home." Rachel's expression spoke volumes, to anyone who chose to notice, but only Adam did.

Adam climbed into the back of the car and sank into the cream leather seats. Slim's vast frame, much the same as his uncle's, seemed much more at home in the spacious Rover than in the confined space of Roger's Mini Cooper.

"Damien is going to join us in the pub. He's probably there already" Harry was still in charge of the evening. Adam had not quite worked out how Damien fitted into the picture. He was older than the others, not naturally a part of the 'youth group' and he never attended any of the studies. What he had worked out was that, although the 'brethren' were generally good, clean living people (if not a little puritanical), there were, for some at least, certain acceptable sins. One of which as far as Harry and Slim were concerned, was booze.

Damien had indeed got there before them. He was sitting by the window with two glasses in front of him, one empty and the other heading in the same direction.

"Big day tomorrow for these two lads," declared Harry, skilfully carrying three pints in two hands and setting them down on the table without spilling a drop. "Yours is on the bar Damien. I couldn't carry four."

"What are you hoping for Adam? A's and B's I suppose." Slim laughed out loud and taking a deep swig of his pint said, "What he's really hoping for is three fails, then he won't have to go to university, but he will have to face the wrath of his mother, that's about it isn't it mate?"

"Something like that." Adam confessed, surrendering himself to the pint in front of him.

Harry looked at him with growing interest. "University," he opined, "is not the be-all and end-all of everything. I didn't go, Damien didn't either and we have done alright. Rachel thought she wanted to go and study landscape architecture, but what's the point of that? You don't need to go to university to learn about gardening do you? Slim here wants to be an architect, so I suppose he will have to go."

Turning to Slim he said. "You be careful now. There is a lot of nonsense goes on at those universities." Given he had never been, it was not clear how he knew. "Make sure you remember what your priorities are Slim, remember where we're all going."

He had again seamlessly moved back into preaching mode for a moment and was back in the assembly hall holding forth. Adam was often struck how Harry could switch so easily between the one world, and the other. He switched back again, "So what are you going to do Adam, what do you want to do with your life?"

Adam suddenly realised that no one, certainly not recently, had asked him that question. His mother and sister both thought they knew what he should do. He assumed his father was 'on message', but no one, not even Slim, had asked this simple question, *what do you want to do*? He knew what he didn't want to do. The answer that had probably been there for some time, drowned out by all the surrounding noise, suddenly presented itself.

"Really, I'd like to get myself a job, and I'd like to earn some money of my own."

"Well," declared Harry, "there's nowt wrong with that", and picking up the empty glasses, handed them to the Damien, "Get us another round in lad." He turned back to Adam, "I think it is time we had you around for Sunday lunch." It was not just Rachel, Adam noticed, that Harry felt able to order about.

Damien was the dogsbody this evening, and resented it every bit as much.

* * *

The exam results had been more or less what he had expected. The reactions and consequences were not. An A in maths and two Es in physics and chemistry. None of this was a surprise to Adam, but his mother's reaction was. He was prepared for recrimination, accusation, tears and general grief. The recriminations and grief would, no doubt, come later from Julia. His mother had just sat down at the dining room table, looking again at the piece of paper, trying, perhaps to make it say something different, and then leaning back in the chair, stated the obvious. "Well Adam, you're not going to Sheffield with those results." But then, God bless her, she looked at him with a surprisingly sympathetic smile and asked him the same question that Harry had asked the previous day, "What do you want to do?" It was not accusative. Twice, in two days, the same question.

"Just at the moment mum, I would like to go and cut Pop's lawn."

"Good idea, we can talk about it all later." She gave him a kiss and pushed him out of the door. Life was becoming a catalogue of surprises.

Later in the day, he was sat on the rough bench with Pop at the back of his old, terraced house, looking across the considerable length of the garden, with its newly cut lawn and trimmed hedges. At its far end, the early evening sun was threatening to dip behind a stand of trees, casting long shadows over the grass, and a crimson glow across the low horizon. Horticulture was now Pop's main interest, but, at one stage, it had been his whole life. These days he struggled to keep on top of it all. As he sat on the bench smoking his pipe, feet propped up on the stone planter overflowing with bright red geraniums, he was the image of contentment. Like Hector, contentment was one of Pop's gifts, and sometimes, such as this evening, it was contagious. He leaned back against the warm brickwork of the house, blowing out a steady cloud of sweet-smelling tobacco smoke and said, "So it wasn't quite as stressful a day as you were expecting? You might find that's often the case."

"No, mum was surprisingly cool, although I know I've disappointed her."

"She'll get over it lad, she's a very smart woman your mother, very smart indeed. Your father is a lucky chap to have landed her, so are you." Pop was looking into the distance. "She's a very smart lady indeed."

"Unlike her son then", said Adam.

"Don't give me that self-pitying crap, you are clever enough, as you very well know, and an A and two Es was probably pretty good for someone who actually did zero work, or was it a bit less than that?" Pop grinned.

"Once you have decided what it is you want to do, the rest had better watch out. You are going to be fine, Adam, just fine." Pop had not asked him what it was he wanted to do. He just assumed that whatever it was, he would be okay, and, hearing him say it, almost made Adam believe it.

Pop looked out over the garden with satisfaction. He was more grateful to Adam than the lad could ever have imagined, because he was too young to understand the power of a simple act of kindness from a young man to the old.

"You've certainly got no problem with hard work here. I think you deserve a beer." He wandered into the house, coming back with two bottles of Tetley's best bitter. As he poured their contents into the tall glasses and held one up against the fading sunlight, he said, "Managed to get the MG running yesterday. If you're sticking around for a while we can finish the driving lessons and get you through your test. If you can drive an MG, you can drive anything. It's even got brakes now!"

"That should help in the test", Adam said with a grin and a taste of his beer. Learning to drive with Pop in the ancient car was more difficult, but less stressful, than with his father, in his precious new Cortina. Recently however, they had spent more time underneath the car than driving it.

"Tomorrow night then, I will pick you up at 6 o'clock. By the way, didn't I see you in the Spread Eagle last night, you're keeping very fancy company these days?"

"Oh, you mean Harry Sunderland. Do you know him?

"I have known Harry since he was a lad. This is a small town and you get to know most people. Done very well for himself, has our Harry, very well indeed."

"You sound like you are not so sure Pop."

"No, no! Harry is right enough, he's a bright chap, but not so sure about the son. Not as clever as the father, not as clever as he thinks he is either. He's married to that Gaynor girl now I believe. She's done well for herself too, at least, I suspect that's what she thinks. Harry's a big cheese these days isn't he, in the chapel down by the river? Don't really get that, but each to his own."

"Got a nice daughter, though," Adam said as he got up to leave.

"Has he really?"

"He certainly has and if have my way she is going to be the one for me." He said this with more conviction than he had ever possessed.

"Is she really?" Pop said to nobody in particular. "Is she really?" He went inside and got another beer from the cellar, returning to the bench to enjoy the rest of the evening in the relative bliss of solitude, while wondering about his young friend's future.

Chapter 4

Spring 1966

Harry and Jenny Sunderland lived at Salem, a large house just off the York Road, going north out of Smawthorne. As with most towns in South Yorkshire, the more desirable residential areas were to the north, closer to the Dales, the Yorkshire Moors and the coast. There was no westerly wind to blow the industrial grime from the south-west to the north-east as there was over the Pennines in Lancashire. Smawthorne, like the other towns on the Yorkshire coalfield, was dominated by the winding gear and slag heaps of the local collieries, with the occasional coke ovens and glassworks to give variety. Those who had lived all their lives in these grimy towns, took the coal dust and dirt for granted. Housewives were careful how long the washing was left on the line. If they trimmed the ubiquitous privet hedges, they expected to look like a miner after a shift at the coalface. Blackbirds, sparrows and starlings were all the same colour to a child growing up on the Yorkshire coalfield: grey black.

One of the few consolations of the dirt and grime, was that since most of the industry was below ground, the towns themselves, the urban areas, were relatively compact. There was less of the urban sprawl that characterised the industrial towns of Lancashire, where you could drive 20 or 30 miles across Greater Manchester without leaving a built-up area. The grim pit villages and mining towns of South Yorkshire sat next to some of the most beautiful countryside in England. To the north was the Vale of York, and to the east the Yorkshire Wolds. The Sunderland's house was just where the open countryside began.

It stood well back from the road, behind a large hedge that opened onto a long sweeping gravel drive. The house was very much 'arts and crafts.' If not designed by Charles Voysey, and it probably wasn't, it was very much in that style. It was constructed in soft, red handmade bricks that had mellowed gently over the years. The elaborate hips and gables of the roof were finished in Westmorland green slate and surmounted by richly detailed chimneys in the same handmade brickwork. The entrance was beneath a large oak framed porch, with elegant dormer windows puncturing the line of the eaves above. Unlike much of the inept stockbrokers' Tudor style that characterised most of the other houses on the edge of town, Salem looked like the real thing.

Harry's admiralty-blue Rover was parked in front of a sizeable oak framed double garage. It very much looked the part. Sitting next to it, with deferential feminine elegance, was a small sky-blue Alfa Romeo. As Adam crunched over the gravel in Pop's beat up

MG, he couldn't help thinking of one of Uncle Harry's favourite quotations, 'Seek ye first the kingdom of heaven and all these things shall be added unto you.' He looked again at the front of the house and the elegant cars and thought to himself, added on to you? It certainly has been.

He had already worked out that not all the brethren lived in the same style as the Sunderland's. They seemed to be the economic outliers. Most of the congregation were predominantly, although not exclusively, middle-class. He had wondered whether, "The things being added on to you," were added in proportion, or even inverse proportion to the energy with which they were sought. He was, however, still too young to fully appreciate the chaotic nature of divine providence, or the full effects of time and chance on the Almighty's creation. He would get there eventually.

Before Adam reached the oak framed entrance porch he was greeted by an attractive middle-aged woman, coming around the side of the house and carrying a basket of cut flowers and herbs. She put the basket down and removed her gardening gloves.

"You must be Adam. Harry has told me so much about you, I'm Jenny."

The introduction was entirely unnecessary. Jenny was the image of her daughter with the same straw-blonde hair, if more carefully groomed. She had the same easy grace and confidence, no doubt cultivated in these fine surroundings. Her make-up had been applied with that skill and care unique to the affluent classes, that gives the impression that there is no make-up. Such sophistication was very striking to an impressionable teenager like Adam.

"That's a very interesting car you have there," wandering over to have a closer look. Adam explained who it belonged to and how he had been loaned it for the weekend, as a reward for passing his test. Opening the passenger door and glancing up at him beneath her blonde hair, she said,

"May I?" and without waiting for a reply, elegantly dropped down onto the worn red leather of the cramped passenger seat.

"You must take me out in this sometime. Would you do that for me?" She was looking at him with a charm and intensity he found more than a little disturbing. Had she been younger he would have assumed he was being propositioned. He was too young to recognise when an attempt was being made to suborn him.

To his great relief they were interrupted by other cars coming up the drive. Sadly, these included Roger's Mini Cooper.

Soon, all the guests for Sunday lunch were assembled in the large dining room. Slim and Damien were handing out drinks, beer for the men and a glass of sherry for the ladies. Adam noticed nobody had been asked what they might want, though no one seemed to be complaining. The rugby season had started, and Slim, as usual, was proudly displaying his battle scars, above his right eye and down the side of his cheek. Adam thought he looked a larger, and more imposing figure than ever. Although he had gone to Leeds to study architecture, he was still living at home. Adam was not sure if it was his choice, or the result of combined pressure from his father and uncle. He suspected it was the latter.

Rachel had not yet made an appearance, being heavily involved in the kitchen. Adam would note that there were many differences between Sunday lunch at Salem and 39 Lumley Street, but in both places the kitchen was the exclusive domain of the women. Adam wondered if, later on in the day, Harry would be in there, preparing mushy peas and meat sandwiches like his father. He suspected not.

There were two more significant and serious differences between Sunday lunch in the different locations. One, for which Adam had been prepared, but still found unforgivable, was that the Yorkshire puddings, if served at all, would arrive with the meat and vegetables! The other difference was that everything was on a far grander scale. The large dining room was dominated by a vast reproduction regency table with ten chairs and matching mahogany sideboard, replete with twin multi-branch silver candlesticks. The only things missing were two liveried servants standing on either side of the head of table. The dining room was strangely out of character with the rest of the furnishings in the house, which were much more consistent with 19th century arts and crafts architecture. It suggested there was somebody in the house with a better sense of interior design than whoever did the dining room.

The fake Regency dining tables were a strange feature of the houses of the aspiring English middle classes of post-war Britain. Acquired by people who wished to be thought of as men and women of taste and judgement. Since such furniture in the past was the choice of the aristocrats and the landed gentry, by definition, people of taste and judgement, it naturally followed that if you bought yourself the said dining table, Q.E.D. you were a person of taste and judgement. You did not need to exercise any taste or judgement at all. It was much the same, with the turkey-red hall carpet and the hunting scenes hanging on the walls.

This was the first time Adam had seen all the family together, and very agreeable company they were. Slim's father, although carved from the same block of granite as his brother and son, was quite different. Walter was a quieter and gentler man, who had been playing second fiddle to his younger brother for years, yet seemed entirely content with the role. His wife was less so. Felicity had the same generous nature as Walter, but was clearly less tolerant of her brother-in-law. Harry may have been a great talker, but Walter and Felicity were both good listeners and made Adam feel more welcome than might otherwise have been the case.

The atmosphere, as the food was served in large willow pattern tureens, with the Yorkshire puddings, was relaxed and convivial. The puddings had clearly been out of the oven far too long, but Adam thought it best not to comment. Slim, however, did not let the moment pass and holding his plate with the remaining overcooked objects, said with a mischievous grin, "Pass these down to Adam they're his favourites."

He tried to soften them with the gravy, but that was not much better. There was much knockabout, self-deprecating humour, everything being nudged along by old family jokes and anecdotes that they kindly took the trouble to explain to their guest. Only Damien and his new wife, Gaynor, seemed on edge, if not entirely preoccupied. Adam sensed that she was a little intimidated by the occasion, and who could really blame her. She was quiet for most of the lunch, but to be fair, it was not easy to get a word in with the Sunderland's in full flow. Adam had some sympathy. She was young, not much older than Rachel, and such occasions must have been something of an ordeal.

Gaynor was short and petite. She had clearly made an effort, in her smart lilac two-piece suit and white blouse. She didn't have her mother in-law's talent with make up as it was all a little overdone. Combined with the hair, elaborately piled up on top, she gave the distinct impression of trying too hard. Everyone around the table, except Adam, was a member of the local assembly, some second or third generation. Gaynor however, 'had come in from outside' as indeed Adam might one day. She was the daughter of a local builder in Wakefield. Damien was very smitten, but he knew that if he wanted to marry her, she would have to 'come in.' She would have to join the assembly. Slim had explained the situation with, of course, all the necessary biblical quotes. 'Be ye not unequally yoked together with unbelievers." (2nd Corinthians 6v4.) So, after a brief period of instruction by the kindly Walter, she was duly baptised and married shortly afterwards. Everyone was pleased, particularly Gaynor, who regarded Damien as quite a catch. She may have been a little quiet over lunch, but Gaynor knew what she was about.

The other difference with Sunday lunch at Salem, was that after the opening humour, the conversation changed. Usually prompted by Harry, sitting at the top of the table with the remains of the enormous piece of beef in front of him, but without the liveried servants standing on either side, the conversation turned to 'The Way' – 'The Way' being the definite article. The brethren didn't speak of the church, or the faith, or the chapel. It was 'The Way'. You were either in 'The Way' or not, and Gaynor had joined. They all sought to teach, follow or keep 'The Way'. Some people sadly left it. It only became confusing when Rachel came in with the apple pie and told Slim to get out of the way, much to everybody's amusement. Adam, naturally, was slow to get the joke.

The conversation, often more of a debate, was usually based around the teachings in the assembly that particular morning. Today that had been the increasingly familiar subject of watching, 'The signs of the times, watching Israel.' This was of course Harry's great theme that Adam had heard him speak of on previous occasions. Harry warmed to the subject.

"Mark my words everybody, there are going to be great events taking place in the Middle East in the next few years. The time is short! God's people are threatened on every side, just as Jesus and the prophets foretold, 'when you see Jerusalem surrounded by armies, know that her desolation is at hand.'" He went on in a similar vein quoting various passages of the Bible with an accuracy that Adam thought impressive, although he had no way of checking it.

"We are living in the last days, Adam." Harry turned his gaze on him,

"The King of the North will come down on Jerusalem to take a great spoil, Gog and Magog and all the armies."

"Who is the King of the North?" Adam asked innocently, worried that he was probably supposed to know by now.

"Russia, of course!" Harry exclaimed. "Moscow is directly north of Jerusalem." Adam thought to himself, so are Lebanon, Syria and Turkey, but Walter mercifully interrupted the conversation,

"Leave the lad alone Harry, you haven't invited him here just to give him a lecture." Rachel leaned across to her mum at the other end of the table, and in a whisper that she clearly intended everyone to hear, said,

"I am not sure Uncle Walter's quite right about that." The two women looked even more alike as their heads briefly came together, obviously of the same mind. Jenny, smiling, put her hand gently on her daughter's as if to say, 'leave it there'.

"Well," Harry concluded, "you just watch what's going to happen."

Walter took charge of the conversation for a while and matters turned to issues more pastoral, who was well and who was not, who needed a visit or some other help. These seemed to be more the concern of Walter and Felicity than they were to Harry. Adam had noticed that there was always mutual help and support amongst the members of the assembly. Few lived like Harry and Walter, but nobody seemed to be left behind.

It wasn't clear if Slim's architectural studies came under the subject of welfare but Uncle Harry raised it any way.

"How's university treating you Slim, what's the world of architecture like?"

"Well, it's certainly different from school."

63

"How's that?" Adam asked.

"Well at school, most of the time, you go to lessons, try to remember what you hear, read the books, learn your stuff and put it down in the examination when you are either right or wrong. There is still some of that kind of stuff, but the course is more about ideas, imagination and creativity, it takes some getting used to. I've been spending most of my time on the drawing board for the last three months. It's quite challenging and some people find it easier than others." The implication was that he was one of the others. Pausing, he added, while pointing to the cuts and bruises on the side of his face,

"The rugby is good, though."

"You be careful at that university," Damien interjected, "there's plenty going on there that can lead a young man astray." Gaynor, at his side, dutifully nodded in willing support. Damien's attempt at Gamaliel like wisdom sounded somewhat unconvincing and prompted one of the few awkward silences of the afternoon. Damien, presumably, was keen to diminish the value of anything he was not likely to possess. Walter rescued them both.

"Slim's okay, aren't you lad, he knows where his priorities are. Slim knows 'The Way'." There's that phrase again Adam thought. The language did take some getting used to. Changing the subject, to everybody's relief, Walter asked,

"How about you Adam, have you decided what you're going to do? I mean, you're not going to spend the rest of your life digging holes for street lamps and cleaning traffic signs?"

"No, I don't think so, but it certainly keeps me fit for rugby."

"Harry and I have an idea that you may be interested in. Let's go and sit in the drawing room and let the ladies get on with their clearing up." A number of ladies' eyes met, the older ones with patient resignation, one of the younger ones with obvious resentment.

The four men made themselves comfortable among the floral cushion covers of the large drawing-room sofas. Roger had been unusually quiet all afternoon, and making his apologies had shot off early in his usual shower of gravel. Adam sensed that there had been something of an issue between him and Rachel and there was an atmosphere around the two of them throughout lunch. He hoped it was nothing trivial.

"Come on Harry, tell him what we've got in mind."

"Well, Adam," Harry began, "we have been thinking, Walter's side of the business is a bit under pressure at the moment, he is inundated with a lot of surveying work, and we need more help. We need someone to hold the other end of the tape, carry the ranging rods, help with the driving and record keeping. We wondered if you might be interested. If it suits you, if you enjoyed it, you could think about taking it up full-time and train to be a chartered surveyor. We will be happy to sponsor you. There are correspondence courses, night-school classes and day release available. Slim says you're clever enough to do whatever you like. I hear you did well in A-level maths, which is perfect for surveying. What do you think? We reckon it might be just the thing for you, don't we Damien?" Damien didn't say much, but he probably didn't have much he wanted to say.

Adam was taken aback.

"To be honest I have not much idea what a chartered surveyor does."

"Spend a bit of time with us and you will find out. You will be working with Damien and he can show you the ropes, or more accurately, the level and the theodolite."

"You might even learn something about development," added Harry, "what have you got to lose, the Street-lighting Department's loss could be our gain."

Adam had to admit, he had nothing to lose, nothing at all, other than blisters on his hands and a sore back.

"It sounds good, interesting. I might as well give it a go. Thanks very much."

"You'll probably find it pays better than labouring for the council." That sounded good were it not for Harry adding, "Eventually!"

Later, when he reflected on what had happened, he felt it was all very sudden. One minute he was having lunch with a bunch of relative strangers, the next he had accepted a new job. He had spent the last three and a half months fending off his mother's and father's questions about what he was going to do with his life, so he didn't regret saying yes. In fact, the more he thought about it, the more interesting the idea became. And the idea of being a chartered surveyor would probably be just the kind of thing that would placate his parents' anxieties. His anxieties, if he had any, were just that he felt he was being swept along with the tide of Harry's latest plan. He didn't want to say no to the offer, but if he had, he was not sure he would have known how. "Excellent," Walter had said, "that's settled then." And Slim, right on cue, had stood up and demanded that Adam show him the amazing car he had arrived in.

"It will be a tight fit for you, mate" Adam suggested, heading for the door. As they were leaving, he sensed the other three men were moving on to the next item of Harry's Sunday afternoon agenda. Damien was opening up a set of drawings and laying them out across the coffee table.

Wandering out across the gravel together, Adam suggested that the others looked like they had more important matters to discuss than an old car. "Looks like serious business in there."

"It's certainly serious business to Damien and Gaynor. They have found a plot of land north of Wakefield, near to Gaynor's mum and dad. They think it might get planning permission for a new house. Damien is trying to get his dad to buy it cheap, without planning permission and take a risk."

"Do you think he will?"

"Uncle Harry rarely takes risks. He may look like he does, but usually there is far less risk than might appear."

"I don't understand." The big prop put his huge arm across the flanker's shoulders and said with a wry smile,

"If you do spend a bit of time with the two of them at the office, I am sure you will get the idea."

Adam was right about Slim and the car. He just about managed to get into the passenger seat, but in truth, only part of him was actually in the car, the rest was hanging out over the low slung door and the spare wheel at the back. The car was definitely a better fit for his auntie.

"Come on," said Slim, ever the optimist, trying to find somewhere to put his left leg, "take me for a quick spin down the road."

* * *

Pushing a stone that wants to roll is easy, but also difficult to stop. Damien was just such a stone and Gaynor was eager to push. The two of them had lived in the neat little detached house on the other side of the town since they were married. It had been funded by the two fathers, but Damien's father had paid the lion-share of the house and for all of the furnishings. Gaynor had not settled well in the town, but she probably hadn't intended to. Gaynor had her eye on the next thing. She would always have an eye on the next thing, and knew well enough how to adjust her husband's focus. The next 'thing' at the moment was a new house close to her mum and dad in Wakefield. A bespoke architect designed house on its own plot, double fronted, Georgian sash windows and stone columns around the door. She had seen the grotesque design in the Daily Mail Book of House Plans. The precise specifications she was keeping to herself. All Damien needed to know was the location, closer to her mother and further away from her father-in-law.

Father-in-law might have the means to control Damien at work. He and all the brethren might even be able to control him on a Sunday, but at home, Gaynor had all the means of control necessary and intended to exercise them to the full. The extent of her project was not fully understood by Damien's father. Indeed, it was not fully understood by Damien. Only Jenny had an idea of what was going on. She felt that her son and daughter-in-law were well suited to one another. This was the truth, and for many reasons, it left her disappointed. It was not the first disappointment of her married life. Whether their mutual compatibility would make them happy she couldn't say. She doubted it, but happiness from her own experience was a rare flower that rarely bloomed for long. She doubted that her husband was really happy. Perhaps he had settled for success instead.

It said a great deal about Harry and Jenny's relationship, that although Harry was a great fan of new gadgets, the only gadget they did not have in the well-appointed house was a dishwasher. The dishwashers were just finishing their sisterly duties. Collecting the wet tea towels, Jenny suggested it was time they went and found out what the men were up to. She noticed Gaynor had been looking particularly preoccupied in the kitchen and seemed keen to join her husband. There was something else that she had noticed about Gaynor that no one had mentioned yet. Perhaps someone might be mentioning it soon. Taking Rachel by the arm, and holding her back a moment, she whispered, "This should be interesting love," giving her daughter's arm an affectionate squeeze.

The conversation had not gone entirely to Damien's satisfaction. Walter and Harry could both see the potential. It was a good sized, south facing plot backing onto woodland. Although it was not part of the green belt, neither was it within the area included by the

Wakefield Council development plan for residential use. It was something of an anomaly. The elderly couple who had owned it for years wanted to sell. Apparently, they needed the money and although the price was not as low as a basic agricultural value, it was significantly less than it would command with full planning permission.

Walter clearly felt, and almost said, that he thought Damien and Gaynor were getting a bit ahead of themselves, and a little more effort put into the business would be appropriate before these kind of aspirations were realised. Harry didn't entirely disagree, but it was unquestionably a good opportunity and well found by Damien, or was it Gaynor? A vendor needing to sell a prime piece of land at a low price was difficult for any developer to ignore. It was contrary to Harry's natural instincts. He knew Walter was right about the children, but Damien was his son, and not for the first time in his life, he felt himself conflicted. It wouldn't do the two of them any harm to wait a few years, but there was the opportunity, a ripe plum waiting to be plucked.

The ladies came in just as the debate had reached this awkward impasse. Gaynor sat down beside her husband, taking his hand and looking at him for some indication of how the conversation had gone. Rachel perched herself on the arm of the sofa next to her mother, wondering what was going to be so interesting.

"All done in there? "Harry asked, somewhat obviously. Rachel was tempted to say, "Hell no Dad, we've been smoking dope in the back garden for the last hour and thought we would leave the washing up to you! Instead, Gaynor made one of her few interjections of the afternoon.

"Well we have got a little announcement to make, haven't we love?" Jenny looked up at her daughter giving her a knowing wink. Seizing Damien's hand again and looking demurely down at the Persian rug at her tiny feet, she announced, "We're going to have a baby."

The news was greeted with customary joy and delight, much hugging, kissing and back slapping, especially from the future grandfather, who immediately went looking for champagne, missing all the women's questioning. How are you feeling? When is it due? Do you want a boy or a girl? Have you told your mum and dad? Most of them were obvious for, of course, she had told her mum and dad first. She looked the picture of health. It was clearly going to be a spring baby, and as for the gender, they would accept anything that divine providence provided.

Harry returned with two bottles. Not many residents of Smawthorne would have had two chilled bottles of champagne and a handful of flutes ready at a moment's notice.

"Rachel love, will you go and get the other flutes?" When all the glasses were charged, Harry and Jenny went to sit down with the two expectant parents and proposed a toast to the new baby, to much cheering and general adulation. It was probably only Jenny who anticipated what came next, although later she wondered if she had imagined her own perspicacity. Before the jubilation had died down, Gaynor leaned across to her father-in-law, placing her little hand upon his enormous knee and quietly said,

"So you can see it would be so nice to have a new house ready for the new family, wouldn't it Grandpa?"

She hadn't actually said, 'Okay, I am going to provide the son and heir, how about your coming up with the accommodation', but there was no need. Harry sipped the champagne thoughtfully and replied,

"I will need to make a few enquiries. There are one or two folk I need to have a quiet word with. It may take a while, but I'll see what I can do." Grandpa leaned back on the sofa, deep in thought. Gaynor looked at her husband for a translation and he nodded to confirm it had been a job well done.

Jenny smiled somewhat smugly at Rachel, but with no pleasure. She was having to confront a truth that she would rather not own. A truth she had hidden for too many years now. She was ashamed of it, deeply ashamed. She wanted to deny it, put it away somewhere, somewhere it could be forgotten and never found. But there it was in the living room, large as life. When she heard the news that Damien and Gaynor were expecting a child, that they were going to be grandparents, she had to admit the truth of it – she did not love her son. She did not love Damien. What kind of a mother she wondered didn't love their own son? Did it start when she stopped loving her husband? In which order had this shameful course of events occurred. It hardly mattered, it had happened.

Perhaps those who knew and disliked Damien, of whom there were a few, might not be so surprised. He was, Jenny had to admit, not particularly likeable. It was unfortunate, but sometimes that's just how it is. He was so much his father's son, but without Harry's redeeming features. Harry may have been self-obsessed, chauvinistic and controlling, but he was also clever, hard-working and a good and generous provider. He truly believed the things he taught and preached. He gave a great deal of time to the brethren with his lecture tours. He was able and in great demand, even if such things only further flattered his ego and his overdeveloped self-regard.

But poor Damien, he had all his father's ambition, self-obsession and arrogant chauvinism, but without the brain or the diligence, and certainly not his father's generosity of spirit. He had joined the assembly as a young man, along with his peers. He wanted to be the powerful orator and teacher his father was. In this he was the most tragic figure of all – the one who doesn't know, and doesn't know he doesn't know. For his lack of self-awareness, Jenny should have felt sorry for him. Perhaps she did feel a little sympathy, but that wasn't the same as loving him.

She sometimes wondered if his commitment to his religion was little more than having got the best of things in this life, he was anxious to ensure that he got the same in the next.

But, for whatever reason, when the news came that Damien was going to become a father and her a grandmother, she was not filled with the joy she should have felt. She could not escape the shameful knowledge that she did not love her son. The only question that remained was, would he ever notice?

The lounge doors opened to reveal two windswept teenagers.

"That's one amazing car Adam has out there…" Slim stopped in mid-sentence, looking at the bottles of champagne and half empty glasses.

"Come on lads," exclaimed Harry, "you've missed all the news."

Adam waited for the celebrations to die down and then felt he should make his excuses and leave the family to their celebrations. He said goodbye to everyone and thanked Harry for the job. It was only when outside that he realised he had only thanked Harry and not Walter, but that was the effect that Harry tended to have on people. As Slim got up and followed Adam out, Jenny grabbed Rachel's arm and said,

"Come and have a look at Adam's brilliant car." Rachel wasn't particularly interested, but was always happy to please her mother, so was drawn along by her enthusiasm. It would also give her a chance to speak to Adam out of earshot of her father. She may not have been interested in the MG, but her mother was full of questions: when was it made, how long had Pop had it, had it always been bright red?

"Come on Rachel," she insisted, "Adam will take you for a spin, won't you Adam?" There was that disconcerting look again, the charming smile and penetrating blue eyes. Of course Adam would, there was nothing he would like to do more. Well, nothing you could do in a MG TA. Jenny expertly helped her daughter into the passenger seat and waved them off for the briefest of trips down the road and back. She was there when they returned, standing on the drive, smiling with her arms folded. Seeing her, Adam said,

"I quite like your mum." In code, "I quite like you."

"I think my mum quite likes you." In code, "I think I quite like you too."

Chapter 5

Spring 1967

Adam had mostly enjoyed his time following Damien around the North of England, learning how to be a surveyor. He liked the work, the freedom and the driving. Damien was hard work at times, needing Adam's help, but not really wanting him around. He had quickly got the hang of it, the ranging rods, the surveyor's chain and even mastered the complexities of the level and theodolite. The brothers had been right, he was well-suited to it. His mathematical skills and orderly and methodical mind would make him a natural surveyor. More than anything, he was enjoying doing something practical. Adam was essentially a practical man, who wanted to know 'what' and 'how', the 'whys' he was content to leave to others, such as his sister.

By the start of the new year, it had become clear that with the minimum of help he could manage the surveying on his own, or at least, without Damien. This suited Damien very well, as his immediate and most pressing priority was to secure the site in Wakefield, which was not progressing as quickly or as smoothly as Gaynor had hoped. Things rarely went as quickly as Gaynor hoped.

The brothers could see Adam's potential, and were keen to take him on as a permanent trainee. They had sponsored him at the College of Estate Management and enrolled him on its correspondence courses where evening classes and day release were available. This was not just self-interest with Walter and Harry, they liked to see themselves as mentors and sponsors of young talent. Harry, in particular, had taken a shine to Adam. As is often the case with intelligent and highly-successful businessmen, their children, particularly the 'heirs apparent,' are often something of a disappointment. Harry loved his son, but he was less than he had hoped for. Whatever he had hoped for, he appeared to find in Adam. It was an inconvenient truth that would not escape Damien or Gaynor, and over the years, would add to a growing resentment.

Adam's mother may have been disappointed at how events were unfolding, but not in her son. She believed he had grown into a decent, caring and intelligent young man, someone of whom she and Hector could be proud. She tried to remember who first said, "Life is what happens, while you're making other plans." Night school and day release at the local college was not what she intended, but then, life *had* happened.

She was pleased about the job and her son's general transformation. The mahogany table in the back bedroom was witnessing a level of endeavour and hard work that had been lacking in earlier years. The shelves around the room were now stacked with books on building construction, land surveying and property law. There was even a drawing board and T-square in regular use. Ring binders, filled with lecture notes, essays and worksheets lined the walls. It was a regular hive of industry. She could not help but be pleased at the Damascene conversion the Sunderland's had brought about, but was, of course, less happy with the other events along the Damascus road.

Cleaning the top of the wardrobe, she felt slightly let down to discover that in place of the Playboy magazine and Lady Chatterley's Lover, there were shamefully hidden copies of Where Christianity Went Wrong, and Israel and Divine Providence in the Last Days. This concerned her far more than she ever been about the erotica and hoped that her son had passed the copies onto some other deserving and curious adolescent, rather than destroy them out of a misplaced sense of shame.

Julia believed that her brother's increasing interest in the Assemblies of Christ and their biblical fundamentalism was down to the new job, Harry Sunderland's influence, and the obvious attractions of his daughter. He had got the lot – romance, religion and employment, 'and these three are one,' she would observe with her university trained wit.

This was true, but it was not 'The Truth!' Not the whole truth. Mother believed that there was something about this particular take on religion, this formulaic fundamentalism, that resonated in Adam's imagination. She was right, but she could not know how she was right. She wasn't there in the study classes at the assembly, she wasn't privy to the long conversations he had with Slim long into the night, and she had not sat there with his new peer group, as they collectively embraced what to them was a clear, reasonable and compelling narrative.

Adam, she tried to tell herself, was no different than any other bright teenager trying to make sense of his life; trying to find order and purpose in a random and chaotic world. Then along came Slim, someone he liked and respected, with nice friends and charismatic leaders, who had said to him "This is it, this is *The Way*." It is neat and tidy, it's in this book, it's in this box, look how it all makes sense, look how it all fits together, check it out...So he did check it out, and it did make sense. And what's more, this was the only way, it was right and everyone else was wrong. That radical idea was particularly attractive to the young teenager. And the more Adam applied his precise, methodical mind, the more it fitted together, within its own terms and within its own box. It was not religion by revelation and blind faith, it was religion by consideration and sound reason. Probably for Adam, it was the only religion that would take hold.

Rachel was yet another problem for his mother. Even if she were the Delilah, tempting her son away from the path she had planned for him, she could not help but like the girl. She was the kind of sweet, intelligent young woman that any mother would be glad to see her son bring home, were it not for the 'religion thing.' She found it difficult to work out exactly what was going on – Adam was clearly smitten, but there seemed to be some kind of ménage à trois. How the eccentric Roger fitted in, she had no idea, and like any mother, hoped her son was not going to get hurt.

Sitting alone at the dining room table, surrounded by the papers and paraphernalia her own passions, she told herself that Adam was not in a bad place. He was working hard and studying, still enjoying his rugby and regularly helping out with Pop. He was keeping out of trouble and might even have a nice girlfriend. If anything, she was becoming more concerned about what Julia was getting up to at university.

It was another Sunday afternoon and Mother was in her kitchen. Where else would she be? Hector was in the Black Horse Tavern with Pop. Where else would they be? All things remained the same, yet everything was changing. With Julia becoming more involved in university life, and Adam his time at work, the Sunday roast was often smaller, and enjoyed by fewer folk at the table. But today, both children had promised to make an appearance. Adam had asked if he could bring Slim along. It would not be the first time he had sat around the dining table at number 39. Both Hector and Mother liked the lad, and usually would have looked forward to seeing him. He was always cheerful, good-natured and careful not to go on too much about religion. This Sunday would, however, be the first time that Slim had broken bread with Julia, and there lay the source of Mother's anxiety. Slim may not be inclined to 'go on' but the same could not be said about Julia.

Mother had sent her daughter to university in the hope she would receive the broad and expansive liberal education she had been denied, and still craved. She had wanted Julia exposed to new ideas, to have an open and enquiring mind and the best of intellectual opportunities. However, she now recalled her own mother's advice, "Be careful what you wish for girl." Julia had thrown herself into university life from day one. The academic work was interesting, but not particularly demanding. Attending the requisite number of lectures and seminars, and submitting the necessary essays each week presented few problems, leaving most of the time for what she described to her mother, as 'growing political interests'. The Daily Mail hyperbole would have described it as student anarchy and Marxist provocation. She had become friendly with a graduate student at the London School of Economics and together they were actively involved in the anti-apartheid movement and anti-Vietnam war demonstrations. The latest adventure had them conspicuously involved in a student sitting at the LSE.

Mother's difficulty was that she approved of most of these causes in principle, but in practice, they could be a bit of a nuisance. Her more immediate difficulty was how she could keep the peace between her children for the next two or three hours over lunch. Julia, who may have been strongly against conflict in Southeast Asia, would be more than ready, nay eager for it this afternoon in South West Yorkshire. Hector had had a Henry Kissinger type word with her about a peace movement at No 39, but he was no more optimistic of success than Henry would been some months later in Hanoi.

Lunch had been put back an hour, to give Adam and Slim time to spend with Hector and Pop in the Black Horse after the service at the assembly. This might also give Julia, who was always late, a chance of being there on time. Sitting in his usual spot by the fireplace, with two bright young men, and one much older, Hector was content. It was the first time that Slim had met Pop, and, keen to show an interest said,

"That's a great little MG you've got Mr Featherstone, you don't see many of those on the road these days." Pop looked suspiciously at Adam, and his usual cheerful demeanour seemed to desert him.

"How do you know about my MG?" he asked, clearly irritated at the enquiry.

"Is it pre-war or the 1940s?" Slim continued innocently, as Adam wondered what had got into Pop. Slim explained how Adam had brought it around to his uncle's house and how everyone loved it. Pop took a deep swig of his pint, and wiping his mouth with the sleeve of Hector's old suit jacket replied,

"I didn't lend you that car Adam for you to go showing off to every Tom, Dick and Harry in the district." Adam and Hector were taken aback, it was all completely out of character. Pop had never spoken an ill word to them in all the years they had known him. Adam looked across to Pop for some kind of explanation, but the old man was fully absorbed in his pint, and his own thoughts.

Slim, as ever, sought to rescue the awkward moment he had unwittingly created, and looking at his watch asked, "What time do these famous Yorkshire puddings you promised me come out of the oven?"

"Crikey!" exclaimed Hector pretending they were late, "Time we were getting back, "Now you two remember what we agreed about Julia and the entente cordiale."

Pop was slow walking back to the house, and Adam and Slim went on ahead.

"Are you okay Pop?" Hector asked when the two were alone.

"I'm fine mate, take no notice of me, I am sorry for snapping, I think I must be getting grumpy in my old age." He had clearly recovered his usual good nature. "It'll be a grand lunch waiting for us, you are very fortunate with that wife of yours and so am I", adding an unnecessary attempt to redeem himself.

The two boys arrived at number 39 just in time to see Julia clumsily exiting the passenger door of a beat-up old Citroen 2CV. She was hampered by the long Afghan goat coat and tweed skirt that were wrapped around her ankles, as well as a bottle of red wine in each hand. Everything had changed about her since going to university. Her hair was all over the place, controlled only by a red bandanna and John Lennon glasses perched on the end of her turned up nose. She hoped to give the impression that everything had just been thrown together, but of course, nothing could be further from the truth. Every item was carefully considered to make just the right statement. A tall, bearded man in jeans and t-shirt was more expertly climbing out of the other side of the car. He carelessly kicked the door shut behind him. Any marks this might have left on the door panel would have been indistinguishable from the myriad of dents and scratches that decorated the rest of the bodywork. This, Adam suspected, was the unlikely, and today, unexpected boyfriend he had heard so much about.

"Hi Sis, you remember Slim." and turning to her companion, "I'm Adam, you must be..." No good, he couldn't remember the name.

"Jerome," came the helpful response. Surely Adam thought to himself, I should have remembered that. Pop and Hector arrived just as the introductions were complete.

"Hi Dad, I hope you don't mind me bringing Jerome along, I would have rung, but you know, it was all a bit last-minute and he's been dying to meet you all, haven't you darling." Darling is it? Hector thought glancing at Pop, whose eyes briefly and imperceptibly looked up to the heavens. Jerome grabbed both men's hands enthusiastically, explaining how keen he was to share in the famous Sunday lunch at Lumley Street.

"Most people are!" commented Pop, smiling and clearly back to his cheerful self. As the two men followed the younger generation into the house, Hector put his arm around his old friend's shoulders,

"Well, it should be an interesting lunch today!"

"I don't suppose we can go back to the pub?" he quipped.

Of all the qualities that Hector admired in his wife, and there were many, her ability to cope with any given situation, without drama or fuss was one he prized above all others. Mother hated fuss, she couldn't do with people who, as she would put it, 'made it too many feet marks'. An extra place was set and the perfect Yorkshire puddings appeared from the oven, along with the massive gravy jug. Producing the corkscrew, which only she would have been able to locate at short notice, she handed it to Jerome, thanking him for the kind gift and asking him to do the honours. Sunday lunch happened, the puddings were consumed and duly praised, the beef was sliced even thinner than usual, and the numerous tureens, now bereft of any vegetables, left abandoned on the table.

There was the usual relaxed air of conviviality around the table as Jerome opened the second bottle of wine, while Mother spread out the cheeses. The conversation had gone well. Adam had enthused about the joys of land surveying, Slim was quizzed on how his studies were progressing, and Jerome was entertaining and voluble about life at the LSE and his postgraduate research into the questionable successes of the World Bank in West Africa. Heady stuff for 39, Lumley Street! Everyone was paying him polite interest and attention except Pop who, as usual by this time on a Sunday afternoon, was drifting off.

Later in the evening, when alone in the peace of the living room, Hector reflected that it was probably the second bottle of wine, on top of the beer in the pub and whatever Julia had consumed before arriving, which had ultimately broached the dam. The pressure had been building, particularly with the unusually subdued Julia. Her restraint was, no doubt, out of deference to Jerome's presence. She did not wish to detract from his opining on the problems of exporting Western economic models into underdeveloped postcolonial possessions, or American imperialist adventures in Vietnam, or whatever else it was he had been going on about. But as Adam and Mother came back from the kitchen with the coffee, Julia was leaning forward, empty glass of wine in hand saying,

"So Slim, tell us what the sermon was about this morning?" The implicit provocation of the question, which was all too obvious to her family was lost on

Slim's good nature. Adam knew what was going to happen because he knew Slim. He tried vainly to avoid the inevitable. "Leave him alone Julia you're not really interested." Jerome, mindful of his status as a guest in his girlfriend's parents' house, tried to appear sociable and engaged.

"No, please Slim, we would be interested to know."

Slim would not presume to use Sunday lunch as an opportunity to preach, or to try to convert anyone. He was not naïve, but there was about him a simple decency and integrity, that if asked a direct question, he would give a straight answer. It was what Adam had first noticed and liked about him at the rugby club and school. He had no embarrassment about his faith as he was proud of it. Adam knew that he would answer Julia's question, convincingly and at length. He also knew that Julia had no interest in his answers.

Slim explained that the theme that Sunday was the outworking of Biblical prophecy in current world events. It was about how the Jews had always been witnesses of divine providence, and that the re-gathering of the Jews back into their ancient homeland in Israel after 2000 years, was proof that the Bible was the inerrant word of God. He added that we were all living at the End of Days. Treading on Jerome's academic toes, Slim had gone on to point out that it was more important to watch what was going on in the Middle East, than in Vietnam, South Africa or at the civil rights marches in the American South. All this was delivered in his easy-going style, complete with much chapter and verse, and to Adam, it all sounded very logical and reasonable. But he knew it was all a red rag to Julia's bull and wished that the ground would open up and consume him, or preferably her, like the rebellious Korah, Dathan and Abiram in the Book of Exodus.

Slim was about to launch onto the Rapture, when the faithful at the End of Days would be taken up into heaven to meet the returning Christ ('Two shall be grinding in the mill, one shall be taken and the other left') and would escape the destruction of the Battle of Armageddon, prior to the final judgement. Julia, however, felt she had sufficient information for her purposes, which were, of course, a good-natured, though scathing cross-examination of Slim's naïve Christian fundamentalism and religious bigotry. It was all rather unfair on him, because it was really her brother that she wanted to have a go at. Adam was the preferred target, Slim his proxy. These and other teachings of the assembly had cropped up in the past among the family, but Adam had hidden behind obfuscation and evasion and declined to engage. His mother and father generally preferred to leave it be as the 'elephant in the room.' But Julia, fuelled in part by the wine, saw this as the perfect opportunity.

To her growing frustration, the interrogation was going less well than she had anticipated. She didn't know her subject, or more accurately, she didn't know Slim's subject, as well as he did. She was a little bit like the atheist who tells the Rabbi all the reasons she didn't believe in his God, only to be told by the Rabbi that he didn't believe in that God either. She thought she knew what the Bible said, and she thought she knew what Slim believed, although she had not really been listening to him. The problem was, Slim knew his Bible better than she did, better than anyone around the table. He was better prepared for Julia's debate than she was, so long as it remained on his terms. Her difficulties were exacerbated by Slim's remarkable ability to stay calm, and not take offence or even notice her barbs of sarcasm. He responded to all her charges and insults in the detailed, logical and rational manner that members of the assembly were used to. Adam was relieved he didn't go and get his Bible and show them the actual texts.

The conviviality of the dining room had gone for the moment. Slim and Julia were centre stage. Adam looked down at the crumbs of cheese on his plate, wishing he was not there. Jerome was holding Julia's hand, whether in support or restraint was not clear. Pop, as usual, had fallen asleep in the chair and Hector was more concerned about the possibility of his sliding under the table than anything else that was going on around him. Mother, on the other hand, was observing it all, as she often did. She was observing Slim and was impressed. She was not persuaded, but neither was she surprised. She had heard similar ideas in the past. It was Slim himself that impressed her; his obvious integrity and sincerity, his gentleness contained within the massive frame, and in particular, his ability under severe pressure to remain calm and argue convincingly for what, to most of them, was an extraordinary and eccentric point of view. She thought he was wrong, but she had no idea how to tell him. Mother, probably, understood for the first time how Adam had been drawn in. She could see how the combination of this likeable lad's friendship, combined with a set of apparently simple and rational ideas might appeal to her son's nature. She could see how it might be the neat set of answers that he was looking for. It surprised her that she did not mind as much as she thought she would.

Julia, on the other hand, was minding a great deal, mainly because she was losing and losing publicly. She turned from questions and argument to assertion and ridicule.

"Palestine wasn't given to the Jews by God," she insisted. "It was given to them by Lord Balfour and Baron Rothschild. A Jew living in France, contacted an English Lord living in London, and gave a land that neither of them owned, occupied by people that they didn't know, to a nation that didn't exist, and landed the world with a problem that would probably never end!" It was clever and it was neat, but it cut no ice with Slim.

"The conflict will come to an end, Julia, and soon, just you watch." Julia was exasperated,

"You can't believe all this stuff just because it's written in an ancient book?" Feeling it was time he supported his friend, Adam joined in.

"Well you do, don't you? What about Dialectic Materialism or The rise of the Working Class, and the Dictatorship of the Proletariat. Didn't all those ideas come out of books, and by the way, have you both actually read 'Das Capital,' the Communist Manifesto, and Karl Marx's other impenetrable works? Or have you just read other people telling you what Marx wrote?"

"Anyway" he added, "parts of the Bible might be difficult to understand, but compared to Marx it is as clear as the Highway Code. And as far as I know Karl Marx has not correctly predicted world history as the Bible has!"

This time it was Hector who was impressed, as he had been having similar thoughts, not about Biblical prophecy, but wondering if he and Mother had managed to produce not one, but two ideological fundamentalists. Adam turned to his mother.

"You always told us to think for ourselves and to keep an open mind."

Julia murmured, not quite under her breath, "Not so open that your brains fall out!"

Hector, sensing that it was time for parental action, gently nudged Pop who immediately woke up.

"Is it time you were getting home Pop?"

"Yes, why don't you boys walk him back?" prompted Mother.

"That would be nice," said a bleary-eyed Pop. "You could have another look at the MG Slim, if you'd like." Pop was keen to offer a further olive branch to make amends for his earlier ill humour. Slim expressed his gratitude to Mother for a splendid lunch, and was surprised to be rewarded with a big hug and a kiss.

"Come and see us again sometime soon Slim, and next time we won't give you the third degree, will we Julia?" Julia knew what was coming next and soon both of them were in the kitchen surrounded by the washing-up. Hector had retreated into the shed and Jerome was left alone in the lounge with the Sunday papers, no doubt greatly relieved.

Both women were content with the kitchen and the time together.

"Feeling better are you love? Got it off your chest have you?" The reproach was gentle and not altogether unsympathetic.

"I don't think Slim minded that much Mum, although Adam probably did. But let's face it, Slim gave as good as he got. I think he was quite happy to talk about it all. But it's a bit weird, don't you think, the chosen few looking for the end of the world, convinced that only they understand it. Only one way? Only one truth? Interpreting everything that's going on in the world to fit in with their particular take on the Old Testament. And the Rapture! What the hell is the Rapture? 'One shall be taken and the other left' You know, I'm only concerned about Adam, he's my brother after all, I'm worried about him." Clearly, Julia hadn't got it all off her chest.

"What bothers me Mum, is his complete lack of interest or disregard for what's going on outside the assembly hall. The Americans are getting deeper and deeper into Vietnam, indiscriminately bombing civilian targets. In Alabama black people are fighting for their rights and look what's happening in Selma. If Adam wants a modern day prophet, he would be better looking to Martin Luther King or Bob Dylan and Joan Baez. Rhodesia is going the same way as South Africa and we are doing damn all about it. Slim and Adam are either disinterested, or see it all as some kind of prediluvian, godless world that foretells the end of the days. They should be more concerned about the plight of the Palestinians than eagerly looking for

Armageddon. Surely you and Dad must be worried about him."

She wanted to tell Julia that she was worried about both her children. She wanted to ask about her and Jerome, and sit-ins at the LSE, and demonstrations in Grosvenor Square. She wanted to know if her daughter was doing any serious work at university, but most of all, she wanted her daughter to get her hair done. Julia looked a mess. She wanted all this and much more, but the sink was empty, the draining board cleared, and she felt there had been more than enough confrontation for one Sunday. Calling Hector to come and say goodbye, she shooed the two of them out of the house and into the decrepit Citroen, where they waved them away. The car swayed alarmingly around the bend at the end of the road, as if it too had consumed a second bottle of wine.

"Well," he said, heading back to the sanctuary of his shed, "that all went off very well." This time the Radio Times found its mark. Picking the crumpled magazine up off the floor and placing it carefully on the hall table, he said to nobody in particular, "Never underestimate the power of the media."

It was a slow walk back to Pop's house as he was clearly tired, notwithstanding being asleep for most of the afternoon. Adam suggested that they forget about the car, but Pop insisted they see if they could get it started as it had not been out since the beginning of the year. It was now one of those glorious, late, warm afternoons that only occurred in June, when the broad orange sun is still high in the sky and has a long way to travel before dusk. Pop removed the padlock and the two boys carefully opened the dilapidated doors, being careful that they did not fall off their rusty hinges.

The battery was flat of course, but Pop slid into the driver's seat, and with the boys pushing it down the garage courtyard they managed to jump start it. Clouds of grey smoke enveloped both car and driver and Pop delighted in blipping the throttle, creating even greater clouds. It was noticeable to them how the tired old man, who had walked so slowly back from lunch, was revived by the sound of his beloved MG. He sat there contentedly, with his hands holding the delicate sprung Bakelite steering wheel, revving the engine down to its familiar, rhythmic soundtrack, no doubt thinking of times gone by. Finally he said, as much to himself as to the boys,

"We've have had some good times in this car you know. Some bloody good times. No doubt it will still be around long after I've gone."

Looking at the two of them, the man and the car, with its fading red paintwork and pitted chrome, the steam and fumes escaping from unknown sources and the fluid dripping from numerous leaks beneath the car, Slim thought it would be a close-run thing which would expire first! Pop was gradually sinking below the level of the steering wheel as if he were being absorbed by the vehicle itself. His fatigue returned. Slowly, pulling himself up on the windscreen and climbing out, he tossed the keys to Adam,

"You put it away lad, I'm knackered." As he wandered back to the house, Adam called out, "I will be over to do the lawns tomorrow night." Without turning he waved a weary arm of appreciation, and carried on into the house, still enjoying his memories.

The evening was too good to waste, so they made their way to their usual position on the bench at the back of the clubhouse and with pints in hand, eavesdropped on the regular Sunday night folk club. Inside, the vocalist was making a credible attempt at Paul Simon's Sound of silence. Slim broke the silence between them.

"I got some news you might just be interested in."

"Go on then."

"Roger, the dear boy, has decided to go off to Jamaica."

"It will be a bit hot this time of year."

"He's not going for a holiday you berk, he is going on the mission. He's been thinking about it for a long time. We have a lot of interest in the West Indies and there is a need for someone who is experienced to go and help out, organise things, lead the teaching and be an elder." Adam couldn't help thinking that Roger seemed rather young to be an elder, nor did he seem the ideal person to organise anything, struggling as he did to organise himself.

"The thing is my romantic star struck friend, he wanted Rachel to go with him, to make up the team."

"You're joking!"

"I think that's what Rachel said, or something very much like it. Roger was thinking a short engagement, quick wedding and long honeymoon in a tin hut in the backwoods of Jamaica. He is a very committed fellow is our Roger." Adam thought it sounded like he needed to be committed.

"So?"

"So, there's been a big bust up which has been brewing for a while, but Roger's off at the end of August and poor old Rachel's left on her own."

Slim looked across at his friend and noticed that a general glow had descended over his youthful countenance.

"I thought you might be interested, surely that's the kind of news that's worth another pint?"

"It certainly is" replied Adam, and they both headed for the bar.

They hadn't noticed him before, but he must have been there judging from the number of empty glasses on the table. In the Committee Room next to the bar, Harry Sunderland was in deep conversation with the club president and a distinguished, elderly gent. The boys looked across at him giving a friendly wave, in return receiving an acknowledgement and look that clearly said, 'do not disturb'. They took the hint and returned to Jerry at the bar, who made it his business to know everyone who set foot in the place. Apparently, the distinguished gentleman was Alderman Hughes, a close friend of the president of the club. He was, Jerry said, something to do with planning in the town hall. Slim clinked his pint against Adam's saying,

"I told you Uncle Harry rarely took risks, Gaynor will be pleased!"

Arthur Hughes had been prominent in local politics for most of the post-war years. He was that very English phenomenon, a politician who had risen almost entirely without trace. His rise was not due to his achievements, it was his achievement. By all accounts, Arthur had had a good war. Most of the time he had spent in the UK, eventually going overseas sometime after D-Day, where he made himself indispensable as a staff officer at company headquarters. He was demobbed in 1945 with the rank of Major, a title he retained until he was able to replace it with 'Alderman'. He had been chairman or vice-chairman of most of the committees at the county council in recent years and currently he was vice-chair of the planning committee.

His grandfather had been a gentleman farmer on the rich agricultural land to the east of the Yorkshire coalfield, sometimes finding and benefiting from the coal under his land. Both father and grandfather were men of property, owning a number of farms, cottages and even malt kilns around Pontefract. All this provided them with the means to live the lives of country gentlemen. Arthur liked to think of himself in similar terms, a gentleman, now giving his time to civic and public affairs. Not too much of a sacrifice given that Monday to Friday he had neither the need nor the inclination for paid employment. He was, however, gradually working his way through the remains of the family fortune. Vain and self-important, privilege and idleness had not served him well. He failed to see how the world around him was changing.

Membership of the county council for Arthur was not just about status and prestige, he liked to be in the know. He liked to know what other people didn't know. It added to his illusion of power.

* * *

Monday, 5th June had been a long day for Adam. He had made an early start, hoping to complete a small land survey in North Yorkshire in a day, having promised Pop he would do the lawns. He had gone there as soon as he got back from North Yorkshire. By the time he got home, having picked up fish and chips on the way, it was after 9 o'clock. He could hear the phone ringing as he put his key in the lock. Knowing his parents were out for the evening, he rushed to grab it.

"Turn the news on, turn the news on now Adam! It's from Dan to Beersheba." It was an excited Slim shouting down the phone. "It's from Dan to Beersheba," he kept repeating.

The television seemed to take forever to come on, but eventually flickered into life, showing pictures of Israeli military jets returning to their bases, followed by images of burnt-out aircraft and wrecked runways. The newsreader was describing a pre-emptive strike by the Israeli Air Force on bases in Egypt, which it claimed had destroyed its counterparts. Israeli ground troops were mobilising. There had also been airstrikes in Jordan and Syria. Adam was trying to follow the newsreader and open his fish and chips at the same time. He had the phone in his left hand and was picking out the hottest chips with his right, having not eaten since breakfast.

Slim, still in a high state of agitation, was saying,

"It had to happen! I told you to watch Israel! It is all coming true, all the prophecies! God's people have to occupy the whole of the land from Dan to Beersheba, and the whole of Jerusalem. By the time this is over it will have happened. We thought it would have taken years, but it is going to be over in a matter of months. We are holding a vigil tonight at the hall, come along if you want, everybody down here is getting very excited." Slim was wrong, it was over in six days. Although quite what Slim meant by "all over" was not clear. Perhaps he had something more apocalyptic in mind. Israel had occupied the West Bank, the Gaza Strip and the Golan Heights, East Jerusalem and the whole of the Sinai Peninsula, from Dan to Beersheba.

The vigil of the assembly in the hall that evening did not concern itself with the controversies of the war. Israel, as the aggressor, had killed 20,000 plus Egyptian, Syrian and Jordanian troops, occupied Palestinian territory and displaced thousands of Palestinians from their ancestral homes. This had to be set against the closing of the Straits of Tehran to Israeli shipping, and President Nasser's repeated threats to drive Israel into the sea. None of these conflicting claims concerned Slim and his fellow believers in the slightest, nor for now, did they matter to Adam. Prophecy was being fulfilled before their very eyes. What they had been looking for had come to pass. Julia might be appalled by Israel's aggression, his father might be alarmed at the consequences of the war for peace and stability in the region, and his mother might be anxious about what her son was getting involved in and how easily he was persuaded by the most extraordinary of ideas, but for Adam Rowntree, Monday, 5th June was the day he finally believed, and his belief would not change.

Just what believing meant for Adam was a question that his mother and sister would often ponder, but he would not. He believed. He was baptised, he had joined the assembly, accepted their statements of faith and got involved. His mother concluded that he had just decided to believe. It was a lifestyle choice, like becoming a vegetarian, joining the Freemasons, or becoming a member of the Conservative Party, (although not quite that bad). She couldn't convince herself that he had gone through a deep religious experience. Nor did she believe that his conversion was the product of a great theological enquiry, for Adam was no scholar. He had made a choice prompted by his charismatic boss, a very decent friend, and seduced perhaps by an attractive young girl. Finally, he was nudged over the top by a war thousands of miles away, that he imagined had been predicted thousands of years ago. He decided to believe! He just decided to believe and his belief wouldn't change. He had found 'The Way, The Truth and The Light.'

Mother tried to tell herself that Adam was no different from her or anybody else who decides what they choose to believe. Julia and Jerome were pretending to believe in the march of history, the class struggle and the triumph of the working class. She believed in liberal democracy, human rights and the rule of law – values Thomas Jefferson may have claimed were self-evident and inalienable. But these liberal values had no more come down from heaven on tablets of stone with divine authority than the Ten Commandments had. They were the narrative that she had inherited and accepted, they were the things she had chosen to believe. Adam had just chosen a different narrative, another story. This was what she told herself, but she was not entirely persuaded.

Chapter 6

Summer 1972

The invitation to Gaynor's new house said 'Housewarming Party', but it had much more the feel of an opening ceremony. It had been finished for some time, but Gaynor had needed to get everything just as she wanted it. It seemed natural to call it 'Gaynor's house', for that's what it was, in its conception, design and realisation, if not in its construction and funding. As is usually the case with such projects, it had taken longer, been more stressful, and cost a great deal more than anyone had expected. Gaynor was, of course, more concerned about the first two issues than the last.

Acquiring the land had taken most of the time and caused most of the frustration. However, it was Gaynor's frustration, not her father-in-law's. He knew that such acquisitions require patience above all else. There had been other parties interested in the site and planning applications had been made, and refused, by Alderman Hughes' planning committee. Eventually, the site was acquired without planning permission, for just a small premium over the agricultural value.

A Mr Spigot had been employed as a consultant. He had retired some years earlier as Assistant Chief Planning Officer at the county council. He now offered his advice and experience to those who understood his true value and could afford it. Eighteen months or so later, the submission of a new application in the name of Sunderland Developments coincided with a minor change in local planning policy. A 'fortunate' small amendment to the local development plan excluded Gaynor's site from the Green Belt. After due process and all appropriate consultations, approval was granted. Local democracy in action! The best in the world, if you can afford it.

Construction of one-off houses for private individuals is always fraught, and Gaynor's was no exception. The builder's principal failing was his inability to understand exactly what Gaynor wanted him to do, particularly when she was telling him to do something else altogether. He was entirely used to this kind of thing and knew that it could all be resolved at an appropriate additional cost. This was one of the few things they could agree on. In time, it was finished, as all things must be, and today was the big day when everyone could come and admire.

1972 was not turning out to be much of a year in Britain, with the miners' strike, over one million unemployed, and the three-day week. Even Harry Sunderland was beginning to feel the pinch. Things were little better overseas with terrorism at the Munich Olympics, and President Nixon embroiled in the Watergate fiasco. But for Gaynor, 1972 was turning out very nicely indeed.

Adam did not want to decline the invitation. Indeed, he was keen to go and see the finished house for himself. He had, however, promised to call in on Pop. Work was taking more and more of his time, and weekends were the only opportunity he had. He planned to get to Pop's early, do the lawns and a bit of tidying up and be on his way. But when he had finished, Pop appeared on the bench outside obviously wanting to chat. His health was gradually failing and these days he rarely managed to do very much in the garden at all. That frustration and the loneliness were beginning to impair even his cheerful optimism. As he had gotten older and more needy, the bond between the two of them had become stronger than ever.

As they sat on the bench together, the midday sun bathing the soft red bricks of the back of the house in the summer heat, Pop said,

"Big do this afternoon in Wakefield I believe. I suppose you will be going now that you're courting young Rachel. You must be almost part of the family?"

"How on earth do you know about that Pop?" He was constantly amazed at how many people Pop knew in the town and how he always seemed to know what was going on.

"I've told you before lad, Smawthorne is a small town and if you live to my age you get to know just about everything that is going on. So what's this new house like?"

"Very impressive, if you like that sort of thing."

"Thought it might be, and do you?"

"Do I what?"

"Like that kind of thing?"

"I am not really sure, but it is very grand." Pop leaned back on the bench, offering up his weather-beaten face to the warmth of the sun, and with a knowing smile said,

"If it's grand I suspect Gaynor will like it."

"Come on Pop, you don't really know Gaynor, do you?"

"Well no, not really, but I did know her mother and father. I used to know them very well. Her dad, I seem to remember, was very chummy with that John Poulson at one stage. He did a lot of work on the architect's house, for free I heard. I hope he got something in return, but I'm not sure he did. They do say the apples don't fall far from the tree." Quite what all that meant, Adam could not fathom. Pop, striking an enigmatic pose, was not prepared to elaborate.

"So how is that girlfriend of yours? I was thinking that you might have had something to announce by now." Adam looked across at his old friend, and then down at his feet, not sure what to say.

"Go and get us a couple of bottles of beer from the cellar while you are thinking about it." The truth was that the Rachel 'project,' had been as drawn out and frustrating for him as the new house had been for Gaynor and Damien. Although the approval of the local planning authority was not necessary, he sometimes wondered if her father's was.

Adam had realised that Harry seemed to be involved in almost everything. However, in the matter of his pursuit of Rachel, he was mistaken. The future father-in-law was not the problem, as he very much approved of Adam. It was, in fact, his approval that was the main stumbling block. One of the things that Rachel first found attractive in Adam, was that he was not a part of her father's world – not part of the fellowship, or the assembly. He was the other boy from 'outside', different from all those she had grown up with. For Rachel, her religion was not just something that happened on a Sunday, it had arrived with her mother's milk, it was everywhere. It was her family, her social life, at times even her work. These days she found it increasingly claustrophobic. Roger's fantasy about her joining him in his sacrificial ministry to the Third World, was just the excuse she needed to dump him. And then what did Adam do, he joined up! He was no longer different; he was threatening to be one of them. He had been drawn in like so many others, into her father's 'sphere of influence.'

Poor Adam understood none of this. He had hoped that the disappearance of Roger, and his own conversion would have paved the way, like Moses opening the waters of the Red Sea. Needless to say, as the prize eluded him, it became all the more desirable.

Adam came back with the beer and glasses and the two men sat together enjoying the sunshine, the company and the cold beer.

"Not a bad life, if you don't weaken, eh?" Pop suggested. Adam found a certain peace here that he rarely experienced anywhere else. Pop's bench was his stress-free zone. Everywhere else, people wanted something from him, or of him. Yes, Pop needed the lawns cut and the hedges trimmed, and it was useful if there was someone to get the beer up from the cellar, but that was all. Pop didn't expect, didn't demand, rarely complained, and wanted nothing. Reluctantly he got up from the bench.

"I need to be on my way, do you want me to get another beer before I go?"

"Aye lad that would be grand." Adam turned to go.

"Well, is it still on, you and Rachel, or is it not?"

"Well, I'm still in the game and nobody else is" Adam claimed, and went to get Pop's beer, before leaving to pick up Rachel.

When they got to Wakefield, most people had already arrived and the party was in full swing. The majority of the guests were from the local fellowship, but the guest list represented the two world's that were Harry Sunderland's life. Interspersed among the brethren and sisters were a number of his business friends and associates. It was a strange, slightly awkward mixture. They were all predominantly middle-class and sartorially, much the same, but the difference between the two groups was obvious, if difficult to define.

Adam was anxious to find Slim. He had promised to bring his new girlfriend and both were about to complete their final exams at the school of architecture, and had a one-year secondment at Leeds City Architects' Department. Adam and Rachel paid their respects to the host and hostess and said hello to the rest of the family. They found Slim and Natalie in a quiet corner of the garden and, after the usual greetings and little small talk, Rachel asked mischievously,

"So what do you two nearly qualified architects think about the new house then?" There was an extended pause, until Natalie carefully suggested that it was, "A remarkable example of mid-20th century eclectic domestic architecture in the pseudo-Georgian come Regency style."

"What does that mean?" asked Adam as innocent as his namesake. Rachel, taking a sip of the cheap German wine, grimaced and said,

"They think it's hideous!... A bit like the wine."

'Hideous' was one word, but vulgar or crass would have worked just as well. It had all the necessary Regency features, but everything was wrong: the bright red bricks, the sash windows with imitation secondary glazing, the mock stone lintels and sills, the imitation stone portico around the front door, and red concrete roof tiles. There was even an attempt at a cornice of painted plywood. Everything was there, but nothing worked, the details, the proportions or the materials. Hideous was probably right. Even the brickwork had been changed at the last minute, in a desperate attempt to keep the cost down. This was now sprinkled with white efflorescence, like icing sugar, over-done on a particularly crude birthday cake. The builder had assured Gaynor that these were natural salts that were leaching out of the brickwork. It would sort itself out in a few months, ideally after he was long gone and fully paid up. The only thing that looked right about the house was the rather splendid landscape gardens in which they were sat.

Slim had gone to the school of architecture expecting to be taught how to design buildings, how to draw, and something about building construction. He was unprepared for the breadth of the curriculum. Its historic, cultural, and social content was a significant challenge to his rather sheltered and narrow upbringing. As for being taught to design buildings – nobody did. The main reason nobody taught Slim and his fellow students how to design was because it is almost impossible to teach. The students who were successful tended to pick it up by doing it, or observing each other, but mainly by cribbing the best ideas from the more obscure architectural journals.

A school of architecture can be a cruel place for bright young school leavers. Usually, the best students, with the best A-levels, will get the best results at law school, medical school and most of the other professions. But this is not always so in architecture, where the brightest can struggle with the challenge of creativity, whilst the less intellectually gifted, but more imaginative, can prosper the most.

Slim had struggled, Natalie was a natural. They both coped perfectly well with mastering construction, structures, specifications and the other practical aspects of the course. The problem was the blank sheet of paper with which every project must begin. For Slim and many other students that was a terror, but for Natalie, it was just an opportunity to shine. The good news for Slim, however, was that the absence of any significant design skills, though an obstacle to an architect's self-esteem, was not necessarily an obstacle to progress or even qualification. The breadth of the subject was such that it provided areas where the academically gifted, but creatively lacking, could still graduate. Furthermore, contemporary architecture was going through something of a hiatus. There was such a collective crisis of confidence that no one could agree exactly what good design was. Contemporary architecture of the

1970s, was to some extent the means whereby modern practitioners, with limited talent, might still become members of the Royal Institute of British Architects. Harry would have said it was a little bit like the way in which contemporary theology allowed Anglican clerics who didn't really believe in God to still achieve ordination and receive their stipend. He was eloquent on the effects this was having on the religious life of the nation. The effects of large numbers of architects who could not design, populating studios across the country, was manifest in the grim concrete hospitals, schools and office buildings springing up across England in the faltering post-war building boom. Gaynor's house was not the only hideous new building recently completed in the decade.

Rachel took an immediate liking to Natalie. She was relaxed, intelligent and plain speaking. Slim was clearly smitten. This was Natalie's first encounter with the family, and the fellowship, which to her seemed much the same thing. She had obviously been briefed by Slim of the unique nature of his family and friends. However, six years at the school of architecture had made him more defensive and self-conscious about his religion.

This was the first opportunity Natalie had had to talk to anyone, other than Slim, about the beliefs that she knew were an important part of the life of the man she had fallen in love with. She wanted to know more and Rachel seemed the ideal source.

"So what is the main difference Rachel, between you and all the other churches?" she asked. Unfortunately, they had been joined by Damien, as wine waiter and genial host. He was eager to answer Natalie's question himself. Refilling everyone's glass with a new bottle of Hock, he explained,

"I suppose Natalie, it's that we take the Bible very seriously and at its face value. We accept that it is the inspired word of God and we read it regularly, both Old Testament and New. We believe it and we live by it." Rachel would have added that, "we try to live by it." She often thought that her brother had that special gift of saying something with which she was in complete agreement, in such a way that she no longer was.

"So you take it literally, all of it, Adam and Eve, talking serpents and asses, the Tower of Babel, turning water into wine?" She could not help wondering, looking at the glass in her hand, if Damien had tried to do the same thing with less success. "Don't you have to interpret these ancient myths in the light of contemporary knowledge, science and evolution?"

"They're not myths, Natalie, they're true. Once you start to pick and choose which bits of the Bible you like and which you don't, you start to undermine the whole authority of God's word. And as for Evolution, well that's just somebody's theory, isn't it?" Damien, with his few extra years on the rest of the company, was beginning to assume some sage-like status. Rachel could see Natalie didn't take well to being patronised as her sociable enquiries took on something of an edge. Rachel could also see where this might be going, but realised she didn't care.

"So if it's in the Bible, plain and simple you believe it, however extraordinary or difficult?"

Damien, trying to speak with all the gravity he didn't possess said, "Natalie, it is a matter of faith." He paused, and with a sincere look repeated, "It is all a matter of faith."

She leaned back in the garden chair, looking around at the house, the beautiful, landscaped gardens, the cars parked along the front and thought, well, If I have got him on the end of the line, what else is there to do but to wind him in...

"Then what about it being 'harder for the rich man to enter the kingdom of heaven, than for a camel to go through the eye of a needle'. And I'm sure Jesus said something about going and selling everything that you have and giving it to the poor?" She was going to ask what the Bible had to say about depriving elderly people of the true value of their land by subverting the democratic planning process, but looking across at Slim, thought she had said more than enough already. Rachel didn't think that, and realised that she liked Natalie more and more as the afternoon went on.

Not for the first time in his life, or the last, Damien was saved by his wife, who fortunately appeared with news that father wanted him and Adam to come and meet Alderman Hughes.

"Many are called, but only two are chosen." Rachel whispered to Natalie. The two boys dutifully reported, and Slim went to look for his mother and father. This suited Rachel very well, as she was keen to quiz Natalie more about architecture and university life in general.

Natalie was, of course, the woman that Rachel wished she was and should have been. She should have stood up to her father when she left school and become

109

the landscape architect she wanted to be. Her mother, who had the same passion for all things horticultural, had done her best to encourage Rachel, but her father would have none of it. What was it he had said, "You don't need to go to university to do gardening." She had allowed herself to be pushed into working at the bank, where she had become increasingly bored and frustrated. Her father had expected her to marry Roger, produce grandchildren, and be a faithful sister, preparing the teas, cleaning the hall and supporting her husband. She had consoled herself by helping her mother to redesign the gardens at Salem and the garden layout for Gaynor's house. Her particular passion though had been transforming the piece of overgrown woodland between the assembly hall and the river. She had commandeered it and created a small piece of urban woodland and a nature reserve. It had taken two years of hard work, with only the occasional help from her mother and a few volunteers, but it was now maturing nicely. Accessible from the riverside footpath, locals were beginning to use it for picnics. Mothers with pushchairs would come and sit on the bench and chat whilst their children played among the trees. Even her father approved of this, as it enhanced the setting of the hall.

Natalie was a good listener, and Rachel felt free to express her frustrations.

"You have got to do whatever you want to do Rachel, life's too short. Anyone can see you have got a good eye, look what you've created here." She waved her hands toward the gardens. "Not that though!" she added with a grin, nodding at the house. "Advertise in the local paper, or the Post Office or get some freelance work. Slim and I will ask around, there are plenty of firms who need landscaping layouts and planting schedules. Go for it!" She looked around again and said "It's not as if you're going to starve is it? What have you got to lose?"

There was something very liberating and encouraging about Natalie. Her enthusiasm, confidence and plain-speaking, combined with the numerous glasses of wine, were infectious.

"Let's go and find the boys and check out what Alderman Hughes is all about."

"Oh," Rachel said, "I have a fair idea."

Harry liked to show off his young protégés to the likes of Arthur Hughes. "This is Adam, he is one of our bright young stars, just about to complete his finals in double-quick time. It will soon be Adam Rowntree, member of the Royal Institute of Chartered Surveyors, and since Walter's little heart attack, he has been more or less running the office in town. Damien here is more interested in working on developments with me, aren't you lad?" There followed much handshaking, backslapping, and mutual congratulation, although it was not clear why they were congratulating each other. Perhaps it was for what might be about to happen. As the Alderman made his leave, he called back,

"Don't forget to check out Halifax, Harry."

"What's Halifax?" Damien's antennae were sensing something he needed to know.

"The Welbeck Road Chapel may be coming up for sale and Arthur wondered if we would be interested. They would prefer to sell it to another church rather than see it demolished, or converted for some other commercial use.

"It is too big for us, Dad, we wouldn't fill a quarter of it."

"That's true," Harry replied, looking thoughtful, "but it's a cracking site near the centre of town, right by the river. A site like that could have a great deal of potential in a few years' time, with the right kind of support." Adam said nothing, but noted everything.

Rachel arrived to interrupt the conversation, arm in arm with her mother and Natalie. They all looked sparkling and animated. "What have you three been up to?" quizzed Harry.

"Oh, just women's talk, you know dear, just women's talk." Jenny replied, giving her daughter a knowing wink.

Rachel was clearly ready to go, and changing partners, linked arms with Adam. Saying goodbye to her parents, she led him to the car, demanding, much to his delight, that he take her for a drink as there was something she wanted to talk about. They drove out to Denby Dale and Holmfirth, into the edge of the Pennines, where the grim red brick of the Yorkshire coalfield gives way to the rising hills of millstone grit. The hard-edged pit villages are replaced by the weathered stone-work of the weavers' cottages that line the green river valleys. The woollen towns of Yorkshire, though once the domain of 'dark satanic mills' had been gentler and kinder on the landscape and the people than the pit heads, winding gear, and slag heaps of the coal industry.

Sitting by the river, behind a converted pumping station, Rachel sipped with pleasure the first decent glass of wine she had had all day.

"So what do you want to talk about?" Adam asked, hopefully.

"I am going to jack it in at the bank! Now before you say anything, I've spoken to Mum about it and she agrees."

"So do I. What do you plan to do?"

She looked at him in wide-eyed amazement. She had expected he would try to talk her out of it, as her father surely would. Perhaps it was a mistake, always assuming Adam's views would be those of her father.

"As you know, I've always wanted to do landscape design."

"You're very good at it."

"Thank you, kind sir," she said in mock surprise. "Well, I think it's too late now to go to university and qualify as a landscape architect, but I thought I could try and set up as a freelance designer. I can work from home to begin with, advertise in the local papers and shops. Natalie said she and Slim would ask around the architects and builders they know." She was becoming more excited as the idea began to take shape. "What do you think?" she asked hopefully. Adam took her hand in both of his and smiling said,

"I think it's a great idea!"

"Really! Do you think I could do it, it's all a bit scary?"

"Of course you can do it if it's what you really want. I reckon you could do just about anything you really want to."

"I don't think Dad will agree. How am I going to persuade him? It will be difficult if I can't get him onside."

"Well, I could help you, if you like?"

"How, how could you help me?"

Adam kept hold of her hand. "I could marry you, couldn't I?" Her hand didn't move. "It would certainly help with your dad."

"I think it would too," she slowly nodded her head, smiling but not looking.

"I'd rather you said yes, because you loved me."

She leaned across the table to kiss him, but nearly missed, the table getting in the way, converting the kiss into a giggle.

"Is that a yes then?"

"Yes it is!" She leaned back, still not having recovered from the giggle. "Not exactly the proposal I had been expecting. You will have to do it properly sometime, with the ring, and on one knee."

"It wasn't exactly the form of acceptance I have been expecting", he beamed, "you will have to do that properly too."

"I will!"

They talked in the mellow evening light, of the hows, wheres and whens, until it was time to go. They headed back east, down the green valley, as the low sun was setting behind them over the Pennine Hills.

"Slim seemed very struck, didn't you think?"

"Oh yes," replied Adam, " I can see why, she's an incredible girl isn't she?"

"I should say, but I think there may be problems, don't you. I don't think Natalie is likely to…what shall

I say, comply with what is expected of her, you know, 'being not unequally yoked together.' Adam smiled to himself, wondering if that was what he had just proposed – yoking the two of them together!

"Surely folk will not make a fuss if Natalie doesn't want to join us."

Rachel could think of one or two people at least who would wish to after this afternoon's bruising encounters in the garden.

* * *

He found Pop almost exactly as he had left him, though quite dead. Adam had never seen a dead man before. Pop was still holding the empty glass of beer. Even before he had touched the grey, cold, stiffening hand, he knew that he was dead. Later, he remembered being pleased to notice that Pop had drunk the extra bottle he had got from the cellar before he'd left. He was slumped in the corner of the bench with his head back against the brickwork. His eyes were closed and it was only the gaping jaw that betrayed the ugliness of death. Everything else seemed entirely the same. He liked to imagine that Pop had died just as the sun was setting behind the trees at the end of his beloved garden. According to the doctor's timing, it must have been there or thereabouts. Anyway, that was what he chose to believe. For a moment, he sat down on the other end of the bench beside his old friend, the sadness of the loss not yet having fully registered. Pop, after all, was still there.

It had been a spur of the moment decision to call on his way home. He had dropped Rachel off and driving back, realised he wanted to give Pop his good news.

There was no light on in the house as he pulled up outside. The front door was ajar, just as he had left it, and walking through the house, he had a sense of the thing. Finding him outside was more a confirmation than a shock. It was only when it struck him that he would not be able to tell him about Rachel that his emotions took hold, and he wept quietly.

After a while, he got hold of himself and realised he didn't know what to do. He went back into the house and telephoned his mother, who always knew what to do. On this occasion however, she was more emotional than he expected. He had never heard her so upset and for some time she struggled to say anything that was coherent, eventually handing the telephone to Hector. He told Adam to stay where he was and that they would be round as soon as they had telephoned the police and the undertaker. By the end of the evening, Mother had got herself together and slipped into efficiency mode, doing all that was necessary for her old friend.

Chapter 7

December 1973

Walter's heart attack had put him in hospital for the two weeks before Christmas. It was taking him and Felicity more time to get over the shock than the heart-attack itself. He had always taken health and fitness as a given, playing rugby well into his forties. In his day, he had been every bit the fearless flanker that Adam was. He was as much offended as worried at being reminded of his own mortality. He was back at work now, if only for three days a week. The offices of Sunderland Developments were low-key and inconspicuous, a small suite located above the estate agency in Smawthorne, on the corner of the main shopping street. It was the only shopping street in the town. The offices were accessed via a narrow staircase on the side of the building, which did little to advertise itself or the company. The brothers had no desire to make a grand statement, or spend the money doing so.

Harry was glad to have Walter back, as there was pressing business demanding their joint attention. The two of them were together with Damien in the small boardroom. Boardroom was a rather grand title for a dingy room with a table and half a dozen leather chairs, surrounded by a variety of framed photographs depicting a selection of the companies rather non-descript developments. There were no photographs of the chairman or board of directors, no drinks cabinet or trophy cupboard. Harry ran the development company, but Walter had an interest, and Damien had recently been appointed a director. Adam had also been asked by Harry to join them, and as he sat down, Damien looked at him as if to say, and what are you doing here?

Rachel had been correct. Marriage, or at least engagement to be, had resolved the 'father problem.' Harry was delighted with the news. Like Adam, he could not understand why it had taken so long. But most fathers tend to be blinded and mystified by the problems they cause their own children. He was perfectly happy with Rachel leaving the bank, to "try to make a go of her little hobby," as he chose to put it. He felt sure that family life and motherhood would soon be consuming most of her time.

Adam was not there just as the favoured son-in-law, Harry wanted him in the meeting. Damien was always a great enthusiast for new projects, and when he was interested he would give it heart and soul. But Adam, Harry had come to realise, was a great man for detail. His analysis was always orderly and thorough. He had a barrister like gift for identifying the key issue of any opportunity, and the crux of any problem. Damien brought passion and enthusiasm, but Adam, in all things, liked order and precision. William Hague, the company accountant, was also present. He worked with Harry on all their developments and was an elder of the assembly in Leeds. He enjoyed Harry and Walter's complete trust, and a small interest in their company.

Harry, as ever, set the agenda. "We need to decide what, if anything, we want to do about the Halifax Chapel. It has been on the market for some time now, but Arthur Hughes was right, the trustees are anxious that the building should continue to be used for Christian services. They have already refused a number of good offers from commercial developers."

"It's a massive building." William had spent time at the site. "It will be the largest thing you have taken on by some margin, and surely it would be too big for the brethren and sisters here." Adam was thinking very much along the same lines.

"I'd like you all to consider two things." said Harry, "First, it's not just the chapel itself, there is the large Sunday school room, the caretaker's house, and a sizeable car park at the rear. Between the car park and the river there is a derelict site, with no access to the highway other than across the chapel site. But even with the chapel remaining, it's a substantial development site, right in the centre of town, and close by the river. Arthur Hughes believes that in time, these sites will be ripe for urban regeneration, possibly with government support."

Damien was becoming interested! "And secondly?" He asked.

"Suppose the elders of the Halifax Assembly and ourselves were to consider merging. Most of our members live between here and Halifax. Sunderland Developments could acquire the site, gift the chapel to the merged fellowship in exchange for our existing site in Smawthorne. Halifax don't own their own building so they would have a significant saving on rent. Our hall is in urgent need of renovation, we could build a couple of houses where the hall now stands, to offset the alterations needed to the chapel.

"What about the land behind..." Damien began to say, but his father's look stopped him in his tracks.

Walter queried how the chapel trustees would feel about the demolition of the Sunday school building and the caretaker's house, not to mention a commercial development on the rest of the site. Damien stated the obvious: they would think the site was worth considerably more money.

"Which they will find out eventually" said Adam.

"Yes" said Damien, "but by then it will be too late."

Walter was not too impressed by the observation of his nephew.

"Don't you feel we have our reputation to think about and the reputation of our brethren and sisters here in Smawthorne?" He wanted to add that they would also be dealing with another Christian community, but thought Harry would not see it quite that way.

Harry could see that Walter had reservations.

"As I understand it" Harry replied, "the trustees will be more than happy if they are confident the chapel will remain a place of Christian worship." The accountant still was not convinced,

"It would be a significant financial risk, alongside everything else that we have on. We would have to increase our borrowings, and we all know where interest rates are at the moment."

"Then how do we mitigate our risks, William?" Adam asked.

"Good lad Adam, that's why you are here. We need a quick appraisal of the two sites. I think we may find, with the right scheme on the rest of the site, the chapel might come in at zero cost. See if you can persuade Slim and Natalie to do a quick layout." Adam suspected that would also be expected at zero cost.

A 'quick sketch' is what all developers call carefully considered outline design proposals, presented with detailed plans, elevations, perspectives and comprehensive schedules of accommodation, all produced at short notice by creative architects usually working through the night for days if not weeks on end. Such sketches are the foundation of any proposed development. Nothing can happen without them and banks require such outline proposals before they are prepared to advance any funding for the development. Developers, of course, naturally expect to get this vital and complex work for nothing.

It occurred to Adam that no one had considered how Rachel might feel if she knew her father and brother were planning to redevelop her precious piece of community urban woodland without her knowledge.

As the meeting was breaking up, Walter asked Harry if he had a spare minute to chat. The others made their way to the car park.

"I have a fair idea what Uncle Walter wants to talk to dad about" Damien said to Adam as he climbed into his new Range Rover.

"What's that?"

"Well, yours isn't the only wedding that is being planned at the moment is it? I can see trouble ahead." And without waiting for an answer he was on his way. Damien could see trouble ahead because he intended to cause it.

"How are the wedding plans going Harry? asked Walter, "Have the ladies got everything in hand, everything sorted?"

"Just about, not quite what I had in mind, but Rachel wants it kept very low-key, family and a few friends, with a service at the hall and a simple reception at the Spread Eagle in Pontefract. I thought we might have taken the banqueting suite at the Seasons, but she wouldn't have it. These days, once my daughter gets her mind set on something there is no shifting her."

"Can't think where she gets it from! Look, I think we are going to have two weddings this year, and the other one is going to be more problematic."

"I thought that might be the case, she is an attractive girl is Natalie and Slim looks enamoured. She's talented, picked up one of the few firsts in her year at Leeds this year and that takes some doing. I have to say, I find her very likeable, so do Rachel and Jenny. Can Slim not encourage her to join the fellowship, here or at Leeds? I'll be happy to lead her through the instruction. If she's as bright as I think, that won't take long. She must know how important it is to Slim, it will be a shame if we had to...well, you know."

Walter explained that what Harry was suggesting was highly unlikely. Natalie was an independently minded woman. She was happy for Slim to continue in the fellowship, but she would not be falling into line, nor was Slim seeking to persuade her. He knew what his brother's reaction would be, but somehow needed to hear him say it.

"It's difficult Walter, you must see that the Bible is quite clear, 'be ye not unequally yoked together', we can't compromise our principles just because it affects one of the family. It is about spiritual integrity, we've got to think of our reputation." Oh yes thought Walter, our reputation again. Harry hadn't seemed as concerned about reputation a few moments ago when property and profit was involved.

"We've always been steadfast in the past, the elders won't want to be seen by other assemblies to be lowering standards, don't you agree" Walter was disappointed in his brother, though not at all surprised. "I am not quite sure what I agree with these days Harry, let's leave it at that. I think I'm going to get off home."

Harry went back to his office, thinking how tired his brother looked, and how much he had changed since the heart attack. But he was mainly thinking about how he would approach the trustees of the Halifax Chapel and the elders of his own assembly. There was also the matter of the many acres of agricultural land behind their hall that Arthur Hughes had mentioned, and Damien had nearly let slip in the meeting. He made a mental note to have a quiet word with his son, about keeping quiet.

* * *

As funerals go, Pop's was as good as they can get and attracted a substantial number of mourners. Adam was surprised to discover that all the arrangements had been set in place by Pop himself. His mother ensured his instructions were followed to the letter. A brief service in the crematorium chapel and as many flowers as people wanted to bring. Pop had told Adam that if you live in a small town for long enough you get to know everyone, and it seemed that everyone knew him, and came to pay their respects. Even the Sunderland's were there, and Gaynor's parents. His elderly sister lived in a care home in North Wales and was not fit to travel.

A number of people offered eulogies, but Adam was proud that the most eloquent and informative came from his father and included much that was new to him. Pop and been a conscientious objector in 1939; his objections were political rather than religious. In the 30s he had been actively involved in the antifascist movement opposing Oswald Mosley and his brownshirts, and Hector believed he was at the famous Battle of Cable Street. Eventually, a tribunal had exempted him from military service and directed him to work on the land as a nursery man.

Sitting at the back of the chapel, his mind drifted back to that evening behind Pop's house, and the brutal transition he had witnessed from life to death. When he had left Pop on the bench with his beer, he was a man full of words, humour, memories and wit. When he returned, there was nothing. Everything that he was had gone, Pop would not speak again, or so Adam believed.

The only religious element to the funeral was the tune to What a friend We Have in Jesus, but the words were those of Alan Price's latest hit.

"Everyone is going through changes, No one knows what's going on
And everybody changes places, But the world still carries on

As Adam made his way to the Black Horse Tavern to drink to Pop's memory (as per his specific instructions), Alan Price's upbeat piano solo at the end of the piece seemed to him entirely inappropriate. Pop would have disagreed.

His friend's death had a profound effect on his religious thinking. It either strengthened his faith, or compounded his fears, it was difficult to say which. In the theology of the Apostle Paul, faith was supposed to cast out fear. However, amongst the apostle's 20th century followers, particularly those of a fundamentalist or literal mindset such as Adam, it often magnified those fears and insecurities. To him, his friend had died without faith in the resurrection. Pop had not known Christ, "who gave his life a ransom for many." Pop had died without hope and it was a tragedy, in Adam's mind, that would stay with him for many years to come.

* * *

Mixed marriages were not just a problem for small fundamentalist sects like the Assemblies of Christ. Such has been the case since the original Adam was a lad, or just after. Whether it be Catholics and Protestants in Ireland, Muslims and Hindus in India, or Jews and Gentiles everywhere, Shakespeare knew you didn't even need religion to create a romantic tragedy, hence the Montague's and the Capulet's. Young love only has to collide with ideology, bigotry and prejudice.

However, amongst the brothers and sisters of the Assemblies of Christ it was almost a defining issue for those who were in '*The Way*'. And being in The Way meant understanding and accepting The Way set out in the Bible and their Statement of Beliefs. They had no clergy, there was no Archbishop, no General Synod, no college of cardinals, only, The Way. In New Testament times there were two big sins, adultery and blasphemy, both attracting stoning. With assemblies, it was divorce and remarriage (which they regarded as adultery) and marrying an unbeliever. Fortunately, stoning was one of the imperatives of the biblical teaching they were able to ignore. Since the communities were made of human beings, problems cropped up with unsurprising regularity. Meetings of elders, such as the one currently convened, often came together and invariably failed to resolve the issue satisfactorily.

The elders of the community, like the monks and friars of the Middle Ages, were brethren, and brethren only, elected by the whole congregation. Simeon Kantalow, as chairman, called the elders meeting to order. He was a man of austere and precise appearance. He favoured the same grey three-piece suit, with all three buttons of the jacket fastened. If three buttons were provided, three buttons should be fastened. Few had seen him with a jacket open, or without the blue tie secured to the white shirt with a simple gold tie clip. So much about Simeon was clipped, from the manner of his speech to his short back and sides haircut. The rigidity and austerity of his tailoring was exceeded only by that of his mind. He was deeply read in the narrowest of canons. When it came to thinking inside or outside the box, Simeon's instinct was to look for a smaller one.

He was also one of the organists and notorious for insisting that the congregation sang the hymns quicker than was their natural inclination, or ability. Rarely did the organist and congregation finish at the same time. It was, however, not only in music that Simeon Kantalow wanted people to sing to his tune. Most of the congregation agreed that he was a difficult character, but he had some influence by virtue of his supposed sincerity and unquestionable biblical knowledge, Simeon Kantalow had little knowledge that was not biblical.

There were twelve Apostles, twelve tribes of Israel, and twelve members of the Council of Elders. Harry and Walter had been members for many years, but Damien had only just been elected. They and the other eight represented a broad range of opinion, being in WS Gilbert's words, "either a little liberal, but mostly a little conservative."

There were a number of items on the agenda, including consideration of the dilapidated state of the hall and Harry's suggestion, at this stage nothing more, that it might be possible to merge Halifax with the Welbeck Road Chapel. Given that this was being generously offered as a no cost option, it was unsurprisingly well received. Harry was gratefully thanked and asked to investigate the matter further and report back. A couple of the elders, who were more elderly than others, wanted to know how something that looked too good to be true, could be that good, or true. Experience had made them more sceptical than the younger brethren, but the meeting moved on.

Slim had not told Natalie that their relationship was going to be discussed on Wednesday evening by twelve men, most of whom she didn't know and didn't know her. He knew she would not take it well. Even by the brethren's standards it was precipitous, as although the family knew that the two were very fond of each other and were making plans, no announcements had been made or a date set. It had been Damien, or rather Damien and Gaynor who had forced the issue, and with the reliable help of Simeon, it had been placed on the agenda.

With a practised hypocrisy that had been refined over the years, Simeon led the discussion by saying it was only fair to Slim that the elders should make their views known so that he would have the opportunity to make a considered decision. In other words, do what he was told. He continued by rehearsing the familiar arguments about the importance of keeping The Way, maintaining standards, and the clear (to him), teachings of the Bible. They should also, he urged, be mindful of their reputation and how other assemblies would view them if they were seen to be, as he put it, unfaithful to The Way. There's that reputation thing again thought Walter.

The 'reputation' issue was a powerful argument for the 'little conservatives' of the assembly, and spoke directly to their self-interest. As there was no clergy, all communities of believers relied upon each other to provide weekly visiting ministers. Being an itinerant minister, which most of the elders were, was a significant status symbol. Walter, Simeon and Harry had been doing this for years. Harry and Simeon were national figures and spoke at major gatherings, consequently enjoying even greater status. Damien was just starting out on his career as a travelling minister, and though he showed little of his father's talent, his father's name would ensure a respectable number of precious invitations. The wrong decision on the Slim issue could result in the cancellation of many Sunday appointments if other communities believed that Smawthorne were letting standards drop. It was a little like collective moral blackmail.

Amongst the Assemblies of Christ, keeping an eye on one another, both individually and collectively, was a compelling and popular pastime. This was remarkable given their attachment to the New Testament, containing as it does the Sermon on the Mount with its injunction to "judge not that ye be not judged!"

Damien, wanting to make his mark, pompously reminded them that it was not just a matter of how they were judged by their peers. "All of you one day, and that day may be soon, will have to give an account of the decisions we make here today to a higher authority." He had had more than one run in with Natalie and the graffiti of her sarcastic critiques had left their mark on him. Now he would do his worst to leave his mark on her. He added with almost enough insincerity to match Simeon,

"I am very fond of Slim, he is my cousin after all, but he knows as well as anyone what the Bible teaches and what we believe. He knows he has to choose."

And so the debate went on, in a language entirely of its own and within its own is esoteric logic, incomprehensible to anyone else outside of their particular religious bubble.

It did not seem remotely odd to those twelve men that they should be sitting around a table, deliberating on whether two intelligent, twenty seven year old architects should get married. At one stage Simeon suggested that they might invite Slim and Natalie to appear before the council.

"To do what?" Walter gently enquired.

"Well," stumbled Simeon "to erm...to..."

Walter helped him out, "To talk them out of it? I think that would be very difficult."

Simeon recovered himself "I suppose a young woman would find that rather intimidating."

"No" said Walter "I think you, all of you, would find it difficult and intimidating." He was looking directly at a more subdued Damien.

But Damien and Simeon had won the day. Walter had nothing else to say and Harry had said nothing at all, knowing that the decision was inevitable. A lengthy letter would be sent to Slim by Simeon assuring him of their fraternal love and concern for his eternal well-being. It would set out the biblical imperatives, including much chapter and verse, but essentially saying 'if you marry the girl, we'll chuck you out.' Slim would be in no way surprised to receive the epistle, he could have written it himself, the only urgent thing for him to do would be to destroy it before Natalie had a chance to read it.

As Harry was leaving, Walter took his arm.

"Quick word Harry, if you have a minute?"

"Sure Walter, I am sorry about all that, but if I had tried to argue the case, it would have made no difference."

"I know that, it is just as it has to be, although I don't think Felicity will see it quite like that."

"No, I don't think she will, Jenny much the same."

"No, it's the Halifax deal. I am not comfortable with things not being out in the open, at least as far as the brethren and sisters are concerned. I think the trustees of the chapel will see they have been cheated. It's not the financial risk I'm concerned about, although it is significant and a sudden downturn in the economy could leave us very exposed, it's the reputational damage that concerns me most. If you want this thing Harry, you will have to set up a new company and do it on your own. Damien I'm sure is up for it, and no doubt Adam will be keen to help."

Harry had been expecting something similar. Walter had always been content with the surveying and estate agency business, and had never enjoyed the more lucrative, if riskier, development work. They were not going to fall out over it. Harry knew that he would be able to raise the capital he needed, even if he would have to put up the house and some of the other assets as security.

"That's fine Walter I understand, I will do as you suggest, but it must remain confidential or it won't happen, okay?"

"I understand" said Walter, who understood Harry all too well.

Although Adam was not involved in the decision of the elders, he would not be able to avoid the issue. A decision had to come before the whole congregation for their approval. They may have appeared to the outside world to be an archaic institution, and so they were, but they were more democratic than many of the established churches, and there lay their Achilles' heel. Adam would have to indicate where he stood. Was he in 'The Way' or not, and faith, or fear, he secretly knew, would make it inevitable that he'd betray him. The friendship would remain for many years, mainly due to Slim's generous, easy-going nature, but Adam would still feel that his friend, who had drawn him into this new way of life in the first place, was letting him down. Adam was fully committed, but Slim's stumble, as he saw it, could undermine his confidence. He would claim as the years went by that his faith grew stronger and stronger, but it would always be vulnerable to his secret doubts and insecurity.

The impasse did not prevent the two of them having a beer together at the rugby club. Both were playing less than before. Work and wedding plans were competing for their weekends, but they remained involved, as members and spectators. Saturday night would often find them in their usual position, on the bench behind the clubhouse. Slim was doing his best to persuade Adam not to worry about him and Natalie, who had made the decision to move to Milton Keynes and work on the new town, where, he explained, there were great opportunities for young graduates to do ground-breaking work that could really make a difference. Both of them felt the need for a change, a need to get away.

"But what about the fellowship?" Adam asked "you can't just walk away from it, I know it's still important to you."

"Of course it is, there are a couple of groups in Buckinghamshire, some of which are, how shall I put it, a little more liberal than we are used to. I am sure someone will have me. And there's plenty of rugby down there, you never know, I might get a game with Harlequins!."

Adam saw a great deal of Natalie and Slim over the next couple of weeks, as the two architects worked up their ideas for the Halifax development and he went through the legal, financial and regulatory issues. Of Adam's many talents, imagination was notably absent, but he could recognise it when he saw it. He thought he understood the opportunities of the chapel site, but Natalie was a revelation. It was not just her ability to produce striking visualisations, she found innovative ways to expand the footprint and floor areas that significantly improved the whole viability of the project. Adam was seriously impressed.

He spent his time immersed in legal documents, land registry plans and appraisals for the bank. As the work was finally coming together, there was an unexpected phone call from a firm of solicitors in Pontefract, Curtis, Bendall and Girdall. They asked if they could come and see him the following day on an urgent matter which they did not wish to discuss over the phone. He wondered what that was all about. Up to now, everything had been going well. Solicitors he thought, rarely bring any good news.

Adam always left a tidy desk at the end of the day; all the documents were put back into their files and locked away for the night. As he was putting together the last of the papers and plans, he noticed that there were two copies of the land registry plan for the assembly site in Smawthorne. The site plans were at a small scale, showing little detail. The main road, the bridge and the river were clearly indicated, but the area of woodland and grass verge, including the three ash trees were only in outline. One plan was in black-and-white and clearly a faded copy, while the older looking document, almost certainly the original, was in colour. Adam held both of them in his hands. The difference was small, possibly insignificant. He returned the black-and-white copy to the land registry file and pushed the coloured plan that had been loose in the bundle of other documents inside a brown manila envelope, before placing it into his briefcase for further consideration. He drove home, trying to anticipate what objections or frustrations Messrs Curtis, Bendall and Girdall may be bringing around in the morning.

Chapter 8

The gentleman sat opposite Adam the following morning was clearly from central casting. Sadly, he was not Mr Curtis, Mr Bendall or Mr Girdall. Mr Soames' smart, pinstripe suit, subdued tie and neat haircut spoke eloquently of his profession. Strangely however, he did not speak eloquently at all. He had, Adam was surprised to hear, a Yorkshire accent so broad it would not have been out of place in the pit-head baths at Ledston Luck Colliery. His conversation was as abrupt as his accent was broad, and what he had to say was even more surprising than the manner in which he said it.

"Well, Mr Rowntree, I've some good news fo' thee. We're executors of Mr Albert Featherstone's estate and I'm pleased to tell ye he's left everything to thee." He paused, waiting for the usual look of astonishment and surprise and was not disappointed. Adam leaned back in the chair, suitably speechless. Whatever he had been expecting from the lawyer's visit, this wasn't it. Mr Soames, experienced in such situations, was ready for the reaction, or lack of it. He continued, "Yes, most people tend to be surprised in the circumstances.

I suppose lack of surprise would, in the circumstances, be..." Mr Soames hesitated, "surprising!"

Adam, recovering himself, interrupted the solicitor's ramblings. "Left everything to me? Why me? What about his relatives? Didn't he have a sister? She was his only relative, I think? I am sure she was. She lives somewhere in North Wales, Colwyn Bay, what about her? Pop told me about her." Now it was Adam who was rambling.

"It's not my job Mr Rowntree, to explain why clients instruct me as they do, but I can tell thee this, she's the same age as Mr Featherstone, and quite frail herself, and no family of her own. It 'int a huge estate. It's mainly the house and contents and a small account in the Yorkshire Building Society. Oh yes, the will specifically mentions a car, I think an old MG, something or 'tother."

"Yes," said Adam, "it's an MG TA."

He had coped reasonably well since the funeral, continuing to cut the grass and trim the hedges. But there was no one to sit with on the bench afterwards and share a bottle of beer, no one to listen to his anxieties and frustrations. There was no one to tell him he would be all right. But he had coped, up to now. It was the mention of the car and the gift of it that was too much. Mr Soames, noticing the emotion well up in his young interlocutor, tactfully began to put his papers back in the briefcase. He did, however, manage to display an empathy that belied his abrupt manner,

"Ay, it's nice to see how much the old man meant to thee. You meant a lot to him and he were very fond of thee. He was a grand old chap, was Albert, we've known him in the office for years. He told us a lot about ye, what a grand lad ye were, and how much ye'd help to keep the garden going, when he could no longer manage it. Meant a lot to him, the garden did. Give us a ring in a couple of days and we'll do all the necessaries." With this, he tapped Adam sympathetically on the shoulder and departed as abruptly as he had arrived.

Adam sat motionless at his desk for some time, his mind reeling and his emotions all over the place. There was muted delight at his unexpected good fortune, confusion as to how and why it had come his way, and sadness when he thought about the car. He was raised from his reverie by the telephone on his desk. It was an excited and animated Rachel.

"You won't believe this love, I have got this amazing new commission. A friend of Natalie's is working on a refurb for the National Trust, they need a landscape consultant and I have got the job! I can't believe it, and if it goes well there's a chance of some repeat commissions, isn't it amazing? Are you proud of me?"

"Rachel, slowdown, it all sounds great, but look, I need to come over and see you. Something's happened. I need to talk to you, where are you?"

"I'm at home, working, what on earth is the matter?"

"I will see you in half an hour and tell you then."

Rachel was somewhat disappointed by her fiancé's response to her good news. She had expected rounds of applause and roars of congratulations. Since leaving the bank, she had set herself up with a small studio at home and work had gone well. The room was complete with drawing-board, phone line and second-hand photocopier, all put to good use. Even before any marketing was done, she was surprised how many people were eager to help get the new business off the ground. But a job for the National Trust would be her first big break. Her mother was as excited as she was, and doing everything she could to help. Her father, on the other hand, never failed to live down to her lowest expectations. He was more concerned that the two of them were spending more time on the business than planning the wedding. Adam's response on the telephone had been significantly less than what was expected.

When he arrived, her first reaction on hearing his news was, "Well, at least we will have somewhere to live now!"

"Have you seen the state of the place, it's as old and rundown as he was."

"Well, I'm sure you will be able to knock it into shape love in no time."

"What about you?"

"Me!" Rachel smiled, "I am not sure I am going to have the time now!"

When they had managed to take it all in, the obvious thing to do was go and celebrate. Adam suggested driving out to the Chequers in Ledston, a beautiful country pub midway between Leeds and York. It was hard to believe it was only a few miles from the pit-heads of Smawthorne or the coke ovens of Glasshoughton. The drive out through the late autumn colours would have been idyllic, were it not for the driving rain and mist. Walter and Harry had finally been persuaded to provide Adam with a decent company car, though not the Lotus

Cortina which he had hoped for. The GT badge on the side, the rev counter on the dashboard and the leather steering wheel were enough to let Adam feel he was not in the basic rep mobile. He enjoyed the journey, in spite of the rain, imagining he was on the Yorkshire stage of the RAC Rally. Rachel was always a relaxed passenger, not surprising, given her previous experiences with the erratic Roger. At least with Adam, she was not facing oblivion every time she got into the car.

One of the many things that pleased him about his future wife, was that she was more than prepared to drink beer in a pub. There was none of the fuss and expense of, "I'll just have a G&T love, or a Snowball, or a schooner of sherry would be nice." She was, in his eyes, a proper Yorkshire lass. They drank pints of William Younger's Number Three and chose chicken and chips in the basket, with Black Forest Gateau to follow. Sophisticated dining in South Yorkshire, or anywhere else!

It had been one hell of a day, and would have ended perfectly, drinking coffee by the fire in the pub lounge, had the subject he had been desperate to avoid not been raised by Rachel. She had heard about the decision of the elders, and wanted to be sure Adam would join her in opposing it at the next quarterly meeting. His hesitation was enough to tell her all that she needed to know,

"It's difficult," he stumbled. "The teaching seems clear. It has always been like this hasn't it, you know better than me, don't you?"

"For goodness sake Adam, he's your best friend, you have to stand by him."

"I have spoken to him, and I think he understands. In fact, I'm sure he understands." He sounded feebler to himself with every passing word.

"I'll tell you what I understand Adam Rowntree. This thing with Natalie and Slim is not really about religion at all, or the Gospel. It's not even about the Bible. It's about control. It has always been about control. Men wanting to be in control, mainly men controlling women, but always control. Simeon Kantalow and my father are a pair of control freaks. They see God as the ultimate celestial control freak on high, with them as his controlling representatives here on earth. My father and brother find articulate, intelligent women like Natalie deeply troubling. She challenges their tacit assumptions of male superiority and entitlement, dressed up in New Testament theology. What did the apostle Paul say, 'I do not permit a woman to usurp authority over a man?' Well, given a chance neither would Damien, Simeon or my father. That's why Dad is unhappy with the wedding arrangements, that's why he is uncomfortable with my business and that's why he's putting pressure on Slim, because he's not in control. Well, they are all on the wrong side of history. In the immortal words of the prophet, Bob Dylan, (King James version), 'The Times they are a-changin.' He has controlled my mother for years, but he is not going to control me anymore and hasn't got a hope in Hades of controlling Natalie!"

Adam had never seen this Rachel before. He was shocked and not sure what he ought to say.

"But you are a believer Rachel, you are a part of the fellowship, you have been all your life, surely..." he pleaded. She smiled at him, now with a look of gentle, apologetic reassurance.

"I'm sorry love, it must be a combination of the beer and the excitement of the day. We are not going to fall out over this, but, yes, I believe. I believe in the redemptive power of the Gospel, and that we are all ransomed without a price. But I don't believe in Simeon Kantalow and I certainly don't believe in, 'Our Father who art an elder." She got up, giving him the tenderest of kisses and said, "Come on, Stirling Moss, take me home in that sexy car of yours." He did, but not directly, and wished that he had asked the company for a slightly bigger and more comfortable vehicle.

They didn't fall out over Slim, then or later, but within the fragility of their embryonic relationship, a tiny crack had formed. It was a small hairline fracture, impossible to see, but as is the nature of cracks, their only potential is to grow.

* * *

Harry had been right about the trustees of the Welbeck Road Chapel. They would be prepared to negotiate the sale of the site to a private company if they could be assured the chapel would remain open for Christian worship. The terms, in which this assurance might be set out in any legal documents, would be agreed later, but the principle had been established. Harry would ensure that the content of such a document would be short on detail and long on solicitors' jargon and legal hyperbole. The elders of the assembly were also coming on side, thanks mainly to Simeon's encouragement and support, so now everything depended on Adam's appraisal.

The same group had assembled again in the tiny boardroom, with the exception of Walter, but the addition of Natalie and Slim. Natalie talked everyone through the outline design proposals. The visuals were stunning and not at all what Harry or Damien had been expecting. The chapel was retained at the front of the site, with a revised entrance, allowing the rest of the site to function independently. The remainder of the development, though predominantly in local stone, was a bold, high density and uncompromisingly contemporary scheme. It was mainly residential, but with some offices and workshops. The design revolved around a small public square at the centre of the site which gave access to a new riverside walkway. Car parking was provided in a new undercroft beneath the proposed accommodation and public square.

It was a very accomplished piece of urban planning for someone as recently qualified as Natalie. It clearly was her scheme, presented with Slim's help. The contemporary architecture was challenging, particularly to Damien, but the schedule of accommodation that it generated was compelling. Property Development, in theory at least, is not a particularly complicated process: the total value of the saleable floor area, minus the build and development costs, and the cost of the site, equals profit. The equation really is as simple and neat as that, which was probably why it appealed so much to Adam. Natalie's scheme had created seventy percent more floor area than Harry had believed possible, therefore seventy percent more profit, theoretically!

As Adam took them through the detailed financial appraisal, even Damien's eyes began to light up. If they could acquire the site for close to the figure suggested by the trustees, without them understanding its full potential, it looked like a gift. Adam, being Adam, spelt out the risks. Firstly, it was a complex project and the build costs would be difficult to predict. The undercroft car parking would certainly be expensive. Secondly, they would be buying without planning permission. Would the local planning authority support such a bold and original proposal? Finally, the ground conditions were unknown. The site was part of an old industrial complex, and could be heavily contaminated, needing extensive and costly remediation before any construction work could begin in earnest.

"There is one further risk," added William, the accountant. "This is not like a normal housing development, where you could put in a road and build a few houses, sell them and move on to the rest of the site. A substantial part of the scheme would have to be complete before any sales' revenue would be forthcoming You will have a lot of money outstanding before you see any return and it will need significant support from the bank."

Adam confirmed that the bank was indeed ready to support the project, subject to the normal securities. The accountant concluded that there was a big profit to be made if they built the scheme out, but warned that it was a lot of money upfront, and who knew where interest rates were going next.

There was no way Harry was intending to build the scheme out. Once they had obtained a detailed planning approval, they would sell it on, excluding the chapel, limiting their risk and taking their profit.

Harry was pleased with the whole appraisal. How could he not be! He thanked Natalie and Slim profusely for what they had done in such a short period of time, saying what a great scheme it was. Clearly it was time for the two architects to depart and, taking the hint, they collected their drawings. Saying goodbye, Natalie leaned across the table and placed a small envelope in front of Harry, adding with great charm, "I will leave this with you then. Thank you so very much." Printed on the front was his name and 'Deuteronomy Chapter 14, verses 14 and 15.'

"What do you think that is?" queried Damien, after they had left.

"I have got a fair idea," mumbled Harry to no one in particular, placing it in his jacket pocket and thinking, what a shame, as it had all gone so well up to then.

"Shall I get a firm of quantity surveyors to have a look at these?" Damien suggested, picking up the pile of drawings.

"Why on earth would you want to do that?" Harry asked incredulously.

"To give us an idea of what all this lot might cost," was the not unreasonable reply.

"Well, it will be the first time if they did. Have you ever known a Q.S. accurately predict the cost of a complex scheme such as this, from a set of outline drawings like these? They are brilliant at just two things – one, explaining why the original estimate was wrong, and two explaining why it was not their fault!

You may as well examine the entrails of a dead goat as pay a Q.S. I doubt it would be any less accurate!"

The small, cramped room was getting hot and the windows were steaming up. Harry got out of his chair and stretching his mighty frame, seemed to fill his side of the room. He wandered around the table to open the window, letting in a cool draft of late autumn breeze and the buzz of the tea-time traffic. Taking off his jacket and dropping back down into his creaking chair, he loosened his tie and said, "I'll have a word with Arthur Hughes. He seems to know what's going on in Halifax, and I think we should also involve our friend Mr Spigot. He is very discreet, so get a set of these plans sent over to both of them. Adam, can you ask around, see if any similar projects are going on in the area and try and get some idea of build costs. With this schedule of accommodation, these numbers, and the trustees asking price, we probably have a sizeable margin for error anyway."

"What about ground conditions?" Adam asked, ever the man for detail.

"Difficult. There's no way we can send a ground investigation rig onto the site as that would give the game away immediately. Even if we did, the engineers never want to drill a borehole within the building footprint where it would actually be useful. You pay to have an expert ground investigation telling you everything you want to know about the land you are not going to build on, and nothing of the ground where you might actually put in a foundation." Harry seemed to be in a particularly cynical mood that afternoon, at least as far as consultants were concerned.

Before the meeting broke up, Harry wanted to explain to Adam why Walter was not involved. He emphasised anxieties about his health, rather than his avowed misgivings about Harry's business ethics. "A new development company is going to be set up," he explained. "It will involve myself, William and Damien, but it is also our intention to offer a directorship to you, with a shareholding in the new company." No details or timescale were mentioned, but it still sounded like good news to Adam.

The presentation had gone so well that Adam felt emboldened to raise the issue of Rachel's woodland. He pointed out that if the sale of the assembly hall was included in the project, as it clearly had to be, Rachel was going to be extremely upset if she lost control of her conservation area. It had been her baby, and she had put a lot of time and effort into it over the years. She would not, he emphasised, take it well. From the response of Damien and Harry, it was clear, though hard to believe, that neither of them had given the matter any consideration at all.

"I was thinking," Adam continued, "it might be rather nice if I were to buy the woodland as a surprise wedding present. It is only a small corner of the site next to the river that would never be available for development, and would remove any potential problem."

Harry had to admit he had a point. He would have preferred not to lose control of any part of the site, but Adam was right about Rachel and he couldn't afford to upset her. Confidentiality was everything at this stage, and he could imagine the trouble that his daughter could cause if she set her mind to it. And the wedding present was an excellent idea.

"I see no reason why not and it would probably help the planning application if we were seen to ring fence the woodland as a community benefit." Damien could not help questioning whether Adam could afford it. Given what his father had contributed to his own house, this seemed a bit rich. As it happened, he could, but they had agreed to keep their good news to themselves for the time being.

Harry sat at home in his study, late into the evening, going over the events of the day. The study was on the front of the house, directly next to the front door, with a view down the length of the gravel drive. Its walls were lined with shelves, filled with books and files, both secular and religious. They represented the two worlds that Harry Sunderland inhabited. Both were important to him, demanding a great deal of his time and energy. Some of his critics would accuse him of living a double life, each with its own distinct and perhaps conflicting set of ethical and moral values. To Harry, they were separate, but never in conflict. He had an uncanny ability to move seamlessly between the two worlds without any difficulty. It was a trick that, in later years, his future son-in-law would try and fail to execute with quite the same ease and style.

He was about to wind up for the evening when he remembered the envelope in his jacket pocket. He reached inside, holding it in his hands and looking at the quotation, trying to remember what it referred to. Opening it, he was presented with a precise and detailed fee note – hours spent, expenses incurred, a reasonable hourly charge for two architects and the bottom line figure, not unreasonable in relation to the potential value they had created. It was titled 'For architectural services rendered.' Looking back at the envelope he noticed again the reference, Deuteronomy Chapter 14, verses 14 & 15. Reaching for the King James Bible that was always on his desk, preferring the authorised version for both its poetry and familiarity, he found the passage:

'Thou shalt not oppress the hired servant,
whether he be thy brother or a stranger.
at his day thou shalt give him his wages,
neither shalt the sun go down on it,
lest he cry against thee,'

His first reaction was, "You cheeky bugger..." but then his mind went back to the scheme, and the significant potential value it represented. Looking again at his Bible, he thought, 'this Natalie is surely some formidable woman'. Opening a draw, he took out the company chequebook, making out the cheque to the full amount, but payable to Mr Matthew Sunderland. He put it in a company envelope and wrote the address, again using Matthew's name. Harry went through to the drawing-room, looking to share a night-cap with Jenny, but she had gone to bed some time ago, so, not for the first time, he drank alone.

When the envelope arrived in the post, Slim opened it and, with a smile of surprise and satisfaction, turned it around to show Natalie.

"Well," she said, "it is true what you have always been telling me."

"What's that, love?"

"That the word of the Lord is a powerful thing!"

"Aye," said Slim, "and sharper than any two-edged sword, even to the dividing of soul and spirit." Completing the quotation Natalie had never known.

He greedily pulled his lover on top of him, saying,

"You are a grave loss to the Assemblies of Christ, my darling girl."

"I am sure they can manage very well without me."

"I am sure they can," he pulled her down again, kissing her tenderly, "but I can't." For a couple of young architects, it would appear that there are few aphrodisiacs quite as powerful as a promptly paid fee.

Chapter 9

Rachel and Adam were unprepared that Sunday afternoon for the job of cleaning, clearing and sorting out Pop's old house. Practically they had it covered with cleaning gear, dustpans and brushes, a small skip on the drive and even an industrial vacuum cleaner. But emotionally they were all at sea. The sadness and pathos of the rundown old house, filled with the unwanted possessions of the old dead man, found them totally unprepared.

There had been one or two antiques that had been identified in the will as specific bequests, which the executors had already removed. Everything else – all the myriad of prosaic paraphernalia that had once been his life were as he had left them, waiting around the house, with no more of a future than he had. It all seemed to the young couple desperately sad.

They began carefully, a room at a time, sorting piles of books, crockery, paintings and ornaments. They tried to identify what might be saved, or what might have value to someone else, or what a charity shop would or wouldn't take. Anything that went into the first skip was an agonising decision. Later, when the second skip had arrived, it filled more quickly, with less heart-searching, though no less guilt.

Adam was sat in one of the bedrooms, now devoid of curtains, decorations, and most of the furniture. The more that they removed from the house, the less it felt like Pop's, and the easier it was to clear. He was going through one of the chests of drawers, dropping old papers and magazines into a cardboard box at his feet. At the bottom of the drawer was an old photo album. As he picked it up, a number of them slipped out, as they always do. The largest of the black-and-white pictures caught his eye. There was a young man, standing in front of a wooden hut, full of plants and shrubs. A sign over the top said 'Albert Featherstone Nursery.' Pop was standing there, holding out a glass of wine, surrounded by a small group of mainly young women, similarly with glasses in hand. Clearly, it was a celebration, though of what he could only guess. Even without the sign Adam would have recognised him, just as easily as he recognised the smiling young woman with her arm around his shoulders, pointing her drink at the camera. His mother had changed less over the years than Pop had.

He was about to call down to Rachel but stopped himself. Instead, he sat down on the old mattress of Pop's double bed, looking at the two figures. There must have been 15 or 20 people altogether, but he just looked at the two. Pop's arm was around his mother's waist, pulling her closer, his mother's arm was hanging casually across his shoulders, their heads close together, smiles beaming at the camera. He turned the photograph over seeking more information. It was there, a white label with faded handwriting, 'Open Day at the Nursery, June 1946.' He carefully went through the rest of the album, not sure what he was looking for, but looking nonetheless. There was nothing else of the same, singular interest, so he dropped the album into the cardboard box, but put the photograph in an old brown envelope and took it downstairs, locking it in the glove box of his car.

He found Rachel in the kitchen trying to decide if there was any future life in Pop's eclectic range of cutlery and kitchenware. There was not.

"I think I've had enough of this for one afternoon" he said, "let's go back to mum's for supper." Rachel, looking at the half-sorted collection of knives, forks, ladles and spoons filling the cracked Belfast sink, and then the grimy cooker, complete with a fat encrusted chip pan, the wire basket still imprisoned in the solidified fat, did not require any persuasion.

Adam came up behind her and gave a thank you squeeze. Looking out across the garden, Rachel commented that at least it looked like it was still alive and flourishing. "Perhaps it doesn't know that he is dead yet." The two of them had been coming down regularly to weed, trim the hedges and cut the grass as Adam had always done.

"Yes, " he said, "at least we can retain that in all its former glory."

"What are you going to do about the car, love? Are you going to keep it? Would anyone want to buy it in its current state? Is it saleable?" He had been thinking about the car himself. It was in a sorry state, but the sad experience of dismembering Pop's house had instilled in him a desire not to let the same thing happen to the car.

"Well, what do you think? If we could restore the garden to its former glory, perhaps one day we might be up to doing the same thing with the car?"

"You mean a resurrection of the body?" Rachel asked.

Yes, Adam thought to himself, a resurrection, if not of Pop, at least of his car.

They headed back to Lumley Street and supper. Earlier, Sunday lunch had gone well, in spite of the presence of Julia and her latest man. University had provided Julia with just about everything she needed in life with her two degrees. She had graduated with a first, even though she had not done a great deal of work, and received her doctorate three years later. The university had also provided her with a job lecturing, and a steady supply of partners, none of whom seemed to last long. Richard, the current occupant of the role, was a somewhat quiet, if not morose mathematician, researching chaos theory. The irony of this was not lost on Mother, who reflected that it would be impossible to predict where this relationship might go, ignorant as they all were of the initial conditions!

Peace and harmony in the kitchen, and around the dining table, had been due, in part, to Rachel's presence. Both Mother and Julia found her entirely to their liking. The feelings were mutual. In fact, Rachel enjoyed almost everything about Lumley Street. It was now the home where she felt the most relaxed, as there seemed to be none of the tensions and pressures that she felt were a constant presence at her parents' house.

Adam's mum and dad had accepted her, with their easy generosity, which allowed her to hang around the house, graze in the kitchen, potter in the garden or lounge on the sofas, entirely at her ease. She felt she was going to be far more fortunate in her in-laws than her husband would be. Fortunately, Adam did not entirely share her opinion.

This Sunday she had been determined to try, once and for all, to get the recipe for the Yorkshire puddings. This was problematic, because there was no recipe, certainly not one that was written down in a book. Mother made them the same way she always did, instinctively, almost without thinking. The only solution therefore was close observation. Amongst much giggling and mirth, Mother did her best to cooperate. Two eggs, plain flour measured with the same serving spoon she had used for years, milk and a dash of water, and finally lots of salt and pepper. Then, with a bowl tucked under one arm and a wooden spoon in the other came the beating. There were no whisks, no electric mixers, just a strong right arm. After much laughter, instruction and all three women taking a turn, the batter was done and left to rest under a clean tea towel. The women had then shared the bottle of chilled Chablis that Richard had kindly brought along.

Hector and Adam's timing had been perfect. The opening of the front door coincided, almost exactly, with the opening of the oven. This was further vital information for Rachel, for the fat in the oven trays must be red hot when the batter is poured in. The oven door must not be opened until the very last minute. The puddings and gravy were proclaimed a triumph by one and all. Sunday lunch was exactly what Mother wanted – the family around the table, with the odd stranger (Richard certainly filled that role), good food, good company and good conversation.

Adam and Julia seemed to have agreed on a non-aggression pact for the day which would, no doubt, be as fragile as the original. The conversation had roamed widely. There was Harold Wilson's chance of winning a second election in the same year; Leeds United's chance of being triumphant in the first division and, from Julia's point of view, the chances of the Birmingham Six in the High Court. Richard, knowing of Hector's local government connections, was interested to learn more about the corruption scandal involving John Poulson, but he would not be drawn on the subject, somewhat testily commenting, "There are better things to talk about over Sunday lunch." Realising that he had been unnecessarily short with his guest he apologised, explaining that the disgraced architect had cast something of a cloud over many local authorities in the West Riding of Yorkshire, including his own.

These wide-ranging and informal conversations, sometimes erudite, though invariably uninformed, were a revelation to Rachel. They were usually seasoned with just the right amount of self-deprecating humour to ensure that nothing and no one could be taken too seriously. It was something else that she grew to like about the house in Lumley Street.

When, having served the last of the apple pie, Mother had declared with uncharacteristic drama, "Well, I have an announcement to make", all eyes had turned to give her their full attention. Placing the empty custard jug back on the table like the chairman's gavel she said, "I have enrolled in the Open University, and I am going to get myself a degree at long last." Mother did not say she was going to try and get a degree, or that she had enrolled on a degree course. It had been spoken with a determination, all too familiar, that she was going to get herself a degree.

Julia had looked delighted; Rachel had looked intrigued. Hector, just looked like Hector, resigned but impressed, and Adam had done his best to appear pleased.

"Brilliant!" said Julia, "What are you going to study?"

Hector chipped in, "I don't suppose it is going to be mechanical engineering by any chance?"

Mother picked up the custard jug again with a mock matriarchal menace, silencing her husband. "Not sure, exactly, but something to do with history, I thought it would give me a chance to borrow some of your books and try to get a return on our previous investments, Julia."

Hector had got to his feet looking for a bottle of champagne. It had not been chilled, neither were there any champagne flutes, so wine glasses needed to suffice, but no one noticed that.

By the time Rachel and Adam got back home for supper, Julia and her 'chaotic' mathematician had left. Hector and Mother were waiting in the lounge. The sandwiches were made, the mushy peas simmering on the stove and the glasses were on the coffee table waiting for the beer and the visitors to return. After their sombre labours of the afternoon, the cosy living room with the glow of the coals flickering in the grate was a welcome sight. The two of them sank down together into the sagging cushions on the sofa. Rachel would usually have offered to help, but supper was ready, and they were ready for supper. Hector opened the beer and Mother went to the kitchen to get the peas. It had taken a while for Rachel to get used to the leftover warmed up peas, but eventually she was converted. The four of them sat contented in the warm living room, enjoying the beer and anticipating the sandwiches.

"So how did you get on this afternoon?" Hector queried, "Did you manage to get much done?" His mother and father had shown less surprise than Adam might have expected at his good fortune; Mother had made it clear that neither she nor Hector had any inkling of Pop's intentions. They were clearly pleased for him, and showed no signs of envy, even though his mother had done far more for Pop over the years than Adam ever had. If she did feel a sense of, 'why him and not me?' she showed no sign of it. He was surprised though, when being asked if she would like to help in clearing the house, being the kind of job she would normally have embraced with enthusiasm, she rather abruptly declined, saying, "No it's your house now, you had better get on with it." That seemed to him strangely out of character.

Rachel answered Hector's question, leaving Adam deep in his own thoughts. "We got far less done than we had hoped to do. It was all rather depressing and difficult to decide what to keep, what to sell and what we had to chuck in the skip. Yes, it was all very sad."

"It always is," replied Hector, speaking from experience, "but it has to be done."

Mother, in her usual blunt manner, tried to change the subject. "You're very quiet tonight Adam, what's the matter with you?"

"It's just as Rachel says, it has not been much of a fun-filled afternoon." Hector got up and headed for the kitchen to get the statutory extra sandwiches and beer. Adam, unable to contain himself any longer, turned to the subject that had been preoccupying him. "Mum, how long have you and Dad known Pop? Where did you first come across him?" Mother leaned back in her chair, looking thoughtful, "Oh, it was a long time ago, I'm not sure I can remember when we first met."

"Surely" Adam insisted, "You must be able to remember something?"

"I suppose it would be some time during the War, or just after it. In those days, everyone was growing as many of their own vegetables as they could. The gardens were not green lawns and flowerbeds then, most were well-worked vegetable patches and small greenhouses. Pop, with his work on the land, became something of an expert in the town on how to get the best out of your garden. Most men like your dad were overseas, and we womenfolk had to do what we could. I think that's how we first got to know him, living as he did just round the corner."

"Did he come around in those days for your lunch and tea?

"I am not sure. I suppose he might have done. It is a long time ago now, I can't remember."

"Surely you can remember if he used to come to the house. When did he start coming for Sunday lunch? Was that after the War?"

Adam continued, "I wonder why he never had any family of his own? Did he never marry? He must've had a girlfriend though, surely he would have a girlfriend."

"Well, I am sure I don't know," said Mother, giving her son one of her looks.

"Well, it seems a bit odd if there wasn't somebody." Adam insisted.

"Why the questions all of a sudden?" She was clearly becoming irritated, not taking kindly to being cross-examined by her son, in her own living room.

Hector returned with the extra sandwiches and beer.

"I was just asking about Pop, Dad. I realise I don't know very much about him, do I?"

"You know as much as I do, I gave you as much of his story as I could at the funeral."

"So when did you first meet him? Mum can't remember."

Hector laughed, "Well, I remember when I first saw him. I remember that very well as he was wearing my best wind cheater jacket." He was smiling at the memory. Mother was not.

"I really liked that jacket. I bought it before the War. It had a reversible tartan check on one side and gabardine on the other. Very stylish it was to before the War. It was just after El Alamein. I received your mother's regular letter. We used to write every week although they didn't always arrive the same week. They often came in batches of three or four. Anyhow, Mum included a photograph of herself with a crowd of others on a vegetable patch. And there's this chap, Albert, wearing my favourite jacket. There I was, up to my neck in muck and bullets, and there's this fella wearing my favourite jacket. It made me think I can tell you. I nearly put in for compassionate leave" he joked. Mother had heard this all before and was not sharing the joke.

"He was a grand old chap though, a grand old chap." He raised his glass of beer, in memory, and popped a sandwich into his mouth.

Hector rarely spoke to the children about the War. There were never any tales of adventure or daring do. He never collected his medals and as children they were never allowed to play with toy guns. Hector had seen enough of guns and what they could do. The expression 'up to my neck in muck and bullets' was not bragging. It was his version of humorous obfuscation, a way of not remembering, not talking. He had never shared in the national mood, "This being our finest hour." Too much had been lost, too much had been destroyed. To him, it had been a national tragedy and he would speak about it as little as possible. If Hector could have rerun the tape, in 1939 he would have been standing beside Albert Featherstone, as a conscientious objector.

Tonight, Adam was clearly a dog with a bone and he could not leave his mother alone.

"It just seems very strange, that he left everything to me, why not to you, you did more for him than I ever did, why me? It all seems a bit odd." Mother was clearly beginning to lose her patience and had Rachel not been there she would've expressed herself with greater force.

"If I were you lad, I would leave it alone, count your blessings, and get on with what needs to be done. People who dig around in the past rarely find what they are looking for, or like what they find."

Adam got the message finally and decided it was time he took Rachel home. They got up, making to go, but Mother took Rachel by the hand and led her into the kitchen, "I've got a little present for you, love." While Adam was waiting, he noticed something new on the sideboard in the dining room. It was a mahogany cabinet with two drawers and a lid. Lifting the top, a large canteen of silver cutlery presented itself. Each of the drawers was filled with a similar miscellany of expensive looking silverware.

"This is rather nice." Adam commented to nobody in particular.

"Yes," said Hector peering over his shoulder, "as you can see, Pop did not completely forget your mum. He was a man full of surprises was Albert Featherstone."

"Must be worth a bit," Adam observed.

"I suppose it is." Hector replied, more concerned about where Mother had hidden the Radio Times.

Rachel came back from the kitchen, a beaming smile on her face and a large serving spoon in her hand.

"Look," she said excitedly, "now there's no excuse, we can make Yorkshire puddings of our own. I've got my own spoon now!"

Later, sitting together in the lounge waiting for Sunday Night at the Palladium to start, Mother asked "Why was the Poulson scandal not fit to be spoken of at Sunday lunch? Why were you so sensitive? You were a bit short with Richard, is it going to be a problem?"

"I know, I am sorry about that, but no, it is not going to be a problem, at least, not for us." Mother was pleased to hear it, but Hector still seemed ill at ease with the subject.

"Are you sure?" she insisted,

"Sure, but there are some folk at the county council who are getting very nervous, and with good reason."

For students of the time and chance version of history, the Poulson scandal had to become essential reading. How had an unqualified architect, born in an obscure northern industrial town, created the largest architectural practice in Europe, which then collapsed, bringing down a Conservative Home Secretary and leading to the conviction of numerous public figures? It also fundamentally changed the way members of parliament's interests would be registered for the foreseeable future. The answer is because "time and chance happeneth to them all." John Poulson's corrupt business practices would never have come to light were it not for the coming together of three unfortunate coincidences, the first, of course, being his personal bankruptcy.

While the practice of architecture may be an exciting and rewarding profession, as Slim and Natalie were discovering, as a business model, for commercial success it can be less than ideal. If one is successful in attracting numerous significant commissions (as Poulson was), large offices filled with teams of highly qualified well-paid staff are required. But all commissions come to an end and, unlike other professions, your clients, who may be delighted with your work, rarely have a new commission to offer you immediately. All architects are chasing the next job. The more successful they are the bigger the beast they have to feed. Poulson became the largest beast in Europe. Add to that the regular recessions that blight the construction industry and architecture can become a very high-risk activity. Poulson's businesses became top heavy and unsustainable.

The architect's second misfortune was that Mure-Hunter QC, Council for Poulson's creditors, embarked upon a particularly diligent cross- examination at the bankruptcy hearing in Wakefield. He examined, in detail, Poulson's questionable outgoings and expenses. Most of the media had ignored this 'minor hiatus in the North,' but a number of local journalists and Private Eye, in particular, ensured it came to the public's attention.

Poulson's day of judgement, his Armageddon, was eventually guaranteed by his own hand. He had maintained meticulous records of every gift, every contribution, every overseas holiday, every financial inducement, every bribe he had ever made. Incredibly, he had failed to destroy these records before the investigation began.

Ultimately, his corrupt activities would embrace the great and the not so good of British politics: Reginald Maudlin, Home Secretary; T Dan Smith in Newcastle, Leader of Newcastle City Council; George Pottinger of the Scottish Office and Andrew Cunningham of the GMW Union. A number of MPs were also implicated. He began, however, with local councillors in the West Riding of Yorkshire. Many of them were unsophisticated working men, some decent unpaid public servants who Poulson found easy to corrupt at minimum cost.

Poulson and some of his co-conspirators were unrepentant, claiming, with some justification, that they were only doing what everyone else was doing. His only distinction being that he was more successful than the rest, and got found out. It is certainly true that before the scandal broke there had been informal conversations in the corridors of Westminster as to what might be done for the architect in the next New Year's Honours list.

T Dan Smith, Pottinger and Cunningham we're all prosecuted with Poulson, although the MPs got off on a legal technicality. The police investigation however had a list of the more minor public figures and officials who were being considered for investigation and prosecution. At some point, they would draw a line under any future prosecutions. Some of these officials were Hectors contemporaries in councils across the West Riding and were desperately hoping that their names would finish up below that line.

Mother was still worried, "Didn't he invite you and someone else on one of his overseas trips, somewhere in Spain or Portugal. You didn't go did you?"

"I think you would have noticed if I had gone love. It was 1966 or 67, not sure which, and the invite was really for Jeremy in housing. Open Systems Building, his house building company, wanted to negotiate the contract to build council housing in the county."

"Why didn't you go?"

"I would like to say that we knew that it was corrupt, a bribe, but in truth we didn't. It was all very impressive, with Reginald Maudling on the letterhead. "Come and inspect our developments on the continent." It was all very plausible. I suppose that's why so many were drawn in."

"So why didn't you go?"

"Don't know, it just didn't seem right, narrow escape aye love."

Hector had finished with the subject and turned his focus to the tv, sitting back in his chair with a clear conscience, relaxed. Mother, however, spent what remained of the evening reviewing in her mind the unwelcome interrogation by her son earlier in the day.

Chapter 10

1975

Hector may have been able to relax on Sunday evening with a clear conscience, but Arthur Hughes, Alderman Hughes, could not. He had said, "Yes," on a number of occasions to overseas trips, to favours and emoluments, to generous hospitality and much else. At the time it had all seemed perfectly legitimate, entirely proper, for him to engage with people and organisations who had the skills and experience to provide the developments and improvements that his constituents desperately needed in post-war Britain. Poulson had a track record in all of them – new housing, hospitals and schools. In many respects he was the 'go-to man', a 'blue-chip practice' if ever there was one.

If Arthur occasionally benefited from hospitality and foreign travel, or the occasional modest consultant's fee, wasn't that a reasonable compensation for the many unpaid hours spent on council business? More than anything, it had been the knowledge that many of his peers and associates were ploughing a similar furrow which persuaded him that what he was doing was not only blameless, but in fact admirable, even praiseworthy. Such of course is the collective morality, the herd instinct of the corrupt in every generation.

He had never liked Poulson. He found him an aggressive, driven individual, a workaholic who expected the same of all those around him. Arthur found him to be without charm and always full of himself, although, coming from the vain, glorious Arthur, that was a bit rich. He found T Dan Smith more agreeable. Smith certainly seemed to have the best interests of the North East of England at heart. Nor had he benefited financially to any great extent. None of this had done much to protect him though from the tide of retribution when it broke over them all.

Following the conviction and sentencing of Poulson, what in the late 60s had appeared to be acceptable business practice, now looked different, it looked like corruption. When Arthur had been sitting in the grey, drab, police interview room with his pessimistic solicitor, waiting to be interviewed under caution by the investigating officer, he had feared the worst. He had endured a difficult and stressful time, but it now seemed as though the investigation had run its course and was losing steam. The police were apparently winding down their operation and although he had been on a list of minor players considered for prosecution, his name would now finish up just on the right side of the line. This was less evidence of innocence than fatigue in the legal process. He was not the only council member and official who would be breathing a sigh of relief. Hector knew of a few within his own council.

There would, however, be reputational damage and consequences. Senior members of the local party had suggested, some strongly, that this might be the right time for him to step down, retire from public life and then his many years of service to the council would be acknowledged. This rankled somewhat, as many of those who saw fit to judge him were not without sin themselves. If the Poulson scandal proved anything, it was that the New Testament injunction, 'One should be without sin before casting the first stone,' did not apply to the barrage of stones that might follow.

He mistakenly imagined Harry Sunderland knew nothing of these events. It was he who had later asked to meet him in their usual spot in the corner of the committee room at the rugby club. He sat alone, feeling uncomfortable, in the comfortable leather chairs, reserved for members of the committee. A large measure of Black Label whiskey was on the brass coffee table at his side. The soda siphon beside it was the only thing keeping the two of them company. His small, pink fingers absentmindedly played on the chrome lever at the top of the fountain as he tried to decide which version of Arthur Hughes was going to be present this afternoon. There was less confidence these days. The old swagger and certainties were fading. He was hoping that being free of the restrictions and responsibilities of a local councillor he would be able to help the likes of Harry more directly, as an independent consultant perhaps. It is, however, always harder to judge one's commercial worth when it is in decline. And when the decline is terminal, it's impossible.

Harry was, as ever, punctual and in good spirits. He arrived carrying a pint for himself and a top-up for Arthur's whiskey. Setting the drinks down on the table, he made himself at home in the chair opposite.

"Cheers Arthur!" Harry liked the rugby club. It had all the benefits of a decent pub, but with the privacy and familiarity of a gentleman's club. People would look after you here. Well, they would if you were Harry Sunderland, and Harry Sunderland would look after you.

"That was a grand wedding you had the other month Harry. They looked a lovely couple and you and Jenny seemed to be enjoying yourselves. How are the newlyweds?"

"Yes, thank you, Arthur, it was a good day, wasn't it? Thank you for coming. It was a bit more low-key than I had intended as you know, but it was what they wanted. They've settled into Albert Featherstone's old house. Did you know he left it to Adam? Nice bit of good fortune for the lad wasn't it? Bit of a surprise, though. Strange man was old Pop Featherstone, I never really knew what to make of him. They've put a lot of effort into doing up the old house though and made quite a transformation."

"What about Walter's lad, Slim, a wedding there as well?"

"Oh yes, that was even more low-key. They got married down in Buckinghamshire, just the immediate family and a few friends. They both seem happy. They're working for the New Town Development Corporation in Milton Keynes, so there should be plenty of work there to occupy them. Nice girl, Natalie, very bright, very talented, they'll do well those two."

The pleasantries and banalities over, Harry wanted to get down to business. He thanked Arthur for his help to date and explained that everything was now in place to complete the purchase of both the Smawthorne site and the Halifax Chapel. As he had seen the scheme for the chapel, he could see that it was bold and ambitious and therefore much would depend on the reaction of the local planning authority. Mr Spigot was cautiously optimistic, but his was a professional's view. Harry needed an insight into whether the leading figures in Halifax could be persuaded to get behind it, and what was needed to encourage them to do so.

Arthur had spoken to the chair of the planning committee and the leader of the majority group.

"It is going to be a matter of timing Harry, rundown urban sites like these are going to be ripe for just the kind of regeneration you are proposing. Ultimately, we believe there could be central government grants to pump prime such developments. That though could be some years off. But if you went ahead now, I can't believe that the site will not be worth significantly more in five or ten years' time."

Harry leaned his considerable weight back in the chair, thoughtfully draining his pint. "Want another of those?" he offered, noticing that Arthur didn't seem to recognise that it was his round. "Thank you," he said, oblivious to the niceties. Arthur had got used to other people providing his food and drinks. He was going to have to make a significant adjustment in the not-too-distant future.

Harry returned from the bar and placed the drinks on the table. "There you are Alderman."

"I am afraid it will not be Alderman much longer Harry." Arthur gently splashed the soda into his whiskey. "I am planning to retire from the council in the near future."

Harry was less surprised than Arthur might have imagined. He knew Poulson, as a surveyor and developer in the West Riding, how could you not know him? But Harry's developments, up to now, were small beer compared to Poulson's empire, so their paths had rarely crossed. None the less, he knew enough of what had been going on for the last decade and more to disapprove. He could see a fundamental difference between the way he operated and what he saw as the gross corruption that was now evident in Poulson's operation. Although there was a significant difference in scale, there would be some who would not have found it quite so easy as Harry to identify the 'fundamental difference' between the two men. But as he was often known to quote in his more evangelical lectures, "All the ways of a man are right in his own eyes." Perhaps John Poulson had come across the same proverb growing up in the Methodist Sunday School in Knottingley. If he had, the proverb's exhortation had had no more effect upon him than on Harry Sunderland.

Harry thought of himself as a man of integrity, an honourable man who could be trusted. He saw no conflict or contradiction between his strong religious convictions, his business practices, and the wealth he had accumulated. Harry saw his good fortune not as fortune at all, but as divine providence. From this lofty position, he felt more than able and well inclined to judge Arthur Hughes, and judge him harshly. Even if he was still prepared to take advantage of whatever business intelligence he had to offer.

Arthur was, obviously, not sure how to explain himself. Harry helped him out. "I suppose it's the Poulson scandal is it Arthur?" Helpful but brutal. Arthur bridled. "I haven't done anything wrong, of course. You must understand that Harry, certainly nothing illegal. There's no question of any prosecution."

Not now, perhaps, thought Harry, knowing far more about the thing than Arthur could imagine. "It's just that some of the members of the council seem to think there is guilt by association. Not very fair really, but there's a feeling that I should stand down." There was a moment of embarrassed silence that Harry was not particularly inclined to break. "The good news is that in the future I will have the time and the freedom to become more directly involved in things." Quite what things he had in mind was probably unclear to both parties.

A more compassionate man, such as Walter, might have felt a little more sympathy for the Alderman's dénouement and offered some words of reassurance and even sympathy. There but for the grace of God go I, or something of the like. After all, they had known each other for many years and Arthur had been helpful on a number of occasions, not least over his son's new house. Harry was not that kind of man. He was confident and arrogant enough to believe he knew how God's grace might and might not be bestowed. The Alderman was, in his mind, an unlikely recipient. As far as he was concerned, Arthur Hughes, had been,

"Weighed in the balance and found wanting." Like Belshazzar before him, his power would be taken away and his feasting days were over, at least as far as Sunderland Developments was concerned.

Harry had been relying on him for his political contacts and influence in Halifax and Smawthorne. Unlike Arthur, he had no illusions about the situation. Arthur's stock was in terminal decline. He would soon discover just how quickly he would be sidelined and excluded from the corridors of power and influence. Harry would have to rethink his strategy. There was still a great opportunity waiting to be exploited, but the risks had just ratcheted up a notch or two. Arthur made his excuses, promising to keep in touch and to discover whatever he could about the political scene in Halifax. Harry thanked him, saying how that would be most helpful, and knowing full well it would be no help at all.

Sitting alone, after Arthur's awkward departure, he needed to decide how, if at all, to move the thing forward. Jerry came round, helpfully asking if he would like another pint. "Better not, I'm driving, but a pot of coffee would be good, thank you." He sat there for a while enjoying the fresh coffee and the genial surroundings. What he needed was a sounding board, someone to bounce his ideas off and talk the thing through. Historically this had always been his brother, but Walter had made it clear he did not wish to be involved. He knew what Damien's reaction would be: Go for it! The accountant would give him an accountant's view. The person whose ear he most wished to bend was Adam's. For all his youth and inexperience, Adam would give him a carefully considered, analytical and dispassionate view. Fortunately, they were all due for Sunday lunch this weekend. Gaynor, Damien and the twins would also be around.

Since the twins had been born, Harry and Jenny had not seen as much of them at Salem as he had hoped. Gaynor, understandably, looked to her own mother in the circumstances. When it comes to grandchildren, maternal grandmother's always have the prior claim, but with the unexpected arrival of twins, Gaynor had needed her mother, and the need was still acute. With her help she had coped, just. Although Jenny liked to see her grandchildren, she was content to let mother and daughter do their thing, and see them all as and when. With the children now at school, Gaynor was finding life in Wakefield rather dull. The house was impressive, but the thrill of the new had worn off and she now felt rather isolated. Some days, if her mother wasn't around, she would not see anybody between dropping the twins off at school and collecting them at four o'clock. She had not managed to attach herself to one of the groups of 'ladies who lunch' or the coffee morning set. It was all rather lonely.

It was Harry who missed seeing the family around the table more often on a Sunday lunchtime. But today they would all be there, and he had persuaded Walter and Felicity to come along too, so it would be a meeting of the clans. With two normally noisy eight year-olds, Sunday lunch was less the calm sophisticated affair of former years. Looking across the table, Harry had to remind himself that children do not enter the world with well-developed social skills, they need to be taught, or better still, caught. With Sandra and Darren, the infection appeared to be slow to take hold! Sitting in his usual spot at the head of the table, he tried as ever to be the master of ceremonies, but the twins were serious and persistent competition. What was more, Gaynor was looking increasingly tense and on edge.

Rachel, looking at the diners, couldn't help but wonder if any of the women actually wanted to be there. She would certainly rather have been in the infinitely more relaxed atmosphere of Lumley Street with her in-laws. Gaynor clearly wished she was in Wakefield with her mother and Felicity looked worried to death about Walter. Her own mother, who as usual had done all the work, gave the distinct impression she could have done without the bother. She sat disengaged at the far end of the table, regularly refilling her own wine glass, something she had been doing in the kitchen since 12 o'clock. Rachel had not noticed this before and wondered if anybody else had.

Rachel also noticed the only one keeping pace with her mother this lunchtime was Gaynor. In time, to everyone's relief, the children were freed from the unsuccessful tutorial on table manners, and allowed to go and ransack the garden or play on the Scalextric that Jenny had thoughtfully laid out upstairs. Walter, as was his preference, said he would go and keep an eye on them. He was far more the natural grandfather than his brother and always enjoyed the children's company. There was, sadly, no sign of any grandchildren down in Milton Keynes, so as ever, Walter made the best of things.

Damien was eager to tell them all about their new plans in Scarborough. They had acquired a house, up on the south cliff, overlooking the spa and the open-air pool. They planned to refurbish it as a holiday home/come weekend bolthole and create some additional flats as holiday lets. It was really Gaynor's idea as she knew a number of local people who had done the same kind of thing, spending their weekends there, with or without husbands and children. Damien, who had kept a boat in the harbour for a number of years, was equally keen on the project.

Scarborough had always claimed to be the nation's first purpose-built holiday resort. Echoes of its former regency splendour remained, with the spa and the majestic extravagance of the Grand Hotel. It towered above the more downmarket amusement arcades, freak shows and ubiquitous fish and chip shops, spread out along the foreshore. In truth, the whole town was becoming more downmarket, struggling to compete with package holidays in the continental sun.

To the affluent classes of the West Riding, its principal attraction was proximity. With an early get-away on a Friday afternoon and no hold-ups around York, it took not much more than an hour to get there. You could be sat on top of the south cliff outside the Crown Hotel, or cruising out of the harbour by six or seven o'clock on a summer's evening. That's what Gaynor had in mind.

Turning to Adam and Rachel, Damien said, "You two must come across sometime, and spend a day with us. It's a great spot, just a short walk down to the beach." Then to his father, as ever looking for reassurance, "It's a good location, Dad isn't it?" Harry, somewhat distractedly replied, "It's certainly that, and the views are fantastic. There's only that hotel between you and open country all the way down to Filey and Flamborough Head." Damien had been confident it was a good place to invest his father's money. Perhaps one day they might even buy the hotel.

"What do you think Rachel?" asked Gaynor, keen to show off her new acquisition.

"I certainly will, as soon as I get some time."

She didn't mean it as a dig, or a put down, but it certainly sounded like one, and was probably received as such. She almost regretted it... almost, for her life was considerably different. The business was going better than she could have imagined. They may have been small commissions, but she was surprised how they mounted up. More important than anything, she was enjoying it. Operating from home was going to become a problem though sooner or later, she needed more space both for the business, and the family!

Her mother was the only one who had noticed the subtle changes in Rachel's appearance – the rosy glow, a slight swelling of her breasts and her less than hourglass figure. Rachel had sworn Adam and her to secrecy until she was past three months. There would be no announcements over Sunday lunch on this occasion thank you very much! Motherhood had not been part of the grand plan, though now it was going to happen she was both excited and anxious at the prospect. She was not sure how she would be able to accommodate both motherhood and work, but accommodate them she and Adam would have to, that was clear.

"So how did you get on at Halifax this morning?" Adam said, trying to change the subject. Damien had been on one of his Sunday morning speaking appointments. His chosen theme, not for the first time was, 'Faith in the last days.' It was not so much his favourite subject, as his only subject. Unlike the vicar in a church who has the same congregation every week and therefore needs a different sermon every time, the ministers in the Assemblies of Christ were itinerant. There was a new congregation every time they spoke, so the same 'sermon' could, if they were sufficiently lazy or unimaginative, last most of the year.

When the Halifax service was over, a frail, old brother had come to speak to Damien who asked him how he was and could he hear him alright. He should have left the pleasantries there, but plagued by his familiar insecurities, he went on to ask the old chap, "So how did I do this morning, what did you think?" Sadly, he had chosen a man whose great age had rendered him, like many old men, careless of his words and tactless in his opinions. The old man squinted at him through hooded, watery eyes.

"I'll tell you three things about ye talk lad,

First, you read it.

Second, you read it badly.

And thirdly, there was nowt in what you said."

With this harsh and cruel judgement he started to wander off to find his cup of tea, but hesitating, came back and with a friendly smile, put a frail hand on Damien's arm and said, possibly intending to lessen the earlier blow, "Don't worry about it lad, we don't blame thee, we blame them as sent thee!" And with this, he shuffled away, while Damien absorbed yet another blow to his faltering self-esteem.

It was all rather unfair on the likes of Damien. In most churches and chapels there was some kind of training, some process of selection that would have directed him, and other similar keen young men, to some other form of service more suited to their talents. But amongst the assemblies the pressure on the men to be a 'Sunday Teacher', particularly someone with a father like Harry Sunderland, was intense, and any training or preparation was thin on the ground. So Damien's unfortunate experience, and indeed that of his congregation in Halifax, was not uncommon. Adam continued with his polite question, "Did they appreciate what you had to say?"

"Oh I think so, most of them, at least." he replied, which might almost have been true.

Harry would normally have been happy to remain at the table, quizzing Damien further about what he had been saying, and giving his own particular critique on the altogether more liberal young teacher at their service that morning at Smawthorne. He seemed to believe in some kind of social gospel and had been teaching on the theme, 'A false balance is an abomination to the Lord!' (Proverbs 11 verse 1.) Lambasting bent tradesmen, even if they were from the Bronze Age, was too close to home for some of his Yorkshire congregation. The young brother was not likely to be invited back. It was, of course, twentieth century trade that Harry wanted to talk about, even though it was a Sunday. The three of them congregated in the lounge, leaving the women, as usual, with the clearing up.

Harry brought the two of them up to speed on his meeting with Arthur Hughes and what he regarded as his consequential loss of political connections. He also wanted to express his concerns about the timing of the project and the current rate of inflation, which showed signs of getting out of control. In addition to this, he gave his opinions on weak governments with out-of-date policies and strong unions with overweening powers. He was not optimistic at all about the general economic picture. The rest of the business was fine, the rent roll from the commercial properties was good, but Halifax would be a big step up.

Damien, as expected, was keen to press on. He believed that Arthur could still be useful and he had got to know a couple of new members on the local council. "It is time to be bold," he declared. "The opportunity is good. Adam's development appraisal showed a good margin for error, and a scheme like this would put us in a different league." For all Damien's gung-ho approach, there was a lot of truth in what he said. When the scheme was built out there would be nothing quite like it on the market. Adam, he noticed, was keeping quiet.

As he listened to father and son, Adam's state of mind could have best been described as ambivalent. He was practically running the surveying and estate agents' business, with Walter still not one hundred percent fit. He had produced the development appraisal and yet the directors of the new company were still Harry, Damien and the accountant. There had been no progress with his directorship or shareholding, other than promises and reassurance. But while Damien was doing his man about town act and popping over to Scarborough to sort out his own holiday home, he was doing all the work. He still trusted Harry to honour his promises, but Damien, he was less sure about.

"Come on Adam," Harry insisted, "what do you think?"

"It seems to me, if you're worried about the general economic climate and the timing, it's hard not to agree with you," he said, pointedly looking at Damien. "We only need to secure our position with both sites and then we can wait and see how things turn out. There's got to be an election soon and I cannot believe there won't be a radical change of government."

"But we will have to do something," Harry insisted. "If we move to Halifax, and that is what the elders are now expecting, we cannot leave the old hall standing empty."

"Rachel is going to need more room for her business soon," Adam continued. "There must be lots of people like her in the area, small start-ups looking for low-cost workshops or studios with short term cheap leases. Don't develop the hall site, refurbish it as basic workspaces at economic rents. That income will probably be sufficient to do the alterations needed to make the chapel usable for the two assemblies."

"And what about the rest of the chapel site?" asked Damien. Harry was already reading Adam's mind.

"We take out an option on the rest of the site, for say three years, it won't cost very much, and I suspect the trustees would agree, given that we will be using the chapel for services. Then we would have control of both sites; we control the timescale, and we would have control of the purchase price. We would control everything."

"If I were you though" said Adam, "I would go for a five-year option, three years will pass quicker than you think", imagining this would give him longer to sort out his directorship. He immediately regretted his final comment, realising it would actually give Harry more time to put off the issue.

It occurred to Harry that with his daughter working on the Smawthorne site, she could manage the lettings. Rachel would like the idea as she would be able to keep an eye on her precious piece of woodland, even if it was legally Adam's woodland rather than hers. Adam had never got round to transferring the ownership to his wife and now they were married, he didn't see the need.

Harry leaned back in his chair, pouring cream into the small elegant cup almost lost in his enormous hands. Tapping his spoon on its slender rim, he savoured the strong coffee. He had been contemplating the option idea himself, but the short-term workspaces was a great idea. He could see a way forward. He was pleased, very pleased indeed. Damien, on the other hand, Adam knew, was not. It was not clear whether he resented his interventions, or his father requesting them. Either way, his resentment was palpable. Problems, he knew, would be unavoidable.

The ladies had finished the clearing up and rejoined them in the lounge, minus Jenny, who had gone upstairs to have a 'lie down'. The news caused Harry to raise an eyebrow, but no enquiry.

"Rachel," he said, "how would you like to open your own studio, in the hall after we make the move to Halifax? Your husband has had an idea to convert the place into workshops, studios and offices for business start-ups. You could be the first in and have your pick of the space." She was a little stunned. This was the first time her father had said anything positive about her business since it started, and here he was, encouraging her to expand. Adam had mentioned the idea as a possibility but nothing more.

"Yes," she said, still a little confused, "that would suit me very well, I can't go on operating at home with the business as it is. Yes, that would be a great idea." She was still not sure why the sudden enthusiasm, but thought it would be ideal if she took the corner of the building closest to her conservation area. It would be a great advert for the practice and an attractive place to work. Adam smiled at her, giving a nod of understanding. She returned the look, but with both eyebrows raised.

Damien, noticing that Gaynor was beginning to look tired, suggested it was time they were getting home and went to look for the twins. They were upstairs, still engrossed in the Scalextric that Uncle Walter had converted into Brands Hatch. The British Grand Prix was well underway and understandably the drivers were reluctant to leave midway through the race. Noisy protests erupted. The clerk of the course, namely Walter, suggested a solution. "Why don't you leave them with us Damien? We will finish the race, then they can come home with us for tea. Walter no doubt realised that Jenny had probably had enough of the rest of the family. "I will drop them off before bedtime."

"Yes, yes!" the children cried, "Please Dad, please!"

Damien was only too pleased to lose the twins for the rest of the afternoon and have some peace and quiet, or maybe even indulge himself and Gaynor with the decadent luxury of the afternoon in bed. He would be disappointed, but Gaynor more so.

Chapter 11

Adam's relationship with his sister was close, complex and capable of great contradictions. Their temperaments, ideology and pattern of life diverged to such an extent they could have been living on different planets. Both increasingly disapproved of the other. The disapproval manifested itself in heated arguments on the now rare occasions they got together. Their antipathy was such that one might have expected them to become entirely estranged, as happens in more dysfunctional families. While it may well be true that almost all families are dysfunctional to some extent, the Rowntree clan were less so than most. Hector was often heard to boast, with some justification, "The Rowntree's never fall out with each other." Friends and relatives, particularly those who had joined them around the dining table and witnessed the heated arguments that regularly punctuated their meals, might doubt the veracity of that statement. This was only because they failed to appreciate Hector's definition of the words 'fall out'. The Rowntree's didn't go in for protracted family feuds. Heated arguments over dinner and lunch were the necessary safety valves of filial pressures, an essential feature. Hector believed in the best regulated families.

For all the diverging trajectories of the son and daughter's way of life, they were connected by a fine thread that, though recently stretched to the limit, would always hold. It was the bond of family, of which Hector was so proud. It was seldom spoken of and difficult to define, but there it was.

Julia and Adam were probably typical of the older sister and younger brother's relationship. This is where the younger looks up to and is in awe of the elder, who is always further along the road, always doing the new and exciting things that the younger wishes to copy. They are the first to ride the bike, the first to go to school, the first to have a partner, and the first to know about sex. When there are three or more years between them, it appears to the younger that the older is living in an altogether different and more wonderful world of which they crave to be a part.

Adam would follow her around, wanting to know what she was doing and wanting to do the same things. When boyfriends first came along, he would act as the go-between, especially if Mother disapproved. In return, Julia would mother him, taking her cue from their own mother. She would look after him when he went to school, stick up for him in the playground, protect him when he was bullied and provide a refuge from parental wrath. From this is born a bond of care and affection which, for the lucky ones, will last a lifetime. Of such were Julia and Adam.

Adam's religion was having almost as much an effect on Julia's life as it was on his own. Before his Welbeck

Road conversion, Julie's relationship with religion was, non-specific, probably non-existent. Apart from the occasional visit to the local church, the subject had rarely entered her head. She was neither a believer nor an unbeliever. To call her an atheist would credit her with more curiosity than was warranted. But since her brother's transformation, her interest in religious belief, more accurately her interest in religious unbelief, had become a significant preoccupation in both her private and academic life.

She did describe herself as an atheist, becoming that strange phenomena – the zealous and passionate nonbeliever. She joined the Humanist and Secular Societies at university, becoming one of their more vocal members. She carried out her own research on the history of atheism, particularly in the 18th century, with a view to writing a book. She had become something of an expert on Baron d'Holback, often regarded as the first atheist, who was known to have said, "The course of man's unhappiness is his ignorance of nature, the pertinacity with which he clings to blind opinion...dooms him to continual error." She had tried the quotation out on her brother, but with little effect!

Driven by Adam's preoccupation with predicting the Second Coming, the End of the World and the Battle of Armageddon, she had read widely on the history of eschatology. There was a long list of those who, since the 18th century, had been trying and failing to do the same thing.

There was almost a perverse symbiotic relationship between brother and sister. They were like poles of a magnet driving each other in the opposite direction.

The more that Adam was challenged by his sister's secular humanism, the more entrenched he became in his beliefs, and the more he read of the assembly's narrow canon of literature. The 18-year-old who found it so difficult to prepare for his A-levels now had his own study in Pop's old house, filled with his Bible's and religious texts, where he spent an increasing amount of time studying.

Biblical numerology had become his particular interest, appealing as it would to his mathematical and arithmetical skills. In the ancient text, numbers had a special significance – six days of creation and six thousand years since creation to the present; twelve tribes of Israel and twelve Apostles; forty days and forty nights for the flood and forty days in the wilderness for the temptation of Christ; Jonah was three days in the belly of the whale, Christ three days in the tomb, and so on. Ancient letters and words had numerical values that if interpreted in a certain way could be made to make specific predictions about the end of the world. Adam had begun to study these things, to play with the mathematics, almost as a pure mathematician, like Richard, would play with the mathematics of quantum mechanics or chaos theory.

Julia's concern for her brother was genuine and deeply felt. She worried that he was being taken over by a weird religious sect and brainwashed by a narrow, bigoted and reactionary ideology that was not just his religion, but increasingly becoming his social life as well. Even his work was deeply enmeshed in the same network of individuals. Driving across from Leeds, she had been searching for ways to persuade him of her real concerns and to engage him in a way that was not threatening. Nor did she want it to lead to the usual conflict, where both parties' prime object became winning the argument rather than understanding the other's point of view.

If Adam failed to appreciate the true nature of his sister's anxiety for him, Julia was just as ignorant of his anxieties for her and the rest of the family. Adam did not just believe that everything the assembly taught was true, he believed it was the only truth, the essential truth. All of the other Churches – Anglican, Catholic, Methodist, Greek Orthodox, not to mention Muslims, Hindus or even Zoroastrians, were in error. There was only one way, only one truth, and to Adam, understanding and believing that truth and following in "The Way" was essential to salvation, a literal matter of life and death. Jesus gave his life a ransom, freely given, but only to those who understood His Way and believed it, or so Adam felt. It might sound very strange to the unbeliever, to those unfamiliar with the culture of this evangelical community, but to Adam and his congregation, these were real, tangible, and pressing issues.

Given the strong family bond of affection, it was only natural for Adam to be concerned for their eternal well-being. He was anxious to persuade them of his point of view, just as much as Julia was trying to bring him around to hers.

Julia should have understood her brother's concerns, for she had done enough reading around the subject. The assembly in Smawthorne was not unique. America was awash with a whole variety of Christian fundamentalists and creationists, making their own predictions of the Rapture, the Second Coming and the End of Days. Many of these groups were even encouraged by the prospect of global nuclear war, which they saw as the essential precursor to the Second Coming. The nuclear Armageddon would destroy great swathes of humanity. They, fortunately, expected to escape this cataclysm, by being taken up with the righteous into heaven by the Rapture. All of which may sound incredible, unless you live in these communities in the Bible Belt of the U.S.A, where they are as real as Adam's biblical numerology!

Julia had called round, partly to look at the new house which she had not seen since the alterations had been finished, but also to congratulate them both on their good news. She arrived complete with a bottle of champagne, and a selection of baby clothes in neutral colours. Rachel was working late in her new studio in the village hall and had promised to pick up a Chinese on her way home. Adam, for once, had an excuse to get home early, so unusually, brother and sister were alone together, in the new sitting room by the stylish log burning stove, sharing a decent bottle of white burgundy and the welcome heat of the fire.

She was impressed with the renovation of the old house and it was clear that Rachel had a good eye. There was an elegant simplicity to the whole thing; white plastered walls, decorated with a few carefully chosen contemporary pictures and floors of ash boarding or stone flags They had created additional space by cleverly opening up the cellar as a studio for Rachel, and converted the attic as Adam's study come retreat. The only hint of excess was the stylish kitchen in a new extension at the rear of the house, enclosing a patio accessed from French-windows in the dining room. The old bench was still there, but Adam had not wished to keep the back of the house as it once was. The garden, left well-nurtured but unchanged, would serve as Pop's memorial. Adam could only live in the rest of the house if it no longer retained the ghost of the old man.

Both Julia and Adam had done their best to keep the conversation on an even keel, but were also trying to suppress their aggressive instincts and the family failing of not listening. Adam had done well to listen as Julia went through the long list of people and sects who had been predicting the end of the world for the last two thousand years – but particularly since the eighteenth century. All of whom she emphasised had got it wrong.

"Don't you think it's significant," she suggested, "that no one predicts a date for the end of time that is likely to fall outside of their own probable lifetime. No one says that the Second Coming will be in 250 or 500 years, it is always within 30 or 40 years of the time of the prophet's prediction." Some of the latter-day prophets who were proved wrong, she insisted, were undeterred and kept moving the date forward, while others claimed that Jesus had returned on the specified date, but no one could see him. The comic nature of such claims did not seem to deter them.

The implication for Adam was, of course, if they all got it wrong, why should you be any more successful, given that you have no formal theological or Biblical qualifications. Julia argued that prophesying, 'A time of trouble such as never was' as a sign of the Second Coming (one of Adam's favourite themes), could just as easily apply to any epoch in history. It would certainly apply if you were at the destruction of Jerusalem in A.D. 70, or in Europe when the Black Death arrived and killed between a third and a half of the population. Living in Hamburg, Dresden or Coventry in the 1940s was a similarly 'troubled time.'

The trouble with the troubled times' argument, is that the troubles of the present, to those present, are always more troubling than the troubles of the past, for the obvious reason that the troubles of the past are, to those in the present, no trouble at all. That is why everybody can claim in the words of the song, 'Things ain't what they used to be!'

The ease with which her brother was able to resist her compelling arguments, which she saw as his total resistance to reason, was a source of great frustration. Julia's difficulty, or of anyone challenging such fundamentalist beliefs, was that her arguments were all-too-familiar to the believers. Adam, and the rest of the community, had well prepared and well-rehearsed rebuttals. The essence of which was, 'It is all different now, and now everything fits together perfectly.'

"It has never been like this before," he advised his sister, "the world has never before had the means to destroy itself, as it can today with its nuclear arsenals. The destruction of the world by fire, predicted in the Bible, is only possible today!" as though this was something to be thankful for.

"The children of Israel are back in their own land for the first time in two thousand years. Which country, which people, have ever been destroyed and scattered throughout the world, and then brought back as a nation state after two thousand years of persecution? It is a miracle! And it was all foretold by the prophet Ezekiel's vision of dry bones, "I will place you back in your own land, and you will know that I am the Lord." (Ezekiel 37 verse 14.) He knew the arguments so well and had rehearsed them so many times he now could quote chapter and verse.

"It couldn't be plainer," he insisted, "for those who have ears to hear and eyes to see."

It was sometimes difficult to know whether it was Adam speaking his own words, or quotes from the Bible. He had listened to her, so she felt obliged to allow him to finish, and now he was in full flow. She knew that Adam had begun to do some preaching, as she would have called it, and she was now getting an impression of what it might have been like in the congregation.

"Everything fits together, now, like never before – the numbers and the dates. God made the world in six days." he continued.

"Surely not?" She couldn't stop herself. He wasn't insisting on six literal days of Creation! He carried on as if she was nothing more than a heckler at a public lecture. Perhaps dealing with hecklers was another part of the training.

"God made the world in six days and on the seventh day he rested, and from Creation to the end of this century is 6000 years, and the Bible is clear, that with God, a day is as a thousand years. And, just at this time in history, God's people have returned to occupy the whole of their ancient lands, 'from Dan even on to Beersheba.' It all fits together. And when you begin to study biblical numerology, all of the numbers and dates fall into place perfectly. You really should open your mind to these things. It's really important love."

Everywhere Adam looked it was compelling, and everything he read, things fitted neatly in place. Of course they did, as he only looked and read where they did so.

Julia couldn't let the six days of creation thing go unchallenged.

"Surely you don't believe that the earth was created in six days, six thousand years ago? You can't Adam. What about evolution, the fossils and geological records? It is all impossible."

"Evolution is what is impossible. All of this," he waved his arms around, "all by chance? What about the complexity of the human eye and a bird's wing, or what about the second law of thermodynamics?" The last one was a bit unfair, as he was fairly certain that Julia had no idea what the second law of thermodynamics was. "Evolution is as likely as a tornado blowing through a scrapyard and producing a jumbo jet!"

So they continued, sharing a bottle of wine, the heat of the fire and their genetic history, but nothing else. Brother and sister speaking a different language, living in different worlds and failing to connect with each other. The conversation was pushing each of them more firmly into their own ideological redoubts. Speaking to her brother about religion, Julia felt like a tourist lost in an alien country and unable to speak the language. If she was frustrated by what she saw as his implacable resistance to all reason, he was grieved by what he saw as a wilful refusal to consider the hope of salvation he had offered to her, with no less rationale.

They had driven each other to a standstill and during one of the long pregnant pauses, they were interrupted by a small pregnant woman, burdened with chicken and sweetcorn soup, roast duck in orange sauce and chicken Chow Mein. Rachel breezed into the kitchen, greeting them both with a cheerful, "Good Evening!" and demanding to know if Adam had put any plates to warm or laid the cutlery out.

"Of course, you haven't!" She said with a smile, "But I see you managed to finish the wine. It's a good job I'm pregnant." Unwittingly, yet mercifully, she lightened the mood of the evening, and both brother and sister relaxed, though Julia more so than her brother. Shamelessly, considering Rachel's condition, they opened a second bottle of wine.

The two women chatted away happily as they consumed the food. Rachel spoke of the excitement of her work, Julia of the frustrations of university life, and both of the delights of converting old houses. Julia wanted to know how Rachel was coping with pregnancy, but she waved the question away, saying it was all too boring.

Julia had moved on from the frustrations of her earlier conversation as easily as she would after a seminar with a particularly unpromising and unimaginative group of undergraduates. Not so Adam, for as the women talked, he sat amongst them in solitary silence, going over in his head what had been said. He was hearing again Julia's challenging, dismissive critique of his core beliefs. He was trying to persuade himself that he was as certain of them now as he had sounded earlier in the evening, trying to hide the secret doubts that would always plague him.

Of the two diverging ideologies that Adam and Julia had clothed their lives with, there was little doubt that hers was the more comfortable fit, even if it would prove to be the least hard-wearing.

There was a third component to the ideological and religious journeys of the Rowntree family members, every bit as surprising as Julia's and Adam's. Mother had rediscovered the Church of England, or more accurately, the local parish church had discovered her. The long-serving incumbent had retired, to be replaced by a new priest, taking over in his first parish. Trevor had come to the priesthood late in life. He was highly intelligent, taking a first-class degree at Durham University after which he was fast-tracked into the MoD following a brief commission in the Army. In his mid-40s he had given it all up – the London life, the corridors of power, not to mention the salary, to become a local parish priest in the backwaters of the West Riding of Yorkshire. He had a radical take on Christianity but was blessed with such warmth and so great a generosity of spirit that, even the most traditional Anglicans found him irresistible and had supported his quiet revolution.

His take on religion was a rich mixture of music, mystery, and social engagement. Of his numerous talents, he was a capable musician, often running up and down the aisle to play the organ, accompanying a reinvigorated choir. The greatest change however, was the transformation of the church hall into the quasi-social centre of the town. There were youth clubs, two or three nights a week, mother and baby groups, O.A.P. coffee mornings, and the local centre for the family planning clinic.

To begin with, it was just a matter of Mother, in her role as Secretary of the FPC, agreeing with Rev Trev (as he was now affectionately known), the practicalities of using the hall for the weekly clinics. He was very subtle in his ministry; there was none of the usual clerical blackmail, 'Hope to see you in church on Sunday, Mrs Rowntree.' There was no need, 'I'll try to find a seat for you' would have been more the thing. He was quietly charismatic and spoke in a very distinct and precise way that might have hinted at artifice, but it was more likely that he was just trying to conceal a superior intellect.

Whether Mother had started to believe in God seemed to be entirely beside the point. Trevor never inquired. But she started to believe in Trevor. The first attraction was his breadth of knowledge and ability to engage in an informed conversation on just about any subject she might choose. But it was his take on a Christianity of community engagement, social justice and commonplace charity that drew her more and more into his sphere of influence and she began to attend church services regularly. Trevor's services were a mysterious combination of a music festival, poetry reading and spiritual happening. He could preach, and did, often but briefly. He never gave a long sermon because he hadn't taken enough time to write a short one.

He would often come around at the end of Mother's clinic, as she was clearing up in her usual busy way, demanding a cup of tea, and suggesting that she pause and sit a while. This, Mother began to understand, was how he operated. With all that was going on in the church, one might have expected him to be run off his feet. Yet he always seemed to have time. There was a calm about Trevor and an ability to get other folk to do what was necessary, with the minimum of fuss. Mother liked the minimum of fuss.

Adam and Julia were astonished at the change in their mother. Hector, on the other hand, was not. Neither was he at all concerned about how close his wife was becoming to the new vicar. He was fairly confident none of the husbands in the town need have any concern about Trevor and their wives, daughters, or girlfriends.

Chapter 12

1977

For Natalie and Slim, the move south had gone well and neither felt any regrets. If Slim regretted anything, it was staying at home for too long, particularly whilst at university. He felt he had missed out on much that it had to offer. After graduating there had been a need to get away from Smawthorne, the family and the north of England in general. There was an addictive air of youthful optimism and confidence about the new town project in Milton Keynes. Nowhere was that confidence more keenly felt than in the architects' and planning studios of the new town development corporation. How could you not be excited, as a young architect or planner, with the prospect of designing a place for over two hundred thousand people, on virgin land in the Buckinghamshire countryside?

Without the usual local government structures and oversight of council members, or even the commercial pressures of private developers, the corporation and its architects enjoyed considerable creative and professional freedom. Innovative modern solutions to the problems of urban planning became the norm. Most of the new civic and public buildings were the products of bold, contemporary architecture. Milton Keynes never became the concrete jungle of many people's prejudices, as perhaps had happened in earlier new towns at Runcorn, Skelmersdale and Cumbernauld. It was based on Ebenezer Howard's vision of the garden city, developed before the War at Letchworth and Welling, characterised by low rise, low-density development in generous parkland settings. It became the new garden city of the south. Everyone joked about the hundreds of roundabouts, but it was the only city in England designed from scratch with motor transport in mind. The roads and roundabouts were all tree-lined avenues and it was becoming an attractive and popular place for people to live and work, many migrating up from London, just as Natalie and Slim had migrated down from the North.

Employment was plentiful and varied. Slim and Natalie had managed to buy a small house in one of the new developments, with easy access to work, usually by bike. Socially and culturally there was a great deal going on, and almost everything, including the people, was new.

Even the religious thing had worked out for Slim. The local assembly was much more liberal, progressive and outward-looking than they were used to at home. They would probably have had more in common with Rev Trev than Simeon Kantalow. The assembly had welcomed him with open arms and he had become heavily involved in running the various youth clubs and even doing some rugby coaching with the local club.

These days he almost preferred coaching to playing. If he did play any rugby it was usually for the third team and Harlequins, so far, had failed to get in touch!

Driving north on that wet, Sunday morning in their faithful, ageing beetle, the mechanical beat of the air-cooled engine chattered reassuringly behind their heads, the wipers struggling to keep the rain off the flat windscreen, they knew they were heading back to a former life and another place: 'Smawthorne revisited!' If geographically their new home was one hundred and fifty miles or so south of Smawthorne, its culture, environment and outlook was from another world. Milton Keynes was a place where youth and optimism were creating a modern new city. The mining towns of the West Riding of Yorkshire were dominated by old, declining industries, striving to retain a doomed way of life, mired in social unrest and industrial strife. Radical change was coming and it would be brutal, irresistible and permanent. Lives and communities were going to be changed forever. The affluent Sunderland's may have been above such things, but it was all around them. It was only when the two went home that they were reminded of just how grim and rundown their hometowns had become. Natalie wondered whether it had always been so, but they had just never noticed before.

Slim thought it best to keep these comparisons to himself when later sitting with Walter in the conservatory, looking out at the rain sweeping across the open fields at the back of the house. The wind was rattling the windows and doors with such fury that you could swear it was coming straight off the North Yorkshire Moors. They had been looking forward to spending the day with his mum and dad. Elaborate Sunday lunches with a cast of thousands might have appealed to the Rowntree's, and to Harry Sunderland, but they did not suit Felicity. She found such things something of an ordeal, and far too stressful. There would be just the four of them sharing the usual roast chicken. Rachel, Adam and little Emily had promised to call in after lunch.

Walter, signed off by the doctor, was still something less than his former self. At times, there was a greyness about him, and some of his former vitality had disappeared. Slim noticed his movements were often more deliberate and laboured. Fortunately, his cheerful, optimistic and generous disposition remained undiminished. He was still fulfilling his usual commitments at the assembly and had been "teacher for the day" that morning in Halifax. This was the reason the two had come up on this particular Sunday. Even Natalie was prepared to show a face in the hall, to listen to her father-in-law teach. She was not unimpressed, but neither was she in any way persuaded. Slim was pleased to see that the heart-attack had done nothing to impair his mental faculties or his oratorical gifts.

If Harry was the exuberant, tub-thumping orator, inspiring his congregation with rhetorical flourishes about the Kingdom of Heaven and the Second Coming, in great demand up and down the country, then Walter was more 'The shepherd of the flock' – more thoughtful and empathetic. He saw it as his job, on Sunday morning, to give his congregation enough encouragement, support and if necessary, hope, to get them through to the following Sunday. It would more likely be he, not Harry who would do the pastoral visits in the week, calling on the sick, the troubled and lonely. If someone was relieved to find an anonymous envelope pushed through their door filled with five-pound notes, that would be Walter's work, and nobody, not even Felicity would know anything about it. If Harry was known for inspiring the faithful and distressing the comfortable, Walter was more likely to be taking care of the faithful and comforting the distressed.

Harry had been away since Friday, either inspiring the faithful or distressing the comfortable, at a national weekend conference in Chester. He was the keynote speaker and had taken Roger along with him. Roger was going to lecture on his ministry in the Caribbean. In the past, Walter and Felicity would have gone along and made up a foursome, but this time Felicity had said a firm no. She would claim it was out of concern for Walter's health, but the truth was she had had enough of following her eminent brother-in-law around the country, watching him do the great 'I am' thing, to huge applause and acclamation!

Jenny had been equally reluctant to go, keen to give as much help as she could to Rachel, either with work, or looking after Emily. But Harry, in spite of all his apparent self-confidence and style, liked the reassurance of seeing his wife in the congregation and much to Rachel's disgust, insisted she go along.

When Adam, Rachel and Emily arrived, it was still raining heavily and they came in looking like drowned rats. Emily, dripping wet, shot straight past everyone, and clambering onto Walter's vast lap, began her usual detailed search through his many pockets.

"Let's get this off first." Rachel was struggling to remove the dripping wet coat from the wriggling child.

"Where is it? Where is it Uncle Walter?" she demanded, bouncing up and down on his enormous knees and going through the pockets again.

"That's for you to find out," he teased, "perhaps there is nothing there today!"

But there always was something there, and eventually the prize was located. Emily sat contentedly, and with great care, began to peel the blue wrapping and silver paper off the small bar of Fry's chocolate cream.

"Don't forget to share, Emily," her mother insisted. The little girl's hands slumped down on her knees and her bottom lip popped out. Bending her head forward, her blonde curls obscured the look of total disgust on the cute little face. Dutifully, if somewhat grudgingly, she offered a piece to everyone in the room, all of whom thoughtfully declined, except Uncle Walter, who was compelled to take just the one piece.

When the chocolate had disappeared, except for the remnants spread around her mouth, Felicity took her into the kitchen to get cleaned up and then make jam tarts. It would give the others a chance to catch up, although she knew Walter, as usual, would soon be fast asleep.

Natalie was keen to know how Rachel was coping with both business and motherhood.

"It's okay now, the new studio in the old assembly hall is perfect. There's plenty of space, but the real bit of luck has been the new nursery that has taken over the rest of the space. I drop Emily off in the morning and she can pop in and see me in the studio at lunchtime, or really, at any other time of the day, so it works a treat. That, combined with two grandparents helping out, means she gets spoilt to death, just like today."

The conversation tended to split according to gender, with the girls talking about architecture, landscaping and horticulture, and the boys talking religion and the differences between north and south. Slim was keen to know how the merger and the move to the new chapel had gone. In truth, and it was a truth Adam did not wish to share with Slim or anyone else, as almost everyone was happy with the new arrangement except him, he surprisingly felt guilty about the whole affair. The re-use of the old assembly site was perfect. He had expected he would need a number of short term lets to make it work, but when the children's nursery came on board and wanted most of the space, it was ideal. One of the main reasons they were interested was Rachel's conservation area next to the river. It had been fenced off and was perfect for children's play.

It was the conversion of the chapel about which he felt most guilt. Of the many gifts he had acquired from the Assemblies of Christ, guilt was his speciality. Perhaps Adam Rowntree was already pre-programmed for guilt, but, for whatever reason, it regularly took hold, as had happened now over the chapel. The sale had been agreed with the trustees and a five-year option on the rest of the site was forthcoming at a modest cost. The two assemblies had moved into the chapel. It was still going to be too big and too expensive to maintain, so they decided to seal off the upper galleries. They stripped out the pews and the organ, selling them to an architectural salvage contractor for a tidy sum which helped to pay for the alteration costs. The windows were modified and the new suspended ceiling filled in around the balcony. The reduction in height had achieved a corresponding reduction in heating costs,

So why the guilt? It was the building – that glorious, mysterious chapel, "When steam was on the windowpane and glory in his soul!" The citadel on the hill had changed his life on that Saturday afternoon twelve years ago, when packed with three hundred glorious voices. The majestic organ pipes filling the lofty space with music, and the afternoon light slanting in through the tall lantern windows. It was no more. The atmosphere, the mystery, the magic of the place that for him had changed everything, had gone. They had not just ripped out the pews and the organ, they had ripped out the very soul of the building. He felt he had carried out an abortion on the very place that gave birth to his own soul. And that wonderful, glorious citadel would never be the same again. It wasn't entirely his doing, Harry and Damien had been the drivers of the alterations. The members of the congregation were more than happy with the results, although not all the original trustees were. But he had done nothing to stop them. He did nothing because it was only when it was done that the full extent of the vandalism was grimly apparent.

"Everybody seems to be fairly happy with the arrangement," said Slim, and then, as if reading Adam's thoughts, "I suppose it's not quite what it was, is it?"

"No, not really," he confessed. Perhaps the betrayal of the chapel would, to Adam at least, become a totem of future betrayals.

He needed to change the subject, so tried to encourage Slim to talk about the assemblies in Milton Keynes. The way he described it, it seemed more like a social and community centre than the assemblies with which he had been brought up.

"We still believe all the same stuff Adam, we're still looking, we are still hoping for the same things. There is just a different emphasis, more what you do, less what you think, more action and less study. It's just a different way of engaging people. The youth clubs, the choir, even the rugby and football are great ways to get people through the doors. I can even get Natalie involved in some of the activities, although she doesn't have much time these days. Mum and dad have both been down and they're really impressed."

It was clear that Slim had changed. University, Natalie and working in the new town were all creating a new Slim. His uncle would not have approved: his uncle did not approve! Adam was not sure if he did. Slim's religion was taking him on a different spiritual journey. He had said as much to both Adam and his uncle. Harry's reaction had been predictable. "That's all well and good, but you need to know where it will lead you – the right way or the wrong way!" To the new Slim, not knowing was now the whole point of the exercise.

The conversation left Adam no more comfortable than talk of the chapel alterations. It was sad, if not a little tragic, that for all the effort, commitment and study that he was putting into his spiritual life, it had delivered little contentment or peace of mind. So much of his thinking, his beliefs, his faith even, seemed punctuated by tensions, doubts and anxiety. He did not understand. He would never understand that trying steadfastly to maintain the same fundamental certainties was not the same as faithfulness. Nor did he see that remaining fixed in the same spot, as the river of his life swept past, was both exhausting and ultimately doomed to failure. What was it Voltaire had said, "Doubt is troubling, certainty is absurd!" Adam would, forever, be doomed to absurdity.

The kitchen door was thrown open and Emily, dressed somewhat incongruously and prematurely as a Christmas Angel, complete with halo and wings, swept into the room carrying a plate of jam tarts and looking particularly pleased with herself. Felicity followed behind with a tray of teacups. She gave the sleeping Walter a not so gentle nudge with her foot and said, "Come on Rip-van-Winkle, shift ye great feet!" Tea was poured, and the conversation groups brought together as one. This time, Emily was happy to pass around the jam tarts, remembering to say to everyone, as she had been told, "They're very, very hot."

Outside, the rain and wind were still lashing the back of the house, sounding like a manic snare drummer going berserk on the conservatory roof. There was a kind of primordial comfort about being warm and safe around a blazing fire while the elements were raging, just the thickness of the pane of glass away. Felicity was perched on the arm of Walter's chair leaning against his shoulders, drinking her tea and savouring the moment.

They chatted away about the usual trivialities until it was Emily's bedtime. While Rachel and Natalie took her for a bath, Felicity and Slim went to make the sandwiches, giving Slim the chance to ask in more detail about Walter's health. It also gave Walter and Adam time to talk business, away from the office.

For Walter, Adam had been a great find. He was the natural surveyor, intelligent, precise and conscientious. Since the heart-attack, Adam had stepped into the breach, not just doing the work, but relieving him of the worry and stress when he was unable to get into the office. More than that, Walter knew that he could trust him not to take advantage of the situation. There was a decency about the lad that could only be admired and Walter would always be grateful. Adam, in return, knew that they had given him a great opportunity. Nor did he take for granted all that he had learnt from Walter over the years. It was stuff that he would not have picked up by just attending college and the night school classes.

Walter worried about the intensity of Adam's approach to religion and tried, from time to time, to persuade him that there was more to the Gospel than interpreting prophecy and being right about God.

"Better," he would often say, "to be right with God than right about Him." The subtlety of this was usually lost on Adam's imagination.

Emily was put to bed and Felicity made the sandwiches. Walter had finished reading the story and was coming downstairs when the headlights of a large car suddenly swung into the drive. Adam was just about to say that it was Damien's Range Rover as he appeared at the living room door, soaking wet, dishevelled and clearly in distress.

"What on earth's the matter?" Walter asked, as Damien sank down onto the nearest chair, his head in his hands, in tears and struggling to speak. Walter slowly got to his feet, and put his arm across Damien's crumpled, shaking and wet shoulders, asking again,

"What is it, what's the matter lad?"

"There's been an accident," he sobbed, the words barely audible, then louder, "There's been an accident!"

"Who's had an accident? What's happened?" Walter insisted.

"They're dead! Both of them, they're both dead!"

There are a number of desolate and bleak roads over the Pennines between Lancashire and the West Riding of Yorkshire. Some roads, such as the Floating Light, are named after the pub on the route. This would have been the usual and familiar route home for the three of them – Harry, Jenny and Roger. But having dropped somebody off in Glossop, the less familiar Woodhead pass was the more direct. That was the first of the might-have-beens that night which dialled in the tragedy. There were others, as there always are. Roger was driving. He was trying to be helpful as it had been a busy and tiring weekend for Harry, so he offered. Admittedly, he had wanted to get his hands on Harry's new Rover V8, but he did want to help. Harry had agreed, but added, "Just take it easy Roger, it is going to be a miserable night." Roger had little choice as the roads were busy. Climbing up past the reservoirs on the Woodhead, and then down the other side into Yorkshire, they were crawling behind convoys of HGVs. The spray from the wagons produced monsoon quantities of water, which, combined with the glare from oncoming vehicles, made overtaking almost possible.

Most of the heavy traffic turned right at the roundabout, heading for Sheffield and the A1. They went straight on to where the road opened out for a short while with wide sweeping bends. In later years, this stretch would be regarded as one of the most dangerous roads in England. It was, however, just the one treacherous left-hand bend that earned it its grim reputation. The road looks as if it's going straight on. Even in these conditions, Roger could see a narrow ribbon of wet tarmac stretching away in front of him into the distance, like a faint sliver of moonlight across the darkened moor. It was only at the last minute, as they came over the brow too fast, with the torque of the V8 effortlessly driving the car on, that the left-hand bend came into view. The narrow ribbon of tarmac was the side road. But worse than that, what looked, at first, like a fast-sweeping curve, tightened sharply at the apex just as the camber fell away.

Even then, disaster was not inevitable. If Roger had kept his nerve with smooth hands on the controls, he still had a chance. But he was betrayed, not just by the treacherous bend, but by his own, erratic style of driving. He stamped on the brakes and pulled the wheel sharply to the left. The sudden transfer of weight in the heavy car inevitably caused the rear wheels to lose traction with the wet tarmac and the rear of the car spun around into the oncoming traffic. Jenny, asleep in the back, never saw the truck that killed her. If Harry did, it was his last and most fleeting of moments. The crumpled car finished up unrecognisable, on the side of the road against a dry-stone wall. Roger, the only one wearing a seatbelt, was slumped unconscious in the driver's seat, blood seeping from a gash on his head, dripping onto the mangled leather of the steering wheel. He was, poor chap, still alive. A pillar of steam rose up from the wrecked engine, as if in benediction, as fluids dripped onto the wet verge beneath. The driving rain, unmoved by the tragedy it had caused, continued with undiminished force.

All except Walter were still sat in the seats they had occupied when Damien had entered the room. Walter had stayed with him, in a futile attempt to comfort and gently try and elicit more information. But for most of the time, the poor man had just sat there, with his arm around the wet, crumpled figure. The two great giants were swaying backwards and forwards in a grim fellowship of uncontrolled, almost violent grief.

Rachel hadn't spoken or moved. When Adam tried to comfort her she pushed him away, saying nothing, just staring at her brother. Her face was vacant. Damien had done his best to try and get control of himself, to tell them what little he knew. How the police officers had arrived at the house as if it were a television drama. He tried to explain what had happened, "The car it appeared had gone out of control on a dangerous bend in heavy rain and collided with oncoming traffic. Roger was in intensive care in Huddersfield Infirmary. Mum and Dad......." He couldn't go on and bent over again, sobbing into his hands, strange groans emerging from his heaving chest.

"What did the police say?" Rachel suddenly asked. "What did they say? How do they know it's them? How can they be sure? They can't be sure, can they?" She asked the same question repeatedly, throughout the evening and into the night. Over, and over again, "They can't be sure it's them, can they?"

Adam again tried to put his arm around her, what else could he do, but again she pushed him away, still staring at her brother as if he was in some way culpable. "It might not be them."

But it was them, a mother, father and brother. It wasn't a police drama on television; it wasn't a bad dream; it wasn't something that had happened to another family that they heard about on the television news and tried to feel sorry for people they didn't know. The impossible, the unthinkable had happened. This brutal thing, it had happened to them. They had got up that morning imagining it was just another Sunday, like any other. They had sat happily together all afternoon, carelessly taking their happiness for granted, while the horror was played out on that wind-swept moor. But now, everywhere they looked, was the same hideous, black, impossible reality. Nothing, nothing would ever be the same again.

Emily, of course, woke the following morning as normal, expecting normality, expecting to climb into bed with Walter and Felicity, expecting a story, expecting cereals and milk from her mum. Sensing that something was wrong, she still expected the attention of all the grown-ups. The toddler's unreasonable demands might have helped her mother and later, much later, the little one would be the only balm of healing that had any effect on Rachel, but not that morning. Adam had phoned his mother first thing, and she had come around with her kind, but brisk efficiency, sweeping up Emily up with promises of exciting things to do at Lumley Street, just until mummy was feeling a little better. She, in turn, told her son that everything would be fine at home and to concentrate on Rachel, who at the moment, clearly wasn't.

Mother left the four of them sitting around the breakfast table, staring at the unopened cereal boxes and cups of cold tea. None of them had had much sleep, but the day was now implacably there waiting for them. To begin with, sitting together in silent inactivity seemed to be the only appropriate and respectful response and the only thing of which they were capable.

There were things Adam wanted to do, things he needed to do, but to do anything felt like a betrayal or denial of the tragedy that was crushing them all. But it was impossible to sit doing nothing all day, for Adam and Felicity at least. Cups of warm tea were needed, food had to be prepared and telephone calls had to be made. Arrangements needed to be put in place and there was no one else but the four of them to do it. So slowly and painfully they began to deal with the grim tragic reality of their new lives. The unthinkable had to be thought about and the unimaginable imagined.

Chapter 13

The Welbeck Road Chapel was full for the funeral, with many mourners having to standing outside in the rain. It was unfortunate it didn't have the original capacity, but even that might have failed to accommodate everyone who wished to pay their respects. Folk had come from all over the country, those both secular and religious, inevitably drawn by the tragedy. Simeon had taken the service. He was Damien's choice and he would probably have been Harry's too, if not Jenny's, and certainly not Walter's. At the time, Rachel had been in no state to make any decision.

It was what would have been expected, what Harry would have expected..."Sure and certain hope of the resurrection....As in Adam all die, so in Christ shall all be made alive...A time to live and a time to die... Faithful servants of the Lord awaiting his return...The ransomed of the Lord will return..."

Simeon's eulogy was lengthy and ill-judged. It attempted to provide some hope and comfort in a belief that they would all soon, yes soon, be reunited in the Kingdom of Heaven. Fortunately, most of this went over Rachel's head. She was both there and not there. If she was sustained by anything on the day, it was by a growing and irrational anger rather than Simeon's 'words of comfort and consolation'. There was little evidence that his words had any better effect on the rest of the family. Walter looked an old and broken man, sitting there, lonely in a crowd, clutching his wife's hand. Damien managed to hold it together, through the service at least, breaking down only when he got home to Gaynor and the children.

Roger had been discharged from intensive care, but would remain in the Infirmary for some time yet. Adam had been to see him – the only member of the family who had. He found it difficult, but still, he had gone. He was able at least to reassure the poor lad that it was unlikely the police would be pressing any charges. They had deemed it an accident on a notoriously dangerous stretch of road, in poor conditions. The news seemed to provide Roger with little comfort. Adam wondered if he almost wanted to be prosecuted, needing some form of retribution or mortification to expunge his guilt. Adam left him, a tragic and pathetic figure, isolated and trapped in his hospital bed.

As many mourners as could be accommodated were assembled at Gaynor's house, where she had arranged for caterers to provide refreshments. To Walter, Rachel, and most of the family, it was an unavoidable ordeal. Something they knew had to be done and was expected of them. Felicity and Adam, with his mum and dad's help, did their best to shield the family, fielding the inevitable barrage of well-meaning inquiries and condolences.

Rachel had spent most of the time since Sunday at Lumley Street with Mother and Emily. Julia had been a brick, taking time out of university to keep an eye on her sister-in-law and look after her niece. Rachel's grief had followed the familiar if tragic pattern, from denial, disbelief and shock, through to feelings of great sadness for the loss of her mother and finally, anger. Her anger, at first, was directed at just about everyone around her – people who were carrying on with their lives as if nothing had happened. How could they? People didn't seem to understand! How could they continue with their lives as normal? Later, the anger became more focused and considered.

Strangely, her feelings for Roger were more of sorrow. She knew him well and could imagine how he would be feeling as the sole survivor and cause of the accident. If she could forgive him, she knew that he would not forgive himself. She felt sorry for her one-time boyfriend who would never be the same again, physically or emotionally.

Her anger, her growing and bitter anger, was directed mainly at her dead father, and, of course, at God; The All Knowing; the Omnipotent; the Merciful; He who 'moves in mysterious ways.' He was certainly mysterious that Sunday afternoon on the Woodhead. If her life would not be the same again, neither would God! God though, was a poor and elusive target for her anger. Her father was a better focus for her rage. He was more directly culpable as far as she was concerned. Her mother hadn't wanted to go to Chester. She had made it plain she wanted to spend the weekend with Rachel, planning gardens, playing with Emily, having a tea party with her in the afternoon and drinking wine together in the evening. That's what the weekend could have been, that's what the weekend should have been. But oh no! Her father's wishes must come first, as they always had. He needed his wife's support, for supporting Harry was her job! His needs had to take priority. He was, after all, 'Doing the Lord's work.' Well, the Lord did not seem to have thought much of it, did he. Not on that Sunday afternoon in the rain and mist on the Woodhead Pass.

The period of disbelief and denial may have been brief, but the rage was not. Since her father and God were no longer around to take its full force, it would often be redirected, unjustly, at her brother, and husband, who sometimes had the crass nerve and appalling bad taste to suggest that the divine will, or a perverse version of eternal providence, might in some macabre and mysterious way have been at work that Sunday afternoon.

It is well understood in international affairs, that the funeral of a head of state, which obliges other heads of state to attend, presents excellent opportunities for the pursuit of business and diplomacy. Soundings can be taken, information acquired, and possible future agreements explored. As far as Arthur Hughes was concerned, what was useful in international affairs would serve just as well locally. He was anxious to catch a word with Damien, to express his sympathy and deep condolences. No doubt they were sincerely felt, but also to assure him and Walter, that if there was anything he could do to help, he would count it a privilege. He assured them of the mutual admiration and respect that he and Damien's father had shared over so many years.

Arthur had judged the situation well. Amidst all the grief and shock at the loss of his parents, Damien was acutely aware of the responsibilities that were now laid at his door. Having been frustrated over recent years by his father's measured and cautious approach, particularly over the development of the Halifax site, it would now be for him to make the decisions. Being free to do all the things he had been urging upon his father, he now felt uncertain, vulnerable, and far less sure of himself. Sound advice and support were there if he wanted them, in the form of his brother-in-law. But deep-seated resentments and jealousy that had festered over the years would preclude that possibility. He would tell himself that Adam had more than enough on his plate, running the surveying side of the business, and coping with Rachel. He had appreciated Arthur's kind words, and they had agreed to get together when the time was right.

Arthur was keen to be helpful about one issue in particular. He had found it difficult to adjust to his new life outside of local politics. Harry had been right, and he had been surprised at how quickly he was excluded from the company and the confidences of his former friends and colleagues. He had established his consultancy business, but was finding the role of a supplicant both necessary and unappealing. He may not, anymore, be privy to the current and future policies of the local council, but they could not exclude him from the privileged information he already possessed and that he believed still had value.

The land in Smawthorne behind the assembly hall and along the banks of the river had been of interest to himself and Harry for some time. He knew that this land was the next logical step in the provision of residential development in the area. He was certain it would be included in the next revision of the local plan, which was imminent. The problem was its access and multiple ownerships. Arthur had spent a considerable amount of time and effort with the various landowners, most of them local farmers, trying to create a consortium of interests that would smooth the process of acquisition and development. It would be in everyone's interests, including his own. He had had a number of conversations with Harry over recent years, since the assembly hall site was the only possible point of access to the land beyond. It was, in effect, a ransom strip, and following the judgement in Stokes versus Cambridge in the High Court, a ransom strip was worth between a third and a half of the increased development value of the land it served. Even to Damien, this would represent a small fortune.

Later, some of Harry's former brethren and sisters would want to know what Harry knew and when he knew it. Was he aware of all this when the site was sold? It was now a question that only Arthur Hughes could answer. He would have to decide when and how much to tell Damien. There was also the matter of the redevelopment of the rest of the chapel site in Halifax, where the option had not long to run. Knowing that Damien had been excited about the opportunity and impatient to press on, he wondered if there might also be a role for himself there. Harry's businesses he suspected, would be of such complexity that it would be some time before any new arrangements were in place. So for the present, he would bide his time and keep his finger in as many pies as possible.

He was certainly right about the complexity of Harry and Walter's business arrangements. The estate agencies were relatively straight forward, with the brothers the majority shareholders and Damien and Adam having a minority stake. However, as Harry had left his interest in the business to his son, and his son alone, Damien would now have the major share, yet be entirely dependent on his brother-in-law to run it. Damien had become so detached from the surveying business over the years that Adam was now indispensable.

The development company and Harry's share in the property portfolio had also been left entirely to Damien. Rachel was not surprised. If she could not have anticipated recent tragic events, she would have anticipated this. For her father, it was entirely in character. There were compensations, for she had been left the house and its contents. Her mother also had assets which would come to her. In the context of the events of the last few weeks, Rachel had little interest in her father's businesses. Damien was welcome to them. Adam would have to accept this, but as far as the businesses were concerned, the changes would have a far greater effect upon him. He was less than happy with the new arrangements and he could imagine the difficulties and problems that lay ahead.

* * *

Adam would look back on 1977 and the beginning of 1978 as the darkest and most difficult period of his life. Rachel was a constant worry as she was beginning to show the classic symptoms of clinical depression. She was experiencing violent mood swings and periods of physical exhaustion when she could not, or would not, get out of bed. It was only his mother who kept despair away from the door, spending time with Rachel and looking after Emily while Adam was at work. She had them both to stay at Lumley Street, keeping company through the sleepless nights. Eventually, Rachel began to turn the corner and started to take more interest in Emily and herself. As spring turned to summer, in and among the vegetable patch and the flower beds of their back garden, the three of them would spend time together. They would be doing stuff, or not doing stuff, often just being. Slowly the darkness began to lift from her soul and something of her old self returned.

There had been times when even Mother had flirted with despair. But she had Hector, her rock, and the unobtrusive and surprisingly well-informed support of the Reverend. He seemed to have the uncanny gift of arriving unbidden when most needed and then disappearing unnoticed, like the Lone Ranger or Mary Poppins. Later, Rachel would spend more time alone with Trevor. It seemed to do her good, talking with a stranger, someone unconnected with her family and recent events. Adam could not help but be thankful, but was becoming increasingly concerned as Rachel began to spend more time on a Sunday morning in the parish church than with the assembly. Like it or not, it was one of many changes he would have to get used to in the coming years.

Adam had to work through all of this. There is a brutal imperative about any business, particularly small family businesses. Tragedy may occur, people may die, others may grieve, but a business has an implacable life of its own. Staff have to be paid, rents have to be collected, clients require attention, contracts have to be honoured and obligations discharged. Other people's livelihoods depended on keeping things going. As far as the surveying businesses was concerned, this was all down to Adam as there really was nobody else.

Walter had insisted, and Damien grudgingly agreed, that Adam would have to be given an equal share of the business.

"If Adam were to go Damien, I doubt we would have much of a business in a couple of years. You really don't have a choice, unless you want to come and run the thing yourself." Damien knew this and resented it. Adam knew it and exploited it. No one could blame him. He had never received his promised shares and directorship in the new development company. He now knew he never would. From here on, Adam understood that he would have to look after himself, something he felt more than able to do.

Mother realised Rachel was going to be okay, not the same okay as before, but okay, when sitting in the back garden of Number 39 in the late Autumn sunshine. They were watching a carefree Emily kick around the fallen leaves the two of them had spent the previous hour sweeping up. Rachel suddenly said, "It seems a long time since we had a proper Sunday lunch." Glancing across at her daughter-in-law and putting her dirty hand over her eyes to shield herself from the low setting sun, she considered with some relief the subtle changes that had come over her.

"Is that what you would like to do love?"

"I think I'd like to do that very much. Could we invite Trevor?"

"If he's around I am sure he would come. For all his many talents, he is a hopeless cook. I will give Julia a ring too. We might get a chance to meet her new fella."

The pattern of Julia's love life had not changed, to the extent that the men were continually changing. New men were generally sourced from the academic staff of UK universities. Mother speculated that her daughter might have a plan to cover the entire higher education curriculum with her lovers. Her current partner, James, was something to do with neuro-psychology. She couldn't help thinking that he would have a field day with the diners at Lumley Street. Hector wandered out from the shed, with part of a stripped-down carburettor in his grubby hands, absentmindedly polishing it with an oily rag. His glasses were perched precariously on the end of his oversize nose.

"Rachel thinks it is time we had a proper Sunday lunch," she called across the denuded vegetable patch, "what do you think love?"

Looking up from the shiny piece of metal, he said, "I think it's time we had a proper Sunday lunch, I always think it's time for a proper Sunday lunch, who's coming?" Smiling to himself, he wandered back into the shed looking for his screwdriver, content, as ever, for others to make the decisions.

Arrangements were changed at the last minute. Mother was delighted when Rachel decided that she would like to do it in her own house, with Mother's indispensable assistance she had tactfully added. Sometime after 12 o'clock, Adam and Hector were standing at the bar in The Horse, where their pints, unbidden, appeared before them. Rev Trev was not a drinking man, so was going straight to the house when he had finished his duties at church. Father and son went to sit by the fire, away from the regulars, where Hector would have a chance to find out how Adam was coping at work.

"How're things going at the office lad, got plenty of work on and enough folk to do it.?"

"It's steady Dad," replied Adam, "fairly steady. It is a strange time, but there are still buyers and sellers out there. Inflation seems to be coming back under control, but mortgage rates are starting to crank up again. That's the worry, I suppose, but people are still seeing the value of their houses rising in my considered opinion." He took a deep and a welcome swig of his pint, adding "I have no idea though what Jim Callaghan is playing at."

"No," his father said, "I thought we would have had a general election by now, although I can't see the Tories doing much good with a woman in charge!" His son smiled and nudged his father's elbow,

"Oh I don't know Dad, you've done all right!"

"You cheeky sod!" he replied, checking his watch carefully. "Your mother has only me to deal with, sonny Jim has the whole trade union movement on his back. I can only see trouble ahead in that department."

"How are you getting on with Damien?" His father did have the knack of putting his finger on things.

When Adam didn't know what to say, he usually said nothing. "You have to feel for the lad," he continued, "it is not just Rachel who lost her mum and dad. I suspect he relied on his father more than he knew. It won't be too easy stepping into those shoes. Isn't there anything you can do?" Standing up and collecting the empty glasses, Adam suggested "I can go and get us another pint... I don't think he wants my help Dad." And then over his shoulder heading for the bar, "He seems to be spending a lot of time with Arthur Hughes at the moment. Arthur seems very keen to help."

Of course, Hector thought to himself, Arthur Hughes would be keen if there was something in it for him. Arthur, he knew, was the kind of friend who would always be there when he needed you. He certainly didn't want him offering to help his son. He sat back in the comfy chair, enjoying the warmth of the fire and looking across at his grown-up son standing at the bar. He was pleased to see Adam looking at ease with the locals and the landlord. He liked to think that he was also much more at ease with himself these days. He mused with some satisfaction and pride that the lad had turned out all right. In truth, he was proud of him.

By the time they got home, the three women were united in the kitchen around a bottle of Chilean red something or other. Emily was having a play day with her friend down the road and would reluctantly be back later. Trevor and James were deep in conversation in the front room and had been for some time, both holding glasses of Harvey's Bristol cream, but neither showing any inclination to drink it.

It was a different location, a different dining table and the cast of characters had changed somewhat, but the food and the convivial atmosphere were much the same. There was one further innovation, Mother, in deference to Trevor's clerical presence, wondered if Rachel would mind if they asked him to say Grace. Julia bridled with embarrassment, much the same as Hector, but Rachel, who was all too familiar with such things, happily acquiesced. The Reverend, sensing the divergence of feelings, handled the situation with his typical finesse and wit, offering them all the unfamiliar, though brief Yorkshire Grace,

"God bless us nar,

And meck us able

Te eat all stuff,

That's on this table. Amen.

"Not forgetting those who haven't got a table or much to put on it," Trevor added in parenthesis.

The grace and the food were both well received. Rachel could not help remembering her father's more lengthy and pompous petitions, regularly offered around the table on a Sunday morning at Salem while the vegetables went cold. They were not missed.

James, in appearance at least, was not what Mother had expected. His smart blue blazer, fine grey flannel slacks and black brogues were different from Julia's usual companions. He looked more like your local bank manager dressed for a weekend at the country club. He seemed to have had some effect upon Julia, who had obviously taken a little more care of her appearance than usual. James' sartorial standards seemed at one with his fine aquiline features and large grey eyes, framed in expensive-looking silver-rimmed glasses. His long, elegant hands, neatly manicured, suggested that whatever work his head might have done, his hands had not been involved in any serious labour.

Being born and bred in Cheshire, and having not been warned in advance by Julia, he looked somewhat nonplussed when a plate of puddings and gravy were set down in front of him with nothing else on the table but pickled onions and cucumber. Hector, noticing his confusion, unhelpfully suggested, "You had best make a start lad, that's all you get here on a Sunday!"

"Take no notice James," said Rachel, putting a friendly hand on his arm, "I found them difficult to begin with."

"And now?" James asked, in confident good humour,

"Now, I find them impossible."

"Who's going to carve the meat?" she demanded. Adam had home advantage, but tradition was with Hector.

"Give it to Hector," Adam suggested, "but for goodness sake Dad, can we have it a bit thicker than spoke shavings?" There was a general roar of approval, leaving Hector looking distinctly hurt. He soon recovered.

James may not have been warned about the Yorkshire pudding ritual, but Julia had explained to him that in accepting an invitation to lunch at Lumley Street, he was deemed to have given informed consent to being cross-examined by the whole family on any subject of their choosing. Mother decided to chip in first, sitting with both elbows on the table and red, chapped hands, supporting her chin,

"So James, what are you researching at the moment and what exactly does a neuropsychologist do?"

Trevor was worried, as he knew something about neuropsychology (well he would, wouldn't he?). He had an idea where this all might lead. Julia knew where it would go, and was not in the least bit worried. Later, he even wondered whether she had only taken up with James so she could bring him home for this very conversation! But perhaps that was his own paranoia getting out of control.

James had enjoyed his lunch and the wine and, like most people, was happy to talk about himself. He explained that he was currently researching cognitive dissonance and confirmation bias. Trevor's heart sank. The brain, he explained, was an amazing organ, which up to the age of our late teens is malleable and plastic. By adolescence, it has created its own model, a discreet map of the world for each individual. By then it knows what a chair is, or a table, a motorcar, or a tree. It has a model of everything, and from then on, the brain and the senses just scan the world to check it against its model. This, he said, was a very energy-efficient way of operating, a miracle of human evolution. Adam resisted the temptation to object to the reference.

"And what happens when the brain comes across something that doesn't fit the model?" Julia asked, like a barrister who only asks questions when they know the answers. "Does it rerun the modelling?"

"No, that takes too much energy. There is a tension and discomfort, what we call cognitive dissonance. The brain wants to retain its model and seeks to deal with the dissonances and maintain its original bias. It looks for evidence to support its view and ignores evidence to the contrary. That's what we call confirmation bias. We all tend to see what we are looking for. That's why a driver at a junction pulls out in front of the motorbike, because the driver is only looking for a car.

"So," Julia chipped in again, looking directly at Adam, "Does this explain why perfectly intelligent, rational people can believe extraordinary things that defy all logic?" The Reverend thought it was time he got into the game, in defence of Adam, if not his own church.

"Had you any particular extraordinary beliefs in mind Julia?" He asked with a twinkle in his eye, casually sipping the last of his wine.

"Well Trevor, your church does maintain one or two extraordinary ideas, doesn't it – The Immaculate Conception, the virgin birth and resurrection from the dead?"

"Tell me James," Trevor asked, "which kinds of people are susceptible to cognitive dissonance and confirmation bias?" Now Trevor was looking directly at Julia. James smiled at him, his company and conversation he had greatly enjoyed earlier in the day. He too was asking questions for which he already knew the answers.

"Well, generally speaking," James observed, pushing his silver-trimmed glasses back onto his elegant nose, "they tend to be human beings."

"Any in particular?"

"All of them!"

"Does it even apply," Trevor asked in mock curiosity, "to academics, solely committed to objective reasoning and empirical research in the venerable courtyards of our great universities?"

James laughed out loud, "Oh they're the worst of the lot, there is more confirmation bias per square metre in your average university department than anywhere else on God's earth!"

Mother glanced across at Rachel, who she was pleased to see looking more relaxed than she had in months and clearly enjoying the exchanges.

"Joking apart," James wanted to make a serious point, "the better the intellect, the more able the mind, the more skilful it is at finding clever reasons for maintaining its original bias and sticking with its original internal model." Adam had followed the conversation with more equanimity and satisfaction than Julia could have imagined. As with so many of her strategies, her brother proved himself impervious to the traps that she tried to set. He was pleased to hear of the bias and prejudice of intellectuals in the academic world, something he had always suspected. He took comfort from the knowledge that his own beliefs were not based on the same kind of human reasoning, not reliant, as he would see it, on man's wisdom, but on the revealed word of God. James would not have been surprised to know this and might well have considered Adam as a suitable subject to further his research.

Hector thought it was time he assumed his traditional role as changer of the subject. Looking at Adam he asked, "What about you two guys, what are you getting up to at the moment? Have you any plans, other than working too hard?" Rachel put her hand over Adam's, with a tenderness he had not felt for some time.

"I know what we should do love," giving his hand a reassuring squeeze, "why don't we make a start restoring Pop's MG? We always said we would and it is probably deteriorating sat in that old leaky garage? It would be great to get it running again and restored to its former glory. It would help get you out of the office love." It was some time since that word had passed between them, now twice in two sentences. Trevor's ears pricked up again.

"What's this, what MG?" he asked, looking around the lunch table.

"It is a pre-war TA," Adam explained. "You remember Pop, the old chap who left us this house, well he left us a car as well. It's in the garage around the corner and in pretty poor condition. We've been meaning to restore it ever since he died. It looks like now might be the time.

"I used to have a TD, when I was in the army. I loved that car, should never have sold it. Complete death trap, but great fun to drive."

"This one is much the same. I learnt to drive in it!" Adam said. "Space, that's the problem. If we are going to strip it down, we will need a decent sized garage." Hector had reluctantly suggested that they might use his garage, but it was really too small, and besides, everyone knew he would hate to leave his new Cortina out on the road. The garage at Salem would have been ideal, but that, and the house, were currently rented out.

"I have a better idea," suggested Trevor, "there's a large space at the back of the parish hall that's only used for storage now, so we could use that. How

232

would you feel about involving the senior youth club? It would be a great project for some of the older kids. What do you think?"

Mother thought to herself, this is just how Trevor operates, everyone's problem was his opportunity.

"Sounds great to me!" said Adam.

"Count me in as an assistant mechanic," Hector said.

"And me," insisted Rachel, "as chief tea maker."

So there it was, the decision made by the men. They would go and inspect the said vehicle and once again, the three women were left with their hands in the kitchen sink.

Chapter 14

1979

The 'winter of discontent' was over, and so was Jim Callaghan's Government. It had taken the greatest number of days lost to strikes in British history, rotting piles of rubbish in the streets, the dead left unburied and the sick excluded from hospital to get the desperate electorate to vote for the first woman Prime Minister. At the time, they didn't know they had voted for a social and economic revolution that, like it or loathe it, and many would loathe it, would sweep the country. Its effects would be felt on the Yorkshire coalfield as much, if not more, than anywhere else in the country.

South Yorkshire was the bedrock of the National Union of Miners. The miners' solidarity was legendary. They claimed to be doing the hardest, dirtiest and most dangerous job in industry, something construction workers and their accident rates might query. Yet the miners were prepared to fight and fight to continue doing the hardest, dirtiest and most dangerous job in industry. The solidarity of the mining community was just that – the solidarity of the mining community, not the solidarity of the whole community. There were others living on the Yorkshire coalfield, working men and women, who believed the miners had been well paid for some years now, though few of them would have crawled on their hands and knees to work a three-foot seam of coal for seven hours a day. The mining community looked after its own. There were others, a minority perhaps, but others, who voted for change and welcomed it. Margaret Thatcher could not have won the election without the blue-collar vote.

Arthur Hughes would not have described himself as a working man, nor would anyone else. He had never worked a three-foot seam of coal, nor worn a blue-collar, but he was excited and optimistic about the new radical Conservative government. Like most old school Tories, he had no idea just how radical the changes would be and how painful the short-term consequences. He was confident that Mrs Thatcher would solve the country's economic and industrial woes, even though mortgage rates were sky high and inflation was thirteen percent and rising. By the end of the year, British Leyland would have laid off twenty-five thousand workers, the first of many more redundancies to come in Britain's over-subsidised, inefficient manufacturing sector. He focused on reductions in the top rate of tax and the new administration's clear signal that enterprise and ambition were to be encouraged. Arthur was certainly keen to encourage it that particular evening.

He had been invited round to the house in Wakefield for an early evening drink. Gaynor had arranged it and asked the accountant to join them, but she was now getting impatient with her husband's procrastination.

At home, he would talk incessantly about developing the Halifax site, but seemed incapable of coming to a decision. Gaynor's father, though no longer running his own company, was a marketing consultant for a large construction company in Leeds, keen to take on the work. Damien claimed he wanted to exercise the option, obtain detailed planning approval, and build the scheme out, but he wouldn't get on with it. His father had only ever intended to sell the site on with detailed planning, take his profit, and leave the development profit to others.

The four of them sat together in the living room overlooking the gardens. Rachel's landscaping had matured over the years and presented a striking and attractive aspect to the rear of the house. That evening no one was paying it any attention. Arthur was all reassurance and optimism.

"We are at the start of a whole new era Damien. The socialists have had their day. It's going to be a time for entrepreneurs and men of action. Inflation is serving you well, your option price looks even better value for money now than it did years ago, and look what has happened to house prices over the last ten years." This was all true enough, as there had been some provision for inflation in the option agreement, but nothing like the double-digit inflation of recent years and growth in house prices throughout the seventies had been unprecedented.

What Arthur did not mention, what perhaps he did not even see (confirmation bias being no less effective in Arthur's brain as in any other), was that construction and development costs were rising at similar rates. Nor did anybody mention the universal truth: that what has happened in the past was no guarantee as to what might happen in the future. With Gaynor's approval, Arthur had shown Natalie's original scheme to a partner he knew in a large architect's practice in Leeds, to get some idea of total design costs. These, including as they must the whole design team of architects, engineers, surveyors and other specialist consultants, were eye-watering. A significant proportion would have to be paid upfront before construction began, let alone before any sales income was forthcoming.

William Hague, the accountant, in Adam's absence had rerun the figures of the original appraisal. They still showed a substantial profit, with only a small provision for future increases in house prices. The bank had seen the appraisal, and although it would represent a substantial uplift in the development company's borrowings, they were happy that Damien had adequate collateral to justify the loan. Banks are usually relaxed lending money to people they are confident already have it. What no one said was that Damien was close to "betting the farm" on just the one development.

Arthur had brought him up to speed on the Smawthorne site and its potential value as a ransom strip when the planning authority published its new development plan in around twelve months' time. This was a reassuring financial buffer, known only to the two of them. As Arthur said, "It's a hidden asset Damien that's appreciating every year that goes by."

Damien was like the temperamental horse at York races, down on the Knavesmire ready to go, but reluctant to get into the stalls. Arthur and Gaynor, the handlers, were joining forces behind him, encouraging him forwards, and if that failed, giving him the final push. Arthur was keen to be involved full-time on sales and marketing and, for what it was worth (which these days was not much), political influence. Damien needed his help and was not unsympathetic, but nor was he a fool. If Arthur was so confident and enthusiastic about the scheme, so certain it was a time for entrepreneurs and risk takers, then he too should have some 'skin in the game.' He offered him the Charles Blondin option.

Blondin, the French circus artist, was the first to walk across Niagara Falls on a tightrope. He was as good a showman as he was circus performer. Having attracted a crowd of over a hundred thousand and whipped them up into a state of great excitement by completing a number of nervous crossings, he produced a wheelbarrow and asked his audience if they believed he could also push that across. When they all cheered him on, he invited volunteers to come and sit in the wheelbarrow. Reports vary as to whether it was his manager or his mother who were the only ones who truly believed and took up his offer. Damien invited Arthur, if he was so confident, to climb into the wheelbarrow. It was an offer he found as difficult to refuse, as it was to accept. He had already spent much of his own money bringing together the consortium for the Smawthorne site. He too would need to go to the bank, with some collateral.

* * *

It took some effort, ingenuity and planning to get the MG out of the dilapidated wooden garage and around to the church hall. When they opened the double doors, it was not clear amongst the cobwebs, dust and rubbish, what was motorcar and what was garage junk. Mice had been nesting in the footwells and bird droppings covered the bodywork. Just liberating it from its stygian lair took some head-scratching. The brakes were seized and the tyres flat. While father and son pulled on the tow rope, the reverend, who claimed he had experience of such problems, hammered at the front wheel hubs with a blacksmith's hammer he had found lying around the garage. The vicar's hammer eventually persuaded the brake drums to let go, and slowly they managed to drag the car out, mercifully leaving most of the garage behind. Somehow, Trevor had managed to borrow an old Land Rover and trailer, and they soon had it winched aboard and around to the hall.

Sitting there, against the bare, white-washed walls of the church, it looked even more dilapidated than in the garage.

"Do you think we've bitten off more than we can chew?" said Adam in a crisis of confidence. This time it was Hector's turn to be full of optimism and reassurance.

"No problem," he insisted, "we've got plenty of time and it's all there. Anything we can't do, we will find somebody who can."

"Absolutely," Trevor agreed, as he seemed to have the ability to find somebody who could do anything. When they arrived at the church hall, they were surprised to see lined up along one side, a collection of tool chests, axle stands and an old engine hoist. There was even a workshop manual lying on top of the tool chest.

"Where did this lot come from?" Hector asked.

"Oh, I asked around and one of the local haulage firms, when I told them about the project, said they could let us have a few bits and pieces." Hector looked in amazement, thinking to himself, this is Trevor's idea of a few bits and pieces? There was enough here to build a car from scratch! Rev Trev certainly had his own unique outlook on what form Christian ministry might take.

The MG T series has its own particular place in the history of the motor car. It can rightly claim to be the first of the mass-market sports cars. Austin-Healey, Triumph TR and Lotus, can all trace their lineage back to Morris Garages of Abingdon in the 1930s. The company cemented its reputation in motor racing by being the first, non-Italian marque, to win its class in the legendary Mille Miglia, the gruelling 1000-mile race around the supposedly closed by-roads of Italy.

The TA, however, was born out of compromise and frustration, when the company was sold to Morris Motors. The racing programme was shut down and the new management demanded a more profitable product, based on standard components and simpler engineering. At first, the workforce was unenthusiastic, resenting the loss of their sophisticated race-bred technology, but they still went on to create this landmark in the history of motoring. After the War, MG TCs would be exported in large numbers to the United States by GIs returning home. They had fallen in love with this cute little car and generated an interest in British sports cars that would endure for years.

Not all the GIs took their MGs back home, which was how Pop was able to get hold of one in 1945, from an airman heading back to the States and needing a quick sale. The American did not understand how valuable a car, any car, was in post-war Britain. It still cost Pop every penny he had, and some he didn't have, but he was a singleman and the War was over, so who cared!

Fifty years on, it was the elegant simplicity of the MG's engineering that appealed to frustrated engineers like Trevor and Hector. It was the same engineering, the same skills, that had produced the machines Britain relied on in the grim days of 1939. Mechanics of Hector's generation learned their trade and honed their skills, maintaining tanks, armoured cars, military aircraft and the like. Such cars were an evocation of those dark days and a sentimental bond with a time gone by.

The restoration of the MG would benefit Adam in more ways than one. It would provide an escape from the pressures of the business, and a distraction from what he knew Damien and Arthur Hughes were getting up to in Halifax. There was a growing resentment, he knew there shouldn't be but there it was. He had enough to do and more than enough money and success. He had his work, his wife and lovely daughter. It should have been enough. But the sense of injustice was, at times, overwhelming. He had been excluded from that which he had helped to create, from what had been promised and from what he was entitled to.

But now he could lose himself on an evening or weekend in the company of his father or Trevor down at the hall, methodically stripping down body panels, suspension units and transmissions. The precise, meticulous nature of the work suited his personality perfectly.

The car would also provide a bridge, a necessary bridge between himself and Trevor. The relationship was delicate and complicated. The vicar had become a close friend and confidante of his mother, and could have been something of an adopted family uncle. In many respects they were well suited. The problem was, of course, the religion thing. He could only be grateful for the way in which Trevor had helped Rachel deal with her grief. There had been grim days when despair was not far away. Adam would always remember the vicar's patient, generous and gentle wisdom that helped bring his wife back from the brink.

He was less happy with how this had drawn her away from the assembly and closer to the parish church. These days, to Adam's regret and embarrassment, it was where she and his mother could be found most Sunday mornings. For Adam, Rachel was losing "The Way" and there was little he could do about it.

From time to time he would be alone with Trevor, working on some aspect of the car's restoration, enjoying the work and the company. But hanging over them, more accurately, hanging over Adam, was the spectre of his religious divide. Unlike Julia, Trevor had no great desire to engage with Adam on the subject of religion. He knew enough about the appeal and the dangers of biblical fundamentalism to know that such confrontations would serve little purpose. He certainly had no desire to undermine Adam's faith. Indeed, he believed it was his job to encourage faith wherever it might be found. If Adam's beliefs were a help and consolation, who was he to interfere.

Sadly, Adam could not view Trevor in a similar light. He, who was reluctant to debate the subject with his sister or mother, was, in a perverse way, eager to confront Trevor. The Assemblies of Christ defined themselves as much by what they did not believe as what they did. Pointing out error was as important as affirming the truth. Trevor, representing the established church, was therefore something of a prime target. Adam felt he was on firm ground with the Church of England, as he believed that much of what the church had taught for centuries was not to be found in the pages of the Old and New Testaments. This might come as something of a shock to Trevor's parishioners, particularly as it was substantially true. The immortality of the soul, the Trinity and the christenings of infants, are not readily found in the pages of the Bible. Popes, priests and powerful bishops are equally hard to find. To Adam, the church even seemed to be in two minds about life after death. Do we go to heaven when we die (hardly mentioned in scripture) or is there resurrection at the End of Days?

Adam's instinct was to confront the vicar with this disconnect between church teaching and the Bible. He was like a boxer, or even the rugby forward who wanted to test himself against the strongest of opposition. He could now be as competitive in his religion as he once was in his sport.

Trevor lacked that competitive instinct, but unlike his parishioners, would be neither shocked nor surprised at Adam's revelations. He was well aware of the disconnect that so preoccupied his young friend. He was also aware of the historical context. Adam wanted a Bible based gospel of the first century, but was unaware that in the first century there was no Bible. Church teaching had evolved over the first three centuries of the Christian era and was in effect complete, in the Western Church at least, before the biblical canon was agreed. The two had evolved in parallel, if not always in harmony, and church teachings preceded the finished Bible by many years. This was probably something of an inconvenient truth for both men, but an inconvenience the vicar and his church were far more able to absorb.

It was therefore remarkable that the little MG and the challenges and mysteries of its restoration were able to bridge the theological rift between the two men. Incapable of agreeing on the solution to the mystery of the Divine Creator, they could unite in resolving the many and diverse mysteries of the pistons, crankshaft and non-synchromesh gearboxes that were essential to the little car's resurrection.

Mother was quite happy to lose Hector to the church hall on an evening, or for most of the weekend. She was reaching the end of her studies with the Open University, and was fully absorbed in her final dissertation. She could lose herself in the history of Central Asia, the Silk Road, and the role of the plague in the expansion of Islam, just as easily as the men did in gearboxes, brake assemblies and wheel bearings. Even the Sunday lunch ritual was being neglected. She had found the work, the tutorials and the summer schools every bit as liberating and exciting as she had hoped. It took some time getting used to the idea of submitting her work to be assessed and marked by someone else, but successful results quickly laid such anxieties to rest.

Her only concern now was what to do after graduation. There was no way she was going back to Meals on Wheels and domestic chores. What had one of her tutors said? "Tidy houses are for boring women." There had been a suggestion of working full-time for the Family Planning Association, which was flattering but, like her daughter before her, she rather enjoyed academic life. She may have been looking forward to donning her mortarboard and gown for graduation, however, she quite liked the look of the velvet gowns and floppy hats with tassels that were the adornments and honours of a Doctorate.

It was Sunday afternoon in early December and the church hall was like a fridge. The only effect of the two heaters was to fill the building with the sickly smell of burnt paraffin. Adam and Hector had agreed to make a start on stripping down the interior. They appeared, complete with woolly hats, scarves and fingerless gloves. The engine and gearbox were out of the car, the wheels off and the back axle in pieces. The lonely chassis and bodywork were propped up on axle stands, awaiting further indignities. The parts, carefully labelled, were laid around on the floor, like the entrails and organs of a dismembered laboratory specimen.

They needed to remove the seats, the hood, and carpets to examine the state of the chassis rails and floor. Hector was struggling to lift out the hood frame that was predictably tangled up behind the seat back. Exasperated, he was seeing if foul and profane language would help to shift the offending item, just as Rev Trev arrived to find out how they were getting on. No one, of course, was more amused than Trevor, who enquired if more sacred hands might be of some assistance. Sacred or profane, with much mirth, they managed to lift out the hood and frame, more or less in one piece. The frame itself was in reasonable condition, only needing to be rubbed down and painted, but the hood was in bits and would have to be replaced.

It was Hector who noticed it first, trapped behind and beneath the driver's seat. It was an aged folder with a faded MG logo on the cover.

"This could be interesting," Hector said as he stretched down into the bowels of the car to retrieve it. "And valuable," added Trevor, "if it has the original logbook and some service history." Hector brushed off the cobwebs and dust and placed it on top of the tool chest. It was indeed the original service pack, with the precious logbook, purchase invoices servicing and parts.

"This is great," Trevor said, "it all helps to tell the story of the car and adds to the history, provenance and its value."

They all saw it, but Adam saw it first. A small black and white photograph of the car, with the young couple, squeezed together in the cockpit, arms around one another in a loving embrace, smiling up at the camera. His heart sank. He clumsily tried to push it back into the folder. Here was his mother and Pop, arm in arm in the little MG in 1945, when presumably his father was still away in the War. Trevor noticed Adam's reaction and the worried look.

"What is it, Adam?" he asked, in a tone that said everything. When Adam did not know what to say, as usual, he said nothing. "We've seen it once Adam, so we may as well look at it again." Adam let Trevor take the file from his hand and slowly put the remaining documents on the cabinet, with the photograph and two small envelopes addressed to Albert Featherstone. As James had said over lunch, our brains are miracles of evolution, but at times an unreliable link to the real world out there; we see what we expect to see. Adam expected to see his mother. He was afraid he would see his mother for he'd seen her before in similar circumstances, so that was what he saw. But she wasn't there. When he looked again, it wasn't his mother at all, it was his mother-in-law. There could be no doubt of it, for all the world it looked like Rachel sat there in the passenger seat, but it was Jenny. It could only be Jenny. For a moment, a tidal wave of relief flooded over him, and then his father said, "Good God Almighty!" This time oblivious to the priestly presence at his side.

Silence hung over the three of them in the cold thin air. Hector was staring at the photograph and Adam was staring at Hector. Trevor was acutely aware that he was unwittingly trespassing on an intensely private place. Hector picked up the photo, looking at it closely, though there was no need as the image was perfectly clear. He wished that his wife was there, as she might have known what to say. Adam, still looking at his father, the wave of relief now ebbing away but replaced by new anxieties, said, "Did you know? Did you know about it? Have you always known? Hector made no reply, but looked at his son and then down again at the photograph, trying to hide his indignation at Adam's cross-examination. "So, why didn't you tell us? Why didn't you let me know?"

"Know what Adam? What is it you imagine I know? What is it you think you know now?" There was an edge to his father's voice, an edge he had rarely heard before, and had never been directed at him.

"You thought you already knew, didn't you? You were expecting it to be a photograph of your mother in the car with Pop, weren't you? Of course you were, that's why you tried to push it back in the folder. You're very certain these days aren't you lad about what you think you know. Well, this time you were wrong, weren't you? You didn't know what you thought you knew did you? I think your mother, at least, is due an apology now, isn't she lad?"

The Reverend felt he should intervene. "Look you two, I don't think we are in the best place to talk about all this. Why don't you come into the vicarage. At least it will be warmer there, and we can talk in a bit more comfort." Hector was glad to have Trevor there and appreciated the offer, but it was not the warmth of the vicarage he craved.

"No offence Trevor, but if you don't mind, I think I would prefer the sanctuary of the pub, but I would be very glad if you would come and join us."

Adam, chastened by his father's tone, knew what he had to do. He said, "There's something I need to get from home first, I'll see you in the Black Horse." Picking up the two envelopes, as yet unopened, he gave them to his father. "Look after these will you please Dad, they might be important?"

He knew exactly where the envelope was, locked at the bottom of the bottom drawer of his desk in the attic. He hadn't looked at it for years, nor did he look at it now. He just picked up the faded manila envelope and went to join the others in the pub. The lunchtime crowd had gone and they had the pub to themselves. There was the smell of cigarettes and stale beer. Les hadn't started straightening up the tables and chairs or clearing up the empties, but at least they had the place to themselves. Hector and the Reverend were thawing out in front of a blazing fire they had stoked back into life. Adam sank down into the vacant chair, casually dropping his large envelope onto the table next to the others. He looked at the two of them, then again at the table, still with nothing to say. His pint was waiting for him. There was also half a pint in what Harry would have called a lady's glass. He picked up his drink and nodding at the other said, "Mother's?"

"She's on her way," Hector replied. Then silence again.

Trevor, uncharacteristically unsure of himself said, "Look, are you sure it wouldn't be better if I left you alone?" Adam drained most of his pint in one go. He needed it. He placed the glass back on the table with exaggerated care, saying, "No Trevor, like Dad, I think I really would prefer it if you could stick around." He stood up and casually headed to the bar, asking over his shoulder, "Same again is it?" He didn't wait for an answer.

When Mother arrived, Adam, in a feeble attempt at humour said. "It's a bit like a TV quiz show, isn't it? Shall we take the money or open the envelope." No one laughed. So he opened the envelope, removing the large photograph that, up to now, only he had seen and placed it on the table. Mother immediately picked it up and looked at it for some time with a wistful smile. "I remember this day very well; I was the one who organised it. It was quite an occasion, and there weren't many celebrations around then as there wasn't much to celebrate, but I remember this one. She smiled again at the photograph and then, at Adam, putting her hand over his.

"So you found this. When love? As you were clearing out Pop's house that Sunday afternoon, I suppose." Adam looked down at his pint to hide his feelings of guilt. "I well remember it, and the cross-examination." There was the gentlest look of recrimination. "Presumably, you didn't show it to Rachel?" She looked to Adam for confirmation and received it. "You had just discovered an old man had left you a house, all his savings and a car for no apparent reason. Shortly afterwards you find a picture of him with his arm around your mother and everyone looking happy. We were very happy, all of us." Mother paused and looked again at the photograph. "She looks very happy, too, doesn't she?" She turned the image around and pointed to the young woman standing behind Pop with her hand on his shoulder. Adam had never noticed her before. He had never noticed because he wasn't looking for her, he was always looking at his mother. But there again was Jenny, glass in hand, bold as brass smiling at the camera.

"Yes she does" Adam agreed, incredulous as to what he was seeing her for the first time. Mother thought she also looked very pregnant. Jenny was standing in the familiar pose, familiar at least to other women, leaning slightly backwards, hand on hip, supporting the weight. She kept the thought to herself for the time being.

"Why didn't you show me the photograph Adam? Why didn't you ask me about it?" She realised, immediately, how foolish she sounded. How could he? How does a young man ask his mother who his father was, on a Sunday evening, in the company of his new wife, over beer and beef sandwiches, with or without mushy peas?

The two letters, when read, only confirmed what the photograph had already said. Love letters from Jenny to Pop, both tender and tragic, with the second letter ending the relationship. Broken hearted, the writer insisting that there was no choice, no alternative, a doomed affair with no future. Again, Adam asked the question. "Did you know? Have you known all this time Mum?" She took a while to respond, collecting the photographs, folding the letters, and carefully putting them back in the envelopes, placing them on the table in front of her with all the care and reverence of a priest at the altar rail.

Mother looked wistfully at the documents again, and then directly at Adam, "No love we didn't know, I didn't know. There were rumours at the time amongst the girls. But in the War, there were always rumours about one thing or another. Pop's nursery was a popular place for all the women, digging for victory, as we were. We all had fruit and veg patches in our gardens and he was a mine of information and materials. Yes, he was a bit of a lady's man, charming, helpful, something of a flirt, everybody liked him, we all flirted with him. I knew Jenny vaguely in those days, she was just one of the girls, just one of the mums. There was talk of a romance, a tragic love affair. Nobody knew for certain, and certainly, nobody knew with whom. He was always a very private man was Pop, as you well know. He did get very low after the War and we all noticed that. But many people did, not everybody was dancing in the streets in 1945.

She took a sip of her pale ale and leaned back in the chair, nursing the glass in her lap, her mind drifting back through the mists of the years. "When he died and left you the house and the car, did we ask ourselves the obvious question? Of course we did, didn't we love?" Hector just smiled at the memory. "But we didn't know, how could we? We could hardly have driven around to Salem and asked, "Oh, by the way, Jenny, who's the father of your second child, is it Harry or Albert Featherstone? No more than you could ask me the same question, I suppose?"

"I didn't know quite how to phrase it." Adam observed with the faintest hint of a smile. "We didn't know what to say, so we said nothing."

Mother fell silent, finishing her drink. The silence was contagious. Hector collected the glasses and headed for the bar, a not unfamiliar tactic of his under pressure. Eventually, Trevor broke the spell. "You still don't know, do you? You don't know the thing you want to know, you might think you do, but you don't. I am not sure, now, how you can ever know. The letters speak of an affair, that's all. Unsurprisingly, given that it was the 1940s, they were both determined to keep it a secret. Yes, the dates might fit, but you still don't know if Rachel is Pop's daughter or not." It was a jolt hearing the words that were in everybody's head, spoken out loud. Was Rachel Pop's daughter? Mother was tempted to say what she had noticed, but the men had not. Jenny was pregnant. But again, she kept the thought to herself. Later, she would share the observation with Rachel.

"So," said Adam, "what do we tell her?"

"It's not we," Mother said. "You will have to decide Adam, and you will have to tell her, or not tell her. No one else can."

"Thanks very much" Adam said, looking rather glum. Silence descended again on the quartet...Trevor, God bless him, offered no advice,   only questions.

"What will it be like for you Adam if you don't tell her? How would that go?"

"Do you think Rachel would want to know?"

"What was her relationship with her father, were they very close?" and so on.

Socrates could have done no better. Adam eventually realised what had to be done. When he got home, he found Rachel and Emily happily working in the vegetable patch. They had been there most of the afternoon. It seemed entirely appropriate. They took pleasure getting Emily bathed, fed and eventually tucked up in bed, then went downstairs to open a Sunday evening bottle of wine. As Rachel filled the glasses, Adam laid the folder out on the kitchen table.

"There is something here love that you need to look at."

Chapter 15

1980

The engineer looked up at Damien, grim-faced beneath the mud-spattered hard hat, pushed to the back of his head. The collapse had occurred in the early hours of Monday morning. After a week of heavy rain, the Calder was running high and in full spate.

"How bad is it?" Damien shouted down over the noise of the deluge, trying to keep the note of panic out of his voice. The engineer had got as far as he could, any further and he would be out of his depth. Damien already was. It was not clear whether it had been the cavalier tactics of the demolition contractors, weakening the old stone wall, or the ground workers carrying out remediation to the contaminated sub soil. At this stage it hardly mattered, the breach in the wall was growing wider by the hour. There would be time later for recrimination and litigation.

"What do we do about it?" Damien shouted, again struggling to make himself heard. "Sheet piling!" the engineer called back. "We need tons of sheet piling.

We need to build a cofferdam and quickly, the river authorities are going nuts."

"What's that going to cost?"

"I have no idea, but we don't have much choice unless you want to convert this thing into the first marina in Halifax!"

Everything had gone well, up to the start on site. The revised designs, if not as elegant as Natalie's original, had gone through the planning process with remarkable speed. In this, at least, Arthur Hughes had delivered. When the approval came through, there were, as expected, a number of offers from national house builders, keen to take over the project, and still deliver Damien a handsome profit. Against William's advice, but with much encouragement from Arthur, Gaynor and her father, Damien had chosen to build the scheme out, looking to maximise his return.

The full extent of the ground contamination had been a shock. The additional costs were significant and would swallow up most of the contingency budget. The collapse of the river wall was a disaster, as contaminated ground was being washed into the river at an increasing rate. Pollution was as much a problem as structural stability, but the collapse was now in danger of undermining some of the new foundations. Damien had no choice, the site would have to be stabilised, the dam built, and the additional costs absorbed.

A number of apartments at the front of the site were nearing completion, and could soon be released for sale. However, with mortgage rates at a record high, unemployment approaching two and half million, and an unprecedented slump in house prices, the viability of the whole project was in serious jeopardy. It was haemorrhaging cash and the bank was becoming difficult. A development project going bad is like buying a fake painting: the more you have spent on it, the harder it is to see the problem.

By the end of the afternoon, Damien had the design team and contractors assembled in the site office. Arthur and William joined them. Gaynor's father was no longer involved with the contractors, having received his commission for helping to secure the job. He was last seen with his wife boarding a flight to Alicante.

The engineer brought them up to speed on the design and costs of the cofferdam. They were even worse than Damien had anticipated. The contractor explained he was doing his best to placate the National Rivers Authority and Her Majesty's Inspectorate of Pollution, assuring them they were acting as quickly as humanly possible. He cheerfully added, "Some form of prosecution seems inevitable!"

When all the technical stuff was finished, the consultants and construction team left the three of them alone to discuss development and finance. William was for closing the site down and cutting their losses. He could afford to, as his investment was modest. Damien and Arthur could not, or would not. They were both clinging to the belief that their painting was genuine. Arthur, as ever trying to sound optimistic, said, "The apartments on the front are nearly finished and the sales unit will be ready by the end of the month. We only need to shift fifteen or twenty units, and we can be back on track." Arthur did not say how easy it would be trying to sell houses on a site that was in process of being washed into the river. It was certainly not part of his original marketing strategy.

"We still have to pay for the cofferdam and rebuilding the river wall," the accountant reminded them.

"You and I William" said Damien," need to go and talk to the bank."

"They will want some more collateral," said the accountant, stating the obvious.

"I know that," Damien said testily. "I do know that William."

There was some good news. The local authority had published and approved its revised regional development plan. The value of the twenty or so acres of agricultural land behind the old assembly hall and along the river in Smawthorne had increased exponentially. It was now identified as 'Land for residential development,' Damien and Gaynor knew that fifty percent of that increased value was, by ransom, theirs. At a conservative estimate, even in the currently suppressed housing market, they were looking at a profit of one and a quarter million. Arthur was brokering a draft development agreement with the other landowners that would tie everybody into a legally binding agreement, and outline planning applications were already being prepared by his consortium.

* * *

The Rowntree's had travelled south on mass, and were gathered together in Milton Keynes for the post-graduation celebrations. Hector had suggested that such a momentous occasion justified the family decanting to some posh hotel or restaurant. But when Slim offered to lay it on at his home, Mother said, "Yes, please."

"We don't need to make a big fuss, do we?" she said, to no one's particular surprise. Slim and the family were going to do their best to make as much fuss as possible.

Only Hector and the two children could get into the graduation ceremony to see Mother receive her honorary degree. She looked impressive in cap and gown, having been persuaded by Julia, of all people, to get her hair done and buy a new blue suit and yellow silk blouse, matching the academic colour scheme. No one looked more the part than Sylvia Jane Rowntree, called forward to be presented to the Chancellor of the University. Bachelor of Arts first-class honours with distinction. Who would have believed it? Well, Hector for one. He was thrilled to bits. If only her mother could see her now. They hung around for the photographs, wine and nibbles, as the family of graduates always do, but were soon on their way back to Milton Keynes for the real celebrations.

Slim had taken Emily to the park, thoughtfully leaving Natalie and Rachel time alone to chat. The afternoon was warm and still. It was one of those rare, late September days when the sun shone out of the clear blue sky, days cherished, in the knowledge that they may be but a few left in the year before November comes and ruins it all. The girls lounged together in the garden, making the most of the sun. Though now living miles apart, the two women were closer than ever.

"I suppose it's the not knowing, that's so difficult," Natalie said. "Would it be different if you could be sure, if you knew exactly what had happened?" They had spoken over the phone about the revelations of that Sunday evening, but this was the first time they had been together. Natalie was anxious to know how her friend was coping.

"No, not really, I thought that to begin with, but not now. I am pretty sure I do know, don't ask me how, I just know. It feels right, and it answers so many questions. So much just falls into place. When Adam showed me the photograph and the letters, it was more a matter of confirmation than revelation. I did cry when I read the letters, though. They were heartbreaking. I can't help feeling my mother had something of a tragic life, to go with her tragic death."

"You don't blame her for not telling you?"

"Hell no, living in that community in the 1940s, she really had no choice." She looked thoughtfully down the length of the garden trying to imagine a time that never was.

"I do sometimes wonder though if she would have told me one day, given time. But she didn't get much time, did she? So that's something I will never know."

"But you know Pop is your Dad?"

Rachel leaned back on the sun lounger, closing her eyes, feeling the comforting warmth of the afternoon sun and eventually said, "I believe Pop is my Dad."

That was really Trevor speaking, not Rachel. She hadn't told Natalie the whole truth. Not knowing had been a big problem. She wanted to know, she believed it was true and she wanted it to be true. She wanted to be Albert Featherstone's daughter. If only so that the man she still blamed for her mother's death would no longer be her father. She hadn't told Trevor that, she hadn't confessed it to anyone. But she wanted it to be true. She had sat with the Reverend in his lonely vicarage, late one night, raging against her doubts and uncertainties. Trevor, having listened patiently at some length, began to enquire what it was, exactly, that she believed she did know with complete certainty. As the evening wore on and his questions wore her down, there appeared to be little Rachel knew for certain.

"But Trevor," she said in exasperation, "you're supposed to be a man of faith, you're supposed to know. Surely you've got to know what's right and what's true?" It was getting late. He was tired and stood up, indicating it was time to call it a night. Putting his hand on her shoulder, something only he could do with total impunity, he said, "Rachel, faith has never been about knowing, faith is the doing." As she got up to leave, he added, with only a tinge of sarcasm, "You're supposed to know your Bible, check it out, girl. 'The substance of things hoped for, the evidence of things unseen.' So if you want to believe Albert Featherstone is your father, then for goodness sake get on with it." She did, and she had.

Mother, that is Sylvia Jane, had intended, like most graduates, to hire her academic garb for the day, and then return home with only the memory of her celebrated status. Plus, of course, the obligatory photograph, holding the fake scroll. It was a piece of cardboard rolled up in gaudy red ribbon. Mother noticed it was rather grubby by the time it was her turn with the photographer, so declined the cheap prop and arms folded, stared defiantly into the camera lens, challenging it to do its worst. Hector, however, wanting a memento of such a special day, had bought her the whole outfit, cap, gown and sash. So when she got back to Milton Keynes, her arrival was suitably dramatic. Emily was the most impressed, and demanded Granny's silly hat, adorned with which she began parading around the garden. Adam and Slim opened the champagne, while mountains of food miraculously appeared on the terrace. The company settled in to spend the remains of the day basking in the reflected glory of the family's most recent scholar.

The light quickly faded, the twilight more so, but a sufficient amount of the day's warmth remained to keep them comfortable in the garden. Emily had helped Slim to light the Chinese lanterns and see them sparkle in her clear brown eyes. The little girl was now on Granny's lap, curled up in her academic gown, becoming heavy with the onset of sleep.

The day would be memorable for more than just Mother's graduation. Hector announced that he was taking early retirement in the new year. He was delighted, Mother was non-committal. "For richer for poorer, for better or worse, but definitely not for lunch," was all she had to say on the matter! As Mother was gearing up, Hector, most determinedly, was slowing down. The real surprise, though, was Natalie and Slim announcing that they were both leaving the New Town Development Corporation, and planning to start their own practice.

"We may as well," Natalie said "there's going to be precious little money for public buildings with the current government, so we may as well take our chance in the commercial jungle." Adam hunted around for what champagne was left to celebrate Hector finishing work, and hopefully, Natalie and Slim finding some.

The end of the evening found Adam and Slim alone in the garden.

"How's my cousin getting on in Halifax?" Slim's question was, as ever, genuine and very much to the point.

"I have no idea mate. It is nothing to do with me these days." Adam lied, "I haven't been involved in that for the last couple of years. Arthur Hughes seems to be his right-hand man and confidant. Best of luck to him is all I can say." He may not have been involved, but he had made it his business to know precisely how Damien was or was not getting on. He knew about the issues with contaminated land, and everybody in the town knew about the collapse of the river wall. He knew from his own business what little confidence there was amongst the house-buying public. It did him little credit, but schadenfreude best described his mood. Slim was sad to see this hard edge to his old friend, and the obvious traces of bitterness that were beginning to mar his usually generous nature.

As for Adam, he also knew about the change in planning policy, as it affected the chapel site in Smawthorne, and the preparation of the outline planning application. He might not be involved in Damien's plans at the moment, but that was likely to change in the near future, and then it could all have a great deal to do with him. The night had suddenly turned cold and chill, and the wind sent the two friends inside to join the others, knowing each other a little less than before.

* * *

"Why are these places always like this William?" Damien was feeling hot and nervous and resented being kept waiting.

"What do you mean, like this?"

"Well, look at it! All banks are the same, the marble floors, mahogany panelling, elaborate chandeliers and all this leather furniture. How do they get away with spending so much money on themselves.? How can they be so lavish and extravagant?"

"Oh, I see what you mean." William Hague sipped his coffee from the elegant Thomas China he had been handed by the equally elegant secretary when they had arrived 20 minutes ago.

"Some would say, and the bank certainly would, it's to give the impression of sound money, solidity, reliability and respectability. But really, it's the same reason they pay lavish and extravagant salaries and bonuses for mediocre talent. It's because they can, because they're the ones with the money. If you or I want the likes of this…" he waved his arm at the marble and glass staircase rising up to the executive floor, "we have to either earn it, or borrow it. We're all limited by cash flow, otherwise, we wouldn't be here now. But the banks have the cash because we all give it to them, and if they run out, they don't go bust like the rest of us, the government tops up the coffers."

William's gentle tirade was interrupted by the area manager's secretary returning, carefully tiptoeing across the polished marble in her impossibly high heels. Tall, blonde, beautiful and no doubt, William suspected, even more inaccessible than the extended loan they were seeking. The two men dutifully followed her into the equally elegant and oversized boardroom.

The meeting went much as expected. The bank was as worried about the general economic outlook and the downward spiral in consumer confidence as they were about the increased costs and disasters on site. They would extend the loan to cover the cost of the cofferdam and repairs to the river wall. Why wouldn't they? The original loan was partly secured on the site itself and it was hardly in their interests to see part of it wash down to the Humber. In return, they wanted weekly reports on house sales and a charge against Damien's interest in the Smawthorne consortium. In connection with which, they also wanted sight of all the documents: draft contracts, title deeds and planning applications.

"That seemed to go well," William suggested as they stepped out onto the Headrow in Leeds city centre, joining the Friday afternoon shoppers. Damien thought, if that went well, he did not want to be there when it went badly. He felt as if he had just stepped out of the headmaster's study after being informed of yet another failure to come up to expectations. "Make sure you get the documents to them as soon as possible, and that they are all correct," William insisted.

It was going to go badly, and soon. William knew it would, Damien was afraid it would. When it did, most people would blame Damien. They would put it down to his impulsive and headstrong nature, his youthful naivety and limited intellect. But the truth was, Damien's greatest failing was being unlucky, that was all. In property development, as in most things in life, timing is everything. Damien's timing was awful, but it wasn't his fault, it was just bad luck.

Five years earlier, or three or four years later, he would, even with contaminated land, collapsed river walls and the dead weight of Arthur Hughes, still have been successful. Later in the decade, many impulsive and headstrong young developers, with no better intellects than Damien, proceeded with equally flawed development plans, and overly optimistic viability studies, and succeeded. Most of them were bailed out by escalating house prices and rising land values. Many captains of industry would gain reputations as visionary pioneers, experts in urban regeneration, some even knighted, for nothing more than being there at the right time and riding a tidal wave of other people's enthusiasm for urban living. Halifax was by no means the last bit of contaminated ground to blight an urban development site, or the last river or canal wall to collapse into the foundations. Damien was just unlucky, being there too late, or too early. He got caught up in the undertow, the backwash of the previous boom, and missed the crest of the next wave. Such can be the utterly random nature of human endeavour and the arbiter of success and failure.

As someone put it back in 250 BC, "The race is not to the swift, nor the battle to the strong, but time and chance happeneth to them all." Damien was, no doubt, familiar with the book of Ecclesiastes, and may well have quoted from it in his public utterances, but it is doubtful that it would give him much consolation when time and chance finally struck home and swept him away, as surely as the Calder swept away the foundations at Halifax.

Adam's timing, on the other hand, would be perfect. His only difficulty would be finding ways to see it, not as luck, nor even his own ambition, but as the outworking of divine providence, and a blessing upon his righteous head. Divine providence, like good luck, invariably looks like something you deserve.

He knew the crisis was coming. It would not be of his making, though very much to his benefit. It was just a matter of how it was triggered. As it happened, it came from two directions simultaneously. Rachel came home from her studio, having picked up Emily and a friend from school. Emily was having her first sleep over. Adam was home early, but still working on the kitchen table. As the children ran noisily upstairs to play, Rachel dropped the letter in front of him,

"Have you seen this? Have you seen what my brother, my half-brother, is planning to do with my studio and the nursery?"

"Good evening love, and how are you tonight, have you had a pleasant day?" he teased, as he picked up the letter from the planning authority. Rachel, apologetic, flopped down at the table.

"Sorry love, but do you know about this? We have to stop him."

"No I haven't seen it yet, but I have been expecting it." As an adjacent landowner, he would receive a similar letter informing him of the planning application and inviting his comments and observations.

"There must be something we can do to stop him, surely?"

"Well my dear, I am not sure about stopping him, but we can certainly slow him down a bit."

He had had a message earlier in the week, not from Damien himself of course, but his secretary. Damien wasn't sure where the deeds for the village hall were. If Adam knew, could he forward the original copies to the bank and a copy to Damien? Adam knew exactly where they were, and why Damien couldn't find them. They were in his briefcase, together with the deeds of Rachel's woodland and conservation area. Adam would tell himself and others that he was not the one driving events. It was true; events were driving him. He suggested to Rachel that they should discuss things later when the children were settled down for the night. It would give him a little more time to decide how best to tell her the story.

Later, when she came downstairs, Adam had all the documents and plans spread out over the stripped pine of the large kitchen table, along with two glasses of chilled, white, burgundy.

"Sit down, love, have a drink, I need to tell you a story." She sipped the crisp dry wine with satisfaction, but said with trepidation, "Not another story?"

"Yes, another story and I'm not sure what you are going to make of it." He picked up his wine glass, running his finger along the condensation on the outside and tapped the rim against Rachel's. "Cheers love!"

"When your stepfather either helped or persuaded, whichever term you prefer, the assembly in Smawthorne to move to the chapel in Halifax, there was more to it than most people were aware of. The community got a large new chapel at no cost and Sunderland Developments got the rest of the site for development. They also got control of the original site in Smawthorne. I knew about it, Simeon Kantalow and most of the elders knew about it. It was probably a good deal all round, but particularly good for Harry and Damien. It was all proper and above board, or so I imagined at the time."

"There was, however, something else, something I didn't know at the time. Something only Harry and Damien knew. Arthur Hughes, Alderman Hughes, as he was then, let them know that the farmland behind the hall in Smawthorne and along the riverbank, would soon be re-defined by the planning authority as 'land for residential development.' As such, it's value would multiply overnight. There was one problem however. The only access to that land along the river was across the assembly hall site. The owner of that site would control access to the land beyond. They could hold the other landowners to ransom. Legally, it's called a ransom strip. That ransom is now worth between one and a half and two million pounds."

He paused to let it all sink in, something Rachel, unsurprisingly, was struggling with. He gave her time to think. "You mean that Harry knew about this ransom thingy when the move to Halifax was proposed, and what the site was worth? And Damien knew?"

"They knew what the site might be worth, even though it wasn't worth that at the time."

"Yes, but they still knew, didn't they? They still robbed their own brothers and sisters, their own fellowship, of over a million quid, didn't they? Did you know about this?" Her voice was getting louder, "Are you sure you didn't know Adam?"

"I knew about their interest in the development value of the Halifax site. I was involved, and I helped out. I did the viability study and I did most of the work. They promised me a share in the development company, but never delivered. Did they rob the assembly? No, not really. Did they deceive them? Certainly! Were the assemblies cheated? Probably. Harry and Damien would see it as just good business. Knowledge is power."

Rachel was stunned, she had still not taken it all in, certainly not all its implications.

"Is that it, is that the story?"

"That's just the prologue love." He went to the fridge, retrieving the rest of the wine and refilled the glasses.

"You need another drink."

"Do the brethren and sisters know about this?"

"No, not yet, but they soon will. There is a problem, problems plural. Damien is in trouble in Halifax. The job is over budget and there are issues on the site. He is in over his head, he has the bank on his back and needs to extend his borrowings. His only option is to offer the bank a charge against the potential value of the ransom strip as security."

"Well if it is worth a million quid, that should be enough even for that greedy sod. So what's the problem?"

"The problem is my darling wife," Adam said, unable to keep the smile from his face, "Damian knows less than he thinks he knows."

"What do you mean love?"

"Damien doesn't own the ransom strip"

"Then who does?"

"We do."

"What!" she exclaimed, open-mouthed, "We do! How come? Why do we own it?"

"I can tell you how it happened, but as to why it happened, well, that's a far more profound, even theological question."

Adam had been confident the original site plan was correct. But being Adam, he wanted to be sure – sure how the anomaly had come about. He had spent time researching the history of the area and obtained a number of old maps of the settlement at various times in the past. It had taken determination to research the thing properly, the kind of precise work in which he excelled. The issue centred on the building of the new stone bridge across the river in the 1920s. Before that, there had been a Drovers' bridge, and the area around was ancient woodland going back centuries. When the new road and bridge were put through, most of the woodland was cut down. Rachel's conservation area and the grass verge with the three majestic ash trees were all that remained of the original wood. The boundary of the village hall had always been the inside edge of the ancient woodland and the grass verge, not the edge of the road. The grass verge was never part of the village hall site. It was part of the woodland.

He showed Rachel the original site plan, where the two boundaries were shown clearly, if very close together. It was a tiny detail, but the consequences were profound.

"The ransom strip isn't the village hall, it's the grass verge and your woodland." Adam said, unable to keep a note of triumph out of his voice. "The boundary never was the village hall, it's your woodland and the grass verge," he repeated.

"Strictly speaking," Rachel said, "it is not my woodland is it? It's yours." He had never got around to transferring it into her name. When they were married, he saw no reason to. He could only say. "All my worldly goods, I thee endowed." For all the mixed motives and conflicting contradictions of Adam Rowntree's psyche, Rachel knew, in this, he was totally sincere.

They sat together for some time, drinking the last of the wine, neither speaking, each lost in their own silence. Rachel was beginning to comprehend some of the implications for them, for her brother, for the brethren and sisters of the assembly, and for her own conscience.

"When did you first know about the ransom strip and its potential value? Was that the real reason you bought the woodland?" He knew the question would arise sooner or later, better now than later.

"You were involved in the woodland love, long before you met me. It was your project, your consolation, perhaps even an unwitting legacy from your father. How would you have felt if Harry and

Damien had bought the whole lot for development and done whatever they wanted? That's what they were intending to do, if I'd not intervened." The question was, of course, entirely rhetorical. She would have been incandescent, given the amount of time and effort she had put into the restoration.

"But when did you know about the two boundaries and the importance of the grass verge?"

"When Harry asked me to arrange the purchase of the Halifax site and the transfers at Smawthorne. There were two site plans and I noticed the discrepancy. Harry and Damien had the same information, but they didn't notice, I suspect they didn't look. Even then, I didn't know for certain; it took a great deal of digging around in the records to be sure what had happened."

"But you didn't tell them did you, then or later? Why not?"

"Rachel, I knew it would affect what they could do with the assembly hall and your woodland. I was protecting you, but at the time I knew nothing of the potential housing land beyond, or its value.

"You didn't tell them because you didn't trust them, that's it, isn't it?"

"I didn't trust Damien, of course I didn't. But I bought it for you love, no other reason, as your wedding present. And you've got to believe that." She did believe him, others would not, but she did.

"So what are you going to do?"

"I am going to do what I am obliged to do, what I have to do. Damien has asked me to send the documents to the bank. I really do have no choice, it would be negligent to do otherwise. It is much the same for

Damien and he has no choice either. I am also obliged to write to the planners and point out that there is an error in the outline planning application."

"Then what happens? Judgement Day, Armageddon?" Rachel enquired.

"Something like that."

"You could go and tell Damien what you have told me, save him the embarrassment." Adam had thought about doing just that. He felt no great malice and had no desire to make things worse, but, on reflection, he preferred or thought it best that the dramatic revelations should not come directly from him. Far better for the truth to be revealed by other parties through the planning process, or the bank's process of 'due diligence.' Then his good fortune would appear to be just that, or as he chose to see it, the outworking of the Divine Will.

Adam's religion had few rituals. But one was his private Bible reading. Damien and Walter, and in earlier years, Harry, would follow the same plan, that in a year would see them reading the whole of the Bible, Old Testament and New. Adam and Rachel had once read together in the evenings before going to bed. Rachel's reading had lapsed some years ago, along with much of her religion. So Adam would read alone, usually late at night. Later that week, the gospel reading was a familiar parable in Matthew Chapter 18. Adam read, "A King was settling accounts. There appeared before him a man whose debt ran into millions. Since he could not pay, his master ordered him, his wife and children to be sold, to ransom the debt. When the man pleaded for time to pay, his master was moved with pity and remitted the debt. Later the same man came across a fellow servant who owed him a few pounds. Taking him by the throat, he demanded, "Pay me what you owe."

He knew the parable and the message well, including the fate of the principal characters, but left off his reading early that night and went to bed. He did not sleep particularly well.

Chapter 16

Winter 1981

Hector was looking forward to retirement, but not the regular retirement party that had been organised. Concerning engraved brass carriage clocks, in red leather travelling cases, Hector had made his feelings clear: he didn't want one. So when the chief engineer had concluded his obligatory, if humourless oration, enumerating the countless ways Hector had been vital to the running of the roads and drainage of the Borough, and then handed over the retirement gift, there was not the usual inward groan of disappointment. Thanks to Mother's timely intervention, Hector was delighted to receive the large metal toolbox, filled with spanners, socket sets, and just about any tool that might be required in the restoration of the MG.

The council offered counsel, to retiring senior officers. Hector accepted it, more out of politeness than need. He was advised to take his time. He said, "That's why I didn't want the bloody clock." They said people sometimes found it a challenge, the loss of status, not having a role. Hector, who never felt much need for status, and was more than capable of finding a role for himself, viewed retirement as the easiest challenge he had ever faced in his life. Someone suggested it was good to have a new project, to which Hector, of course, replied. "What do you think the toolbox is for?" Few were better equipped for retirement than Hector Rowntree. Being time-rich would be the greatest of luxuries. He couldn't wait to get down to the church hall and finish restoring the old car.

There was a core team now, himself and three keen lads from Trevor's youth club. Rachel, though devoid of any mechanical skills, desperately wanted to be involved, and hung around, making the tea and running errands. Trevor was there, mainly as a cheerleader and Mr Fixer. He would occasionally use the project in his more philosophical discussion groups. Something like 'Christianity and the art of MG maintenance.' Is there virtue in the love of an inanimate object? Can you justify the restoration costs when others are starving? Is there an objective definition of beauty? What, if anything, has it to do with God? and so on. The young people of his senior youth group were more interested in such ideas than anyone might have expected. But then Trevor never was 'expected.'

Most of the oily bits on the car were done. The engine and gearbox had been rebuilt and sat resplendent on top of the newly restored chassis rails. The bodywork was away being painted in its new livery. The lads were on with the rear axle, suspension, and brakes. Hector was entangled, sometimes literally, in the complexities of the electrical loom. It had all been slow progress, but that was no matter at all.

Adam, sadly, had spent little time in the church hall in recent months. Unsurprisingly, it had been a difficult year, though nothing like as difficult as Damien's. They had managed to get twenty or so units ready for sale, and the marketing suite up and running. But the market was dead, killed by the fear of unemployment and record mortgage interest rates. When Damien and Arthur felt that things could not get any worse, the bank phoned, demanding an urgent meeting. If Damien felt the previous meeting had been difficult, this one was infinitely worse.

The revelation of the ransom strip, was, of course, devastating. Their first reaction was shock, then disbelief and denial. Later, Damien would convince himself that it was all a deliberate conspiracy, hatched up by Adam. He would accuse him of fraud and try to mount a legal challenge. However, to his growing horror, it was the bank who were hinting at fraud and would, they said, "Be investigating whether he was guilty of the preparation of a false document." They reminded him it was a criminal offence. In the meantime, there was no possibility of extending the company's loan beyond securing the river wall. To complete the Jobian dimensions of Damien's predicament, the members of the Smawthorne Consortium of Landowners, who had spent time and money on the planning application, were also accusing him and Arthur of acting in bad faith and threatening to sue. Arthur had not been around for some weeks now and was said to be out of the country.

It was early in the morning and Rachel was alone in her studio, sat by the drawing board. Emily had stayed overnight with Grandma, planning to make the Christmas cake and decorate the tree, so Rachel had got in early. It had snowed heavily overnight, but now the air was cold, crisp and still, and the trees were crowned with a heavy, white blanket. Even the smallest of branches retained their delicate frozen tracery. The low morning sun was briefly transforming her woodland into an enchanted world of silver and gold, iridescent in the lifting morning mist. Soon the temperature would rise by a few degrees and spoil the magic of the moment, returning everything to slush.

She was cold, but content. Her studio was her sanctuary, her retreat, and the drawing board her refuge. Sitting there, she was surrounded by the colourful drawings and sketches of her current and past commissions. The walls were decorated with photographs of completed projects and she thought how lucky she was. Someone had said, "Find a job you love, and you will never work again." That was Rachel now. She didn't need to work, and she certainly didn't need the money, but she loved what she did. To her, there was a world of difference between a drawing board and a desk. Desks were for work and she remembered the boring rows of them at the bank, and the boring work upon them. But drawing boards were for fun. Drawing boards were where design happened, a place to indulge yourself in the joy of creativity, where ideas flowed and visions appeared as if from nowhere. At school, children are usually allowed to draw on a Friday afternoon. These days she could draw every day of the week and get paid for it! Natalie would have understood.

Looking out onto the frozen woodland that morning, as the first piles of snow began to drop from the branches, making deep holes in the virgin white ground, it seemed incredible that so small a piece of land could have such dramatic and profound effects on all their lives. It had been her desire, her frustrated need to restore this small piece of overgrown ancient woodland, that had triggered off everything that followed. She wondered how often such prosaic accidents of history and geography had blighted or blessed the lives of others. On a grand scale, these accidents of history were well documented: the French nobility bogged down in the mud, slaughtered at Cressy; the Arch-Duke's chauffeur driving down the wrong street in Sarajevo in 1914. But how often can something as trivial as a two or three-metre strip of grass verge be of such significance, and of such value to ordinary folk like her.

She had only wanted to stop Damien, not to ruin him. But it was difficult not to see it as a self-inflicted disaster. Adam was right though, they were not, nor ever had been in control of events. Events had controlled them. She had accepted his account of what had happened, extraordinary though it was. She knew him to be impossibly, sometimes brutally honest. But she was still conflicted. There was still something underhand, even shameful about the whole series of events. The congregation she was still nominally a part of, the community in which she had grown up, if not cheated, had been used and deceived. But not by her or Adam. Those responsible were either dead or ruined.

Furthermore, Rachel could not deny that these days, she was not particularly sympathetic towards the Assemblies of Christ, in Halifax or anywhere else. Increasingly she resented the time it had taken out of her life. More than that, she resented the space that they had occupied for so long in her head. She had no desire to 'campaign' on behalf of Simeon Kantalow and his fellow elders. If someone should be compensated for what had occurred, she had no idea who. Were they now trapped by their good fortune, just as surely as Damien was doomed in his?

Ultimately, in Rachel's mind if not her conscience, it was the money that settled the issue. She should not have judged herself too harshly. People presented with an entirely legal and undeserved pot of gold, rarely turned it down. She drew herself up to the drawing board, pushing the endless deliberations aside, and as was her way, lost herself in planning for spring and summer in someone else's garden. By the time she looked out of the window again, it was lunchtime and the scene outside had changed. The trees had lost most of their sparkling frozen attire and stood stark and black against a grey, threatening sky. She felt the disappointment of the child seeing the cap and scarf of the now-departed snowman left abandoned on the wet ground.

For all Damien's woes, he did have one rather unexpected piece of good fortune: his wife. Much to everyone's surprise, Gaynor became his principal asset. She knew the rest of the families had always viewed her with casual condescension. Young, dumb and not so blonde, unsophisticated and without much education. An attractive girl on Damien's arm, mother to his children, and on the make? Most of the time she was patronised or ignored, often feeling completely invisible. The family, Adam and Rachel included, had been concerned she might fall apart under the pressure of her husband's downfall. Nothing could have been further from the truth. If anyone was falling apart it was Damien and she, for the present at least, was going to keep him together. For love? For pity? For her children and her survival? She didn't say, but Gaynor was just going to do it.

Unsophisticated and not very bright may have been how the family saw her, but there was a new steel in that short and slender frame. Gaynor was going to survive. She would prove to be shrewder and more determined than any had given her credit for. Her instincts were sound; she was quick-witted and pragmatic. In the situation she found herself, such qualities, such talents, had far greater utility than a degree in history from Leeds University, or a well-stocked library of modern literature.

If she was Damien's one piece of good fortune, Gaynor's was that the Scarborough properties were in her name and the holiday lets had paid off most of the mortgage. They were hers and practically debt-free. While her husband was raging at Adam, the bank and fate in general, Gaynor, once she had recovered from the shock and laid aside her craving for revenge, was pragmatically assessing the situation. There was a stoicism and a cool objectivity that her late father-in-law would have admired.

She quickly realised they had lost the Halifax site and that Sunderland Developments would be wound up. The house would have to go (something that troubled her less than she imagined), as well as a number of commercial properties that were security for the debts. She accepted these blows with surprising equanimity. With William Hague's help, she looked to negotiate a settlement with the bank and voluntary agreements with the other creditors. They offered deals whereby they might get something, rather than nothing if Damien was made bankrupt. She had even made it clear to her father that whatever he had got out of the scheme by way of commission, she wanted it back, and put it into the pot. Her ability to accept the disaster for what it was and to have a clear idea of what she believed was possible impressed everyone. It particularly impressed the bank. They were easily persuaded that no criminal behaviour had taken place and abandoned their investigations. They took what they could, as banks do, and wrote off the rest as just another bad debt. It was by no means the only bad debt they would have in 1981.

Standing on top of the South Cliff in Scarborough on the first decent day of Spring, Gaynor Sunderland looked down with some satisfaction on the sweep of the South Bay, with the Grand Hotel in the foreground and the castle and harbour jutting out into the grey North Sea. Gaynor had loved this rundown seaside resort ever since she first came as a child. Today, she looked not much more than a child in the wide wind-swept landscape of the South Cliff. A slight figure, one might imagine her being blown away by the slightest breeze off the sea. But one would have been mistaken. The defining moment of her life had come and she was up for it, ready, excited even. She had got what she wanted, or as much as anyone could have got in the circumstances. They had moved to Scarborough and were living in one of the small two-bed holiday lets with the children. It was a tight fit but would do for now. The main house was being subdivided to create more properties. In addition to wanting the money her father had received in commission, she strongly suggested that he might get himself across to Scarborough and give them a hand. She pointedly added, "When your Spanish holidays are over." Gaynor was becoming increasingly persuasive. She had always had the ability to get the men in her life to do what she wanted. They would do all the work themselves. Damien would need to learn some new skills and quickly if he was going to remain part of her team.

She was going to make a new life for herself here on the East Coast and for the present, at least, Damien was included in the project. She wandered down through the gardens, not noticing the rich and colourful displays of Spring flowers that would have thrilled her sister-in-law. She was not thinking of her sister-in-law. She was taking the twins down to the spa, for a kick about on the beach before the tide came in, just as she had as a child. They had left Damien in the house, knocking down walls and stripping out bathrooms. They would be back later to check how he was getting on.

The move had also resolved one other difficulty. There was clearly no way that Adam and Damien could break bread together on Sunday morning in the same place. Gaynor would have been happy just to stay away. Her religion was now but a small part of her hectic life. It had come attached to her husband and was now loosely attached to her. She would still occasionally attend, still affirm a commitment, still join in, perhaps even fall back on it in any future crises. Now though, there were more pressing matters demanding her attention. Damien, on the other hand, desperately needed his religion and somewhere to go on a Sunday morning. He was in more need than ever of some hope and consolation. Incredibly, given what had taken place, he was still preoccupied with trying to predict the future and the end of the world. You would have thought it had already happened. His wife however was setting about to organise her own future. He would be able to attend a small assembly down the coast in Filey, where he hoped to find relative obscurity. Gaynor would find little time to accompany him.

The move to the east coast would come as something of a relief to Simeon Kantalow and his fellow elders. No one knew the whole story. Simeon probably did not want to know, nor did he enquire. He had been one of the chief advocates and cheerleaders of the move to Halifax. The community, in general, were more concerned about what was happening around the chapel. Initially they had to put up with the usual noise and dust of being next to a large construction site, but when the wall collapsed and part of the site was washed away down the river, there was understandable alarm. Now that the site had been closed down and temporary repairs carried out to the river wall, they naturally wanted to know how long they would be worshipping on an unfinished building site.

Damien, unsurprisingly, was deemed to be the one responsible for this sad state of affairs, but was no longer around to answer the awkward questions. Adam, on the other hand, was untainted by the disaster, at least as far as the elders were concerned. They were now increasingly looking to him for guidance and advice in matters both temporal and spiritual. The mantle of Harry Sunderland was being passed onto the shoulders of young Adam Rowntree. It was a responsibility he felt able, ready and even duty-bound to accept.

Echoes of Harry's teachings were reverberating down the years. 'Seek ye first the kingdom of heaven and all these things shall be added unto you.' Given the extraordinary events of recent years, how could Adam not be convinced that the power of divine providence was at work in his life? He would ask himself what other possible explanation there could be for the blessings that had come upon them. He was confident that he had not conspired or planned to secure the small fortune that had come his way. He knew he had never been in control of events. Something else, or someone else was in control. He knew none of these things would have happened if he had not first, faithfully committed himself to Christ, and the brethren and sisters of the assembly. His whole life had been turned around, transformed by that Saturday evening with Slim in the Welbeck Road Chapel all those years ago. Removing the original deed plan from the file and keeping it to himself all those years, locked in his desk, was now just a memory, lost in the mists of providence and confirmation bias. Strangely, it never occurred to Adam when he was reflecting on the way divine providence rewards the faithful to ask himself what of Harry and Jenny? How did their untimely, tragic deaths fit into his model of God's blessing on the righteous? God really did move in mysterious ways.

He would accept the responsibilities that that same providence was now placing upon his shoulders. He had gained a growing reputation as a Bible student and teacher and was being invited to speak at the same gatherings that his late father-in-law attended. Though not a charismatic or inspirational orator, he was admired for the depth of his knowledge and his detailed expositions on current world events and 'The End of Days' prophecies in the books of Daniel, Ezekiel and Revelation. The truth was that most of his congregation failed to follow or understand his complex and detailed exegesis of these obscure and arcane prophecies. They did, however, approve of his conclusions. Namely that the 'End was Nigh,' 'The Kingdom of Heaven was at hand,' and the Rapture of the faithful would soon be upon them.

Adam had also acquired something of that remarkable quality his father-in-law possessed, which at first, he had found perplexing: the ability to live two separate lives. He was totally committed to these eschatological beliefs, and at the same time, equally committed to a successful and profitable business life. Some might ask, if the end of the world was indeed nigh, what was the point of making millions out of a housing development in Smawthorne, or sorting out the chaos in Halifax? Surely all this would be irrelevant in the new Millennial Age. But that would be to fail to understand the nature of his and the assembly's beliefs in the afterlife.

They had no hope of heaven, sitting on clouds with the angels, playing their harps for all eternity, nor even some more sophisticated belief in a mystical heavenly dimension. They looked for the Kingdom of God on earth. 'Thy kingdom come. Thy will be done...on earth!' To quote the Lord's Prayer, no less. Adam and his brethren and sisters had a rather earthly view of the Heavenly Kingdom. It being, essentially, a utopian version of the present, with them, the righteous saints in control and the wicked put in their place. So whatever he could do now, by way of setting things right was all to the good. He saw it as his duty, his obligation, given the blessings that had come upon him. If he made a little profit along the way, well that was just more things being 'added unto him.'

Damien would give him no credit or thanks, but he was going to assuage the anger of the Consortium of Landowners in Smawthorne and persuade them to abandon their legal action. He would support their planning application, and propose a joint agreement of his own, whereby they could pay his ransom in stages. It was an offer they could hardly refuse. Adam would then be profitably tied into future increases in house prices when the current slump was over. Exactly what the rate of house price inflation would be during and after the Battle of Armageddon and throughout the Millennial Age, was a question he had not addressed.

Resolving the hiatus in Halifax would be more difficult and take longer, but he was determined, when the time was right, to be the saviour there also. He had given that commitment to Simeon and the other elders, which to some extent had eased their anxieties and further enhanced his own reputation. A visit to Milton Keynes was overdue.

It would be interesting to see if Natalie had any original ideas to improve the viability of the scheme. It also appeared that Slim, since leaving the development corporation had become something of an expert in negotiating and securing central government grants in support of difficult and problematic urban regeneration schemes. It was remarkable and revealing to witness the wonderful ways of providence. The mantle of Elijah was indeed heavy upon him.

Chapter 17

Somewhere, sometime later

The Prime Minister, Ken Clarke, was due to make a statement to Parliament on Monday regarding the crisis in the Middle East. It would be the first test of his premiership since taking over as caretaker Prime Minister following Margaret Thatcher's stroke. The attempted coup in Syria and assassination of President Assad had plunged the administration into chaos, with rival factions fighting for control. The chaos was reflected in rioting on the streets of Damascus, Aleppo and Homs. In the Soviet Union, Gorbachev's authority had been undermined by Yeltsin, and dangerous, old-school communists in the military were flexing their muscles. Naval exercises, so-called, were taking place in the Mediterranean Sea, and large numbers of troops and equipment had mysteriously arrived close to the Lebanese and Israeli borders.

President Reagan had sent two additional aircraft carriers, the Kitty Hawk and Nimitz to support the existing carrier groups in the Mediterranean and the Red Sea. There were already large numbers of American troops and aircraft stationed in Saudi Arabia. Calls from the Director-General of the United Nations for calm and the peaceful resolution of the crisis were not helped by bellicose statements from Hosni Mubarak in Egypt and members of Yitzhak Shamir's supporters in the Knesset.

Sitting in Harry Sunderland's old study at Salem, Adam reflected on these events with a satisfaction that would have escaped the rest of the population. He had, of course, been expecting just such a crisis and been predicting something like it at a number of assembly gatherings around the country for the past few years. Jerusalem surrounded by armies, God's people in peril of their existence. Existential threats. If not now, then soon. "These things must surely come to pass."

He turned the television off in the study and went to look for Rachel and Emily in the garden. Hector and Trevor were bringing the MG over that afternoon for the grand unveiling. They had kept Rachel out of the way in recent months while they fitted the new bodywork and interior. They wanted it to be a surprise on her birthday.

Moving into Salem had not been a simple decision for either of them. Adam had always assumed they would move in one day, but there was always some ambivalence. It was not his house, it was Harry's, Rachel's now, and not all her memories were good. They were both attached to Pop's old house, which they had made their own, where they had started a family and made a life for themselves. There had been lean times and dark days, times when Adam feared he might lose her altogether. But now things were easier;

they had found ways to rub along together. Perhaps they were expecting less and giving more, accepting each other for what they were, not for what they had wanted them to be.

So when the last tenant gave notice that they would not be renewing the lease, it seemed the right time to move on or move back. Rachel's only condition was that the furniture would have to go, starting with the mock regency dining room suite. In the end, she wanted the whole house redecorated, rewired and new central heating. They could afford it. They could afford to do just about anything. The refurbishment had taken some time, with the usual frustrations of getting tradesmen to do the work when they said they would and finish on time. The electrician was the least co-operative and competent. None of the decorations could be finished until the complex and extensive rewire was complete. The 1920s wiring had clearly been a fire waiting to happen, so the work was essential, but the electrician was a nightmare and filled the two of them with little confidence.

Post-Falklands' Britain was booming. Thatcher's vision of a property-owning democracy was dramatically coming into focus, for some at least. The housing along the river in Smawthorne had progressed rapidly and returned profits well in excess of Adam's expectations. Profits he was keen to reinvest in Halifax, where else? He had been careful to keep in touch with the people at the bank who had taken control of the site after Sunderland Developments had gone into liquidation. He knew, at some stage, they would be looking to move it on, find someone to rescue the situation and finish the development. Adam was determined that the someone would be him. After all, and as he would tell them, no one knew the site better than he did. After much haggling and negotiation, he persuaded them to give him three months to put a proposal together before they offered it to the market.

Natalie and Slim had got their new practice off the ground, working out of a small studio in the new town. They had secured enough commissions to give them credibility with future clients. For a new emerging practice, Halifax was a commission to die for. Natalie would redesign the layout to increase the density and scale, reduce the car parking, and return the architecture to its original contemporary style. She was confident this would get a positive response from the planning authority, even without Arthur's questionable influence. The crucial contribution would come from Slim. Urban regeneration were the new buzz words and urban regeneration grants were available, to those who knew how and where to ask. With his public sector experience, Slim had become something of an expert in securing such monies.

Between them, they put together a proposal that the bank was happy to accept. In doing so, it got rid of an embarrassment and recouped most of its losses. Adam had no intention of repeating Damien's mistakes. As soon as the revised planning application was approved, he did a joint venture agreement with one of the national house builders from Smawthorne, who were desperate to get onto the urban housing bandwagon. Adam secured his profit and limited his risk. His late mentor would have approved.

By the time the marketing suite was opened by the Chief Executive of the newly formed West Yorkshire Development Corporation (whose principal job was giving away public money to private developers), prospective house buyers were queueing down the length of Welbeck Road. He hailed the development a groundbreaking scheme and an excellent example of the kind of project that his organisation would be able to help get off the ground. This was a bit rich, given that the scheme had been two years in planning, and his corporation had only been going for two weeks, but in development, as in politics, timing is everything.

The Adam Rowntree who sat comfortably in his upholstered wicker chair in the warmth of his garden that Saturday afternoon in late August, watching his wife teaching his young daughter to play tennis, was a man who had unquestionably made it. He had moved into this fine house with his young family, had two successful housing developments to his name and the estate agencies were flourishing in the current boom. He was now actively looking for the next promising development and, incredibly as it might seem, expecting the end of the world at any moment.

Rachel, who had moved on some time ago from her adolescent preoccupations with the apocalypse, had her own particular take on her husband's schizophrenic, double life. She was, after all, more qualified now than most. She found it hard to believe that he really wanted his comfortable, prosperous lifestyle to be terminated by the Second Coming and the Rapture whisking him up to heaven. She believed there must be something of Saint Augustine's famous prayer in him, "God make me pure, but not yet." Something like, 'Thy kingdom come when the next development's done' or just 'Thy will be done, but not yet.' She suspected his obsession with predicting the end of the world and the Second Coming was as much to do with verification and justification than revelation. A need to be vindicated, proved right in the eyes of those who doubted or ridiculed him. She couldn't help thinking that he would get a terrible shock if it all actually happened.

At two o'clock he called the budding tennis players over for a glass of lemonade. He had been instructed by Hector and Trevor to keep Rachel well away from the front of the house when they all arrived with the car. The refreshments were interrupted by the repeated honking of a thin tinny horn. Smiling mischievously, Adam said, "I wonder who is making that terrible din, Emily? Shall we go and see?" Rachel looked suspiciously at her husband, slowly putting two and two together. "Is that what I think it is?"

"Darling, as you well know, I seldom have any idea what you are thinking these days." Mother and daughter ran off together around the corner of the house, leaving Adam to catch up.

It had not occurred to him before, but the car and house were almost of the same vintage, give or take a decade. It could have been the perfect photo-shoot. A 1930s sports car sat on the pale gravel, in front of the oak framed porch of a 1920s country seat. The MG did look immaculate, in its new two-tone green livery and skinny spoked wheels, painted black. Against the broad frontage of the house and the wider gravel drive, it looked impossibly small, toy-like even. But to Emily and Rachel it looked unbelievably cute. The transformation from the dilapidated, rusting wreck they had dragged out of Pop's garage, to this sparkling re-creation in metal and chrome was stunning.

Emily kept running around it, when not jumping up and down in her excitement, with Rachel just standing there, hands over her mouth, smiling, but close to tears. She was as happy as she had felt for years. Hector extravagantly opened the driver's door, beckoning her forwards,

"Your carriage awaits, madam." Rachel slowly walked around the car, astonished at the glorious transformation and eventually slipped into the narrow leather driver's seat. She thought of her mother, as the bright young girl in the photograph, with her lover, sitting in the very same place. The photograph of the two of them had pride of place over the mantelpiece now, but the car was infinitely more evocative of that other time and place. She rested her hands on the elegant rim of the cream steering wheel, her fingers naturally falling into the grooves, imagining her father's hands in the same place. At that moment, she had no doubt that this was Pop's car, and she was his daughter. It was almost a moment of religious conviction, probably the only one of her entire life.

"Come on, Adam," Trevor said, "climb in, I suspect the driver will need some basic instructions to begin with." And then to Rachel, "Just remember the big one in the middle is the brake and you should be all right." With much grinding of the gears and jerking of the clutch, they set off down the driveway, just as they had nearly twenty years earlier, but in opposite seats. The driver and passenger were looking a little older, but the car, fifty years younger. They waved them away, and Emily dragged Grandad off to the tennis court. Trevor and Mother sat together on the bench inside the porch, waiting for the travellers' return.

"Good day?" Trevor said, looking knowingly at Mother.

"Yes, definitely one of the good days."

The two had become the closest of friends. If Trevor had drawn Mother into his church, then she, in recent years, had drawn him into Lumley Street. For all the Vicar's energetic ministry, for all the many people he knew in and around the parish, Mother recognised the lonely man inside the clerical garb. She recognised it, and she understood it. She knew the cause of his loneliness, though it was never spoken of by either of them. Trevor always appreciated what Mother had to say, but he appreciated even more what she didn't say. If the Smawthorne Church had become her sanctuary, 39 Lumley Street was Trevor's refuge. It was a place he could always go and be welcome. It was where someone was looking out for him, a place he could experience something of family life that he had thus far been denied by his calling and outlook. He had become another of Mother's projects, although with Trevor, much more than a project. Fortunately, from Hector's point of view, the Reverend had more than enough suits and jackets.

"I think those two are going to be all right now, don't you?"

"Perhaps," Mother conceded, not looking entirely convinced.

"I suppose you will always worry about Adam?"

"Yes," she said, looking around her, "strange isn't it, we worry most about the ones who seem to have everything. But I shall still be worrying about you Trevor."

"You do say the sweetest of things, Sylvia." They sat there in the porch together, absorbing the remains of a good afternoon and waiting for the children to return. Neither said very much, but neither needed to.

The car came back up the drive with more speed, purpose and confidence than it had left. Both driver and passenger were windswept but wreathed in smiles. Trevor asked "How did she do Adam?"

"Not bad, not bad at all for a beginner. It won't take us long to rebuild the gearbox and refit the clutch."

"Cheeky sod!" complained Rachel, "It's absolutely brilliant. I haven't had so much fun in years." Hector and Emily had heard the noise and arrived back on the drive, Emily jumping immediately into the passenger seat, demanding that it was her turn next.

"After tea Emily, after tea. I promise you we can go for a long, long drive, but after tea."

Hector and mother made their excuses as they needed to get off home and Trevor had to do some work on his sermon for tomorrow.

"Don't forget all of you" shouted Rachel, "it's Sunday lunch here tomorrow. You too Trevor!"

"Is that builders and electricians permitting?" Quipped Hector.

"Who's carving the meat, Hector?" Trevor demanded.

"Whoever gets there first," replied Adam.

"Then it is going to be a short sermon in Smawthorne tomorrow!"

It was going to be Rachel's first Sunday lunch at Salem since moving back. Slim and Natalie were up for the weekend, and Walter and Felicity had promised to come over. Julia might make it, with or without a partner. James, the psychologist, had moved out, leaving Julia uncharacteristically heartbroken. In the past she would have just moved on to the next promising academic. Mother was concerned that life was catching up with her daughter.

Rachel had been looking forward to doing a Sunday lunch at Salem for some time. It had had to wait until the dining room was redecorated and the new furniture installed. The rewire was eventually finished and all the other decorating complete. The transformation from Thomas Chippendale to Terence Conran was now realised in all its contemporary splendour.

Rachel went to get Emily her tea. She and Adam would share a late supper. Like Trevor, although not like him at all, Adam had retired to his study to write his 'sermon.' These two men, on the same Sunday morning, but in different places, intended to address the same subject, 'Conflict in the Middle East,' from the same Christian point of view. Friends though they were, the common ground between them would be non-existent.

It was nearly 6 o'clock, by the time Adam had finished. He turned the television on to catch the news, surprised that it had already started. A grim-faced reporter was centre screen, over a caption reading 'Breaking news from Jerusalem.' The scene behind was confusing and indistinct, but it looked like part of the Temple Mount or the Wailing Wall. It was hard to make anything out clearly. Adam thought he could spot the Dome of the Rock in the background, but everything was shrouded in mist and black smoke. The reporter was out of breath, trying to remain calm and professional, but there was more than a note of alarm, if not panic, in her voice.

"No one here seems to know what's happening. There are strange and conflicting reports from all over the city. Some are talking of a terrorist attack, or a Russian invasion, although there are no reports of casualties or confirmed sightings of foreign troops. Other sources are talking of an earthquake, or even volcanic activity. Crowds of dazed and confused people are wandering the streets of the old city with strange and bizarre stories, though it is difficult to get anything confirmed. There is a black cloud hanging over most of the city, and although it's only 6 o'clock it feels like the middle of the night. There has been no statement yet from the Prime Minister or his Office. A spokesman for the Army said they were unaware of any attack on Israeli soil, and the Army had not engaged in any military action. Units were standing by, and all reservists had been recalled to their barracks with immediate effect."

Adam sat glued to the television screen. He was now becoming increasingly anxious and alarmed at what he was seeing. "It shouldn't be like this" he told himself. "Surely not like this. Not yet! Not yet!" The television switched to a reporter on the Mount of Olives, "There are strange reports here," the reporter was saying, "graves have been disturbed by what most assume was a violent earthquake, bewildered people have been seen wandering around within the cemetery walls."

He picked up the phone and dialled Walter's number. The call went straight through to answerphone. He tried Slim in Milton Keynes, but realised he would be back at Walter's by now. He tried again, but still no answer. He phoned his mother but no answer there either. He looked down at his watch. It was nearly seven o'clock and Rachel should have been home by now. Matthew chapter 24 kept coming into his head, "One shall be taken and the other left."

Rachel knew where she was going. She headed off through Denby Dale and Holmfirth. It was the same route Adam had taken, the evening he proposed. She was beginning to get the feel of the little MG, learning how to go with the natural rhythm and pace of the car much as she had learned to do with her life of late. They were heading for the Woodhead. She was going to stop at the place, she knew where it was, though she hadn't been in years. She intended to stop there and tell Emily something of what had happened, although quite what, she was not sure, perhaps something about her Grandmother. But just as they approached the infamous spot, Emily suddenly piped up,

"This was Poppa's car, wasn't it mummy?" Rachel looked down at her smiling daughter, sitting bolt upright in the tiny cockpit, holding onto the grab handle and trying her best to look over the dashboard and down the long bonnet. "Yes love, it was Poppa's car, It was very special to him, and now it's ours."

There was a brief pause, and with the hint of a frown the little girl said,

"I didn't know Poppa, did I mummy?"

"No" Rachel replied, a lump in her throat, "you didn't, neither did I really." She was close to tears, but then Emily said with the cheerful innocence that only a child can conjure,

"But I do like his car mummy. I do like his car!"

"So do I love, so do I."

Rachel didn't cry and she didn't stop. She carried on past the tragic grass verge and dry stone wall, straight on through the roundabout, and as they headed up the incline of the Woodhead, expertly doubled the clutch down into third gear, the little car accelerating effortlessly up the hill. The straight road ahead seemed to carry on upwards, as if forever, until car and passengers disappeared into the familiar cloud and mist at the top of the Pennines.

At Salem, the news was no less chaotic and confusing. The bulletin was being extended and future programmes cancelled. Adam grabbed the phone as it rang, hoping it would be Walter. It was Simeon.

"Is that you Adam, are you still there?"

"Yes it's me, and yes, I am still here Simeon. Are you watching this, it's all very confusing. It's not right is it?"

"Not really Adam, I'm not sure what to think, I have been ringing round the elders but most of them have been unavailable."

"You will have to let me go Simeon, I'm trying to contact Walter and the rest of the family." He put the phone down, more abruptly than he intended. He rang round again, but still no replies, He even tried to ring Damien, but Gaynor answered, "Yes, he is watching the news and no, he doesn't want to speak to you." She put the phone down without waiting for a reply. Gaynor and Damien had other things on their mind. The hotel next door was slowly collapsing in on itself. A landslip had undermined the foundations and parts of the building were falling down the South Cliff towards the swimming pool and spa. Their holiday flats could be next.

Adam thought to himself, at least Damien, like Simeon, was still there, but where the hell were Walter and Slim, and Rachel for that matter.

He finally got through to his sister. Julia sounded rough, but it was nothing to do with the news. She was on her own and had been for some weeks now.

"Hi brother," she said, in a feeble attempt to sound cheerful and sober, "and how are you this Saturday evening love."

"Never mind all that, just turn the news on, turn it on now and try and sober up."

"Don't be like that, and besides the news was over an hour ago."

"Just turn the damn television on. It's happening. It is happening now, just as I said it would." Although it wasn't happening just as he said, was it?

He tried again to ring Walter, Slim and his mother. He even tried Trevor, but there was no one there. Julia dragged herself out of the chair and turned on the TV. The scene was much as it had been all evening. She looked on in horror as the reporter was saying, "We have a special report from our correspondent on the

Lebanese border." The image switched to a man in a flak jacket and U.N. blue helmet, crouching behind a crumbling stone wall. "There are confusing reports of an incident close to the border – some kind of explosion or earthquake. It seems to be close to the Russian's military base. There are reports of large casualties and the destruction of military equipment. Some are suggesting that it has triggered a tsunami that is spreading across the Mediterranean towards the Russian fleet. It is all very chaotic and we are still struggling to get any confirmation of the reports we're receiving."

The news returned to the correspondent in Jerusalem, who was saying something about a large flood of water that had sprung out from the base of the Temple Mount and was flooding the valley below, and something odd was happening at the old East Gate of the City.

Julia, through the drunken haze of her brain, was trying to make sense of what she was watching, telling herself that Adam, as usual, was being hysterical and there would be a perfectly rational explanation for everything when the chaos and confusion had settled down and she was sober. Surely it was all a terrorist attack, or some form of natural disaster. The press would soon track the story down and in a few hours everything would become clear. But as she continued to watch the reports with growing alarm and incredulity, she began to feel less sure of herself. There was an insidious fear growing within her. It was, of course, the fear that her crazy brother, who had been predicting such things for years might have been right after all.

Adam, still alone in his study watching the same events, was filled with exactly the same fear as his sister, for exactly the same reasons. He remained transfixed by the images on his television, wondering where everyone was and trying to make sense of it all.

Then the screen became blank, and all the lights of Salem went out. Adam was alone in the darkness. The only light came fom two faint discs shimmering on the driveway.